He s̶ᵗᵒᵒᵈ ... g̶st
a pack of lapdogs,

his dark brown hair brushing his shoulders and his dark eyes surveying the splendor before him with indifference.

Lady Elizabeth watched as he shifted restlessly, moving with an animal sort of grace. He made her think of a dark forest in moonlight and his expression had a strange haunted quality as if he were used to being alert for hidden danger.

There was something wild about him, wild as the wind during a storm, wild like the beating of her heart. An oddly pleasant shiver ran down Elizabeth's spine.

Who was he, and why had she never seen him before?

Dear Reader,

When Catherine Archer's first book, *Rose Among Thorns*, was published, *Romantic Times* called it "Reminiscent of Jude Deveraux…" and "…a spellbinding medieval romance.…" This month, we bring you her new medieval romance title, *Velvet Bond*. It's the story of a noblewoman who is forced to marry an enigmatic stranger and unwittingly finds herself in the middle of a dangerous struggle for land and power.

With *Playing To Win,* author Laurel Ames returns to the Regency period to tell the story of a new wife who will do anything to win the love of her husband, a rakish duke with an uncanny conscience. Don't miss this delightful story of trust and love.

Our featured Women of the West title this month is *Trusting Sarah* by Cassandra Austin, the story of a young woman who heads west on a wagon train, trying to escape her past, only to run headlong into it again, in the form of the man who wrongly sent her to jail years before.

Also this month, *The Magician's Quest,* Claire Delacroix's sequel to her previous story, *Honeyed Lies,* the tale of a man who must come to terms with the legacy left him by his father, and his love for a woman of questionable virtue.

Whatever your taste in historical reading, we hope you'll enjoy all four titles, available wherever Harlequin Historicals are sold.

Sincerely,

Tracy Farrell
Senior Editor

Please address questions and book requests to:
Harlequin Reader Service
U.S.: 3010 Walden Ave., P.O. Box 1325, Buffalo, NY 14269
Canadian: P.O. Box 609, Fort Erie, Ont. L2A 5X3

Catherine Archer

Velvet Bond

Harlequin Books

TORONTO • NEW YORK • LONDON
AMSTERDAM • PARIS • SYDNEY • HAMBURG
STOCKHOLM • ATHENS • TOKYO • MILAN
MADRID • WARSAW • BUDAPEST • AUCKLAND

ISBN 0-373-28882-4

VELVET BOND

Copyright © 1995 by Catherine J. Archibald.

Books by Catherine Archer

CATHERINE ARCHER

has been hooked on historical romance since reading *Jane Eyre* at the age of twelve. She has an avid interest in history, particularly the medieval period. A homemaker and mother, Catherine lives with her husband, three children and dog in Alberta, Canada, where the long winters give this American transplant plenty of time to write.

This book is dedicated to my children,
Catherine, Stephen and Rosanna,
for all their love and support,
with special thanks to my Kate
for all her editorial assistance.

And to my sister, Elizabeth, who cleans when she's
angry and gave me the inspiration for this character.

I must also add a note of thanks to Don D'Auria.
Thanks.

Chapter One

Elizabeth Clayburn sat on the stone window seat, her slender back supported by her brother's broad one. Despite the velvet cushion beneath her, she was less than comfortable. Sighing, she wished herself in her own comfortable house for the third time in as many minutes. But she had promised to stay at Stephen's side until Lady Helen turned her attentions elsewhere, and that she would do. No matter how much she disliked coming up to Windsor Castle.

It wasn't Elizabeth's usual custom to involve herself in Stephen's affairs, but Lady Helen was proving especially difficult to discourage, and Stephen had come near to begging for Elizabeth's help. He hoped that if he was never alone with his former mistress, she would soon give up and move on to greener pastures. Not even Helen was brazen enough to confront him about his obviously cooled interest before his very sister.

Restlessly Elizabeth's gaze roamed the crowded antechamber as she toyed with one of the braided gold tassels that held back the heavy red brocade drapes. The three tall windows let in sufficient light to illuminate the high, wide room, but she saw little that pleased her.

Despite the perpetual chill given off by stone walls, the air was overwarm, due to the presence of so many people.

The high-ceilinged chamber bore no furniture or adornments save the rich curtains, and needed none. Men and women alike displayed their best finery in the forms of colorful cotehardies, tunics and hose. Many of the older men wore a long-skirted cote over the body-hugging tunic called a pourpoint, but the younger or more daring favored the shorter version that was much frowned on by the church. The women wore their cotes slashed at the sides to show off tight-fitting tunics of samite, sendal, and damask. Linen wimples fluttered about cheeks that had been delicately tinted with cosmetics. Jewelry and fur trim were seen in abundance as their wearers moved about, seeing and being seen. And they waited, some patiently, some not so patiently, for a moment to present their case to their sovereign.

Elizabeth looked down with a start as the would-be troubadour at her feet struck a chord on the lute that rested across his knee. She had nearly forgotten Percy.

Eyes of the palest blue gazed up at her with abject adoration as he sang,

> "Oh lips of deepest scarlet hue
> And eyes that sparkle like the dew"

"Sweet Jesu, Beth," her brother Stephen turned to mutter in her ear. "This one is more dreadful than the last."

"Shh, brother mine," she whispered, attempting to prevent him hurting poor Percy's delicate pride.

This was to no avail, for Sir Percy Hustace had indeed heard Stephen's comment. He dropped the lute, which broke a string as it struck the floor. Percy groaned, casting a wounded look toward the other knight.

Rot Stephen, Elizabeth thought. She was of no mind to listen to them quarrel.

When Stephen only stared at Percy with amused contempt, the blue-eyed knight turned from him in disdain. Percy moved forward on his knees to take Elizabeth's slender hand in his. "My lady, do you find my song displeasing?"

As Elizabeth gazed down upon the young man, truth and pity warred inside her. Pity won. "Not at all, Sir Percy. 'Tis most clear you have worked long upon the words and melody. I am flattered by your efforts."

This time triumph lit Percy's pale eyes when he looked to Stephen.

Elizabeth heard her brother click his tongue in disgust. She frowned at him, her sapphire eyes flashing. "If you do not behave yourself, I shall go home and leave you to face Lady Helen alone."

Stephen sat bolt upright. "Now, Beth. I was but jesting with Percy. He should not be so sensitive." Stephen turned toward the other knight so that Elizabeth could no longer see his face, but she knew her brother well, and the expression he was directing at Percy would be unpleasant, to be sure. But she said nothing. Percy could be quite tiresome, with his whining ways. And he did cut a foolish figure in his mode of dress. Every fashion of the day was ridiculously exaggerated. His pourpoint was short to the point of indecency, the gold cotehardie he wore over it sporting tippets that trailed well past his knees, and the points of his shoes extended at least twice the length of his foot. If it weren't for the fact that much of his foolishness was by way of trying to impress her, Elizabeth would have been less inclined to be patient with him herself.

She smiled decisively. "We will forget the matter."

Stephen looked about them to see if anyone else had taken note of Percy's stupidity. As a trusted messenger to King Edward III, Stephen had a certain dignity to uphold.

Few of the other sumptuously dressed occupants of the antechamber paid them even cursory attention. The antics of Elizabeth's most recent admirer were of little interest to them. Sir Percy was new to Edward's court, and like countless others before him had instantly become enamored with Stephen's sister. And Stephen could hardly fault Percy for that. Elizabeth was indeed beautiful, with her deep blue eyes, creamy skin and luxurious black hair.

She was his only sister, and had been dreadfully spoiled by her three brothers, including Peter, who was four years her junior. But Stephen knew it hadn't harmed her. She had a kind and generous nature. She was undeniably patient with each new suitor until he finally gave up after realizing he would get no more than kindness from her. Stephen knew she should be married at twenty, but none had ever stirred her heart, and her brothers were loath to force her into an alliance she did not want.

If he felt that Percy was of any real threat to Elizabeth's happiness or virtue, Stephen would readily take him out and throttle him. But he was not, and Stephen could easily afford to be magnanimous with the lackwit. As long as he didn't become too irritating. So he would do as his sister asked and say no more.

He allowed his gaze to wander freely about the room, then froze.

Elizabeth felt Stephen stiffen beside her as he drew in a sharp breath. Following the direction of his apprehensive gaze, she spied Lady Helen Denfield.

Lady Helen was an acknowledged beauty, and deservedly so. At thirty-two, she managed to look as though she had not seen a day past seventeen years. There was a fawnlike delicacy about her as she came toward them across the bare stone floor. To heighten the image of youth, she wore her golden-brown hair loose down her back in a shimmering curtain, with only a sheer veil to cover it. Her soft brown eyes viewed the world around her with an expression of wonder, and she smiled timidly at whoever she passed.

Elizabeth studied this performance with amusement, having to bite her lip to keep from laughing aloud. For the pose of timidity was just that, a pose. Lady Helen could be more truly likened to the fox than to the fawn.

Peeking over at Stephen to gauge his reaction, Elizabeth found her handsome brother tensed as if to do battle. He ran an agitated hand through his dark auburn hair, his forest-green eyes wary. For three days now she had accompanied Stephen when he came to the castle to await a possible summons. It was his duty as one of King Edward's messengers to make himself available. But that put him into contact with the one he most hoped to avoid, his mistress until very recently, Lady Helen Denfield. The affair had ended the moment he found out that the fair widow had nothing short of marriage on her mind.

Lady Denfield stopped before them.

As if sensing some threat to his goddess, Percy leapt up to stand at Elizabeth's shoulder. It was a clear but unnecessary demonstration of his devotion.

"Lady Elizabeth." Helen nodded, without looking at her. The woman's attention was completely centered on her prey. Though she tried to hide the feral gleam in her eyes as they rested upon Stephen, it was all too obvious.

"Lord Clayburn." The greeting sounded like nothing so much as an endearment.

Stephen ran a large hand over his muscular thighs in their dark green hose. "Lady Denfield."

Helen's eyes followed the path of his hand hungrily.

Watching the proceedings with interest, Elizabeth was hard-pressed not to laugh aloud.

How amusing that Stephen should be working so desperately to extricate himself from the affair that a fortnight ago had been his greatest pleasure, Elizabeth thought. Widowed for a year, Helen Denfield had been

ripe for the picking. But it was Stephen who would end by
being the harvest, did she have her way.

Elizabeth could see that Lady Helen had no intention of
remaining a widow for long, and Stephen had clearly been
chosen as the honored bridegroom. As she had been unable to produce an heir during her fifteen-year marriage to
Lord Denfield, Helen's husband's lands and money had
passed to a distant cousin, and she was nearly destitute,
living on her meager dower funds. When Stephen began to
pursue her, she had put all her not inconsiderable charms
to luring him to the bait.

Not only was Elizabeth's brother a fine specimen of a
man, he also had a large income left to him by their
mother. And, to add cream to the strawberries, he had,
according to court gossip, brought Helen to fulfillment for
the first time.

If truth be told, Elizabeth had no personal experience in
carnal matters, but she did know that the court ladies set
much store by prowess in the bedchamber. To Elizabeth,
it seemed they made a great deal about naught. She had
met no man who stirred even the least bit of feeling in her.
And from what she had heard, she wasn't sure she wanted
to. It was beyond her how one could allow oneself to be
made such a fool of over copulating.

Helen's gaze took on a desperate expression as she
watched Stephen.

Elizabeth could not imagine prostrating herself the way
Helen was now, no matter how much pleasure a man could
bring. She nearly succumbed to sympathy for the other
woman. Stephen was always one to pursue a female with
everything in him. Then, once he had succeeded in his
quest, he lost interest, especially when the idea of marriage was broached.

If Lady Helen had been wiser, she would have allowed
Stephen to go on thinking he was the aggressor.

Elizabeth understood this much about her brother.

But Stephen was of her blood, and she owed her allegiance to him first. So thinking, Elizabeth hardened her heart and reminded herself that Helen had her own agenda as far as Stephen was concerned. The fact that she had fallen in love with him was incidental.

At that moment, Elizabeth noted that a hush had fallen over the room. She looked up, surprised to find everyone watching the entrance to the chamber. It was unusual for anyone to cause a stir among this lot, who had seen some of the most important men in the world come and go on a regular basis, and she wondered idly who had arrived.

At that moment, the crowd parted, and Elizabeth saw him.

The man was tall and wore his acorn-brown tunic, pourpoint and dark hose casually, seeming completely unconcerned with the way the fabrics hugged his wide shoulders and muscular legs. He had made no effort to garb himself impressively, and thus stood apart like a wolf among lapdogs. Dark brown hair brushed his shoulders, and his equally dark eyes surveyed the splendor before him with indifference. Even as he shifted restlessly, first running a darkly tanned hand through his hair, then clenching that same hand at his side, he moved with an animal sort of grace. He made her think of a dark forest in moonlight, and his expression had a strange haunted quality, as if he were used to being alert for hidden danger.

The man seemed unaware of the stir he was causing. It was as though his mind were on other matters of greater importance than what he saw before him. He turned to the equally broad-shouldered blond man at his side, who was also dressed in subtle forest shades.

They seemed of like taste, but Elizabeth hardly noticed the lighter-haired of the two. It was the other one who drew her, though she couldn't have explained it if given a thousand chances, and so she didn't try.

There was something wild about him, wild as the wind is during a storm, wild like the beating of her heart. An oddly pleasant shiver ran down her spine.

Who was he, and why had she never seen him before?

Without even thinking, Elizabeth rose and moved toward him. A narrow path parted for her, as if those in her way seemed to sense her need to get closer to this man, to speak with him.

Elizabeth stopped before him, her gaze taking in the strong features of his face, straight nose, hard, chiseled jaw and high cheekbones. In the pit of her stomach, something fluttered, like a butterfly emerging from its protective sheath.

He glanced down at her with eyes as dark as burnt umber, then away, dismissing Elizabeth as he scanned the room behind her.

Piqued, Elizabeth simply stood there, a knot of irritation replacing the excitement in her belly. Never in all her life had any male looked through her that way.

The man smiled as his gaze came to light on someone behind her. "Clayburn," he said. Elizabeth closed her eyes, unable to halt the tingling along the back of her neck that hearing his voice brought. The sound was rich, like rough fingers in brown velvet. Then she realized that he had spoken her own surname, and she turned to see her brother standing there just as Stephen answered him.

"Warwicke. How do you?" Stephen was nodding, his smile one of welcome.

The man shrugged. "I could be better. You know how I hate coming to court."

"Aye," Stephen agreed. "So what could have brought you to Windsor?"

Elizabeth could only stare at her brother. He talked as if he and this incredible man were long acquainted. And never had he so much as mentioned the friendship to her. Of course, she did know that Stephen met many people in his duties as the king's messenger. But he might have at least thought to speak about this one.

The brown-eyed man looked around them with a frown. "I would rather not speak of the matter in the midst of so many. It is somewhat private."

"I understand," Stephen said. "Do you need to get in to see the king?" He nodded toward the closed door at the other end of the chamber. "I may be able to help you there."

"My thanks," the other man answered, "but King Edward has arranged this audience himself. Methinks he will see me as soon as he learns I am here."

Stephen only nodded.

Elizabeth had had quite enough of this. She wanted to be introduced to this man Stephen had called Warwicke, and she meant to see that she was. "Stephen," she said with a smile for her brother, "you do not behave very well. Where are your manners? You must introduce me."

Both men looked down at her, as if suddenly realizing she was there.

Stephen hastened to do as she asked. "Lord Raynor Warwicke, let me present my sister, Lady Elizabeth."

Her heart fluttered in her breast as his deep brown eyes settled upon her. "Lady Elizabeth." This time there was a faint hint of recognition in them, but his gaze did not linger as most men's were wont to do.

"My lord Warwicke," she replied.

But he had already turned back to Stephen. "Mayhap you could help me by finding a cleric who could tell the king I am here?"

"Of a surety," Stephen replied, and they moved off through the throng.

Elizabeth stood there in surprise. Then she looked down at herself, wondering if she might find the answer to Lord Warwicke's rudeness in her mode of dress. But she could find no fault with the scarlet gown. The sides were slashed wide to show off the black tunic beneath, which fitted her narrow waist and gently curving breast and hips most becomingly. The sleeves of the tunic were fashionably wide and embroidered with a pattern of musical instruments in gold and scarlet threads. She ran her hand over her gold veil and found it to be securely in place.

No, it was not her attire that had caused Warwicke to look through her as if she had no more substance than the contents of an empty cup.

In her twenty years upon this earth, never had she been so summarily dismissed. He had completely failed to acknowledge her. Even her brother seemed to have forgotten her presence. And after she had come to the castle to help him.

But what made the insult doubly hard to take was the fact that never had she reacted to any man the way she had to Warwicke.

A deep flush stained her cheeks as she recalled her actions. Elizabeth had felt drawn to the man by some force outside herself, going to him without even pausing for thought. And had, in doing so, made a complete and utter fool of herself.

Surreptitiously she looked around the room, but no one seemed to be paying any attention to her. Now that Warwicke had left with her brother, they seemed to have gone back to their own interests. Even Percy was busily fixing the string on his lute.

Then her gaze came to rest on Lady Helen, who was standing close by, with cruel amusement in her eyes.

Elizabeth flushed, but forced herself to raise her head high. She would not allow the other woman to think she had been bested.

Lady Helen smiled thinly. "He cuts quite a figure, does he not?"

Raising finely arched brows high, Elizabeth asked, "Who?"

But the other woman was clearly not fooled. "Why, my Lord Warwicke. I felt certain that you took particular notice of him, Elizabeth."

She shrugged with as much indifference as she could summon. "Nay. I took no particular note of the man. He is my brother's friend, as I'm sure you heard."

"Oh, methinks there was more to it than that," Helen countered.

The spite in Helen Denfield's voice was discomfiting, even though Elizabeth sensed the cause behind it. She was not so simpleminded that she was unaware of the fact that most folk thought her beautiful. It was not her fault that her looks drew so much attention, but they had made her more than a few enemies. There were many who would be happy to hear of her embarrassment. Elizabeth was a very private individual and did not care for the idea that idle court gossip would be turned her way. This was one of the reasons she and Stephen had a house in the village instead of residing at the castle itself. If she did not do something to silence Helen now, her encounter with Lord Warwicke would likely have become an affair by nightfall. Court gossips never hesitated to embellish a story beyond recognition.

But Helen Denfield had her own vulnerability, in the form of Stephen, and Elizabeth wasn't above reminding her of this.

Helen did not know her well enough, and so could not know Elizabeth would never actually spread tales. But Elizabeth was aware that most people were apt to judge others by themselves, and so Helen would likely believe otherwise. The widow would surely hold her tongue, if she thought Stephen's sister might talk about her affair with him. Rumor of the liaison would not aid her in her quest for a husband.

Elizabeth said, "My dear Lady Helen, I'm most certain you misunderstood. After all, you seem too much fixed on the things my brother does and says to take note of aught else.''

Lady Denfield gasped, and raised her hand as if to slap Elizabeth. Then, as the younger woman continued to return her stare, the widow seemed to realize that her genteel pose would not be served by such an act. Helen turned and fled the room.

Elizabeth arched a brow, watching as the brown-haired beauty lifted a delicate hand to wipe away nonexistent tears, just in case someone had taken note of their exchange.

But Elizabeth didn't really care. She had already forgotten Helen as she turned toward the other end of the room, where the door to the king's audience chamber lay. There was no sign of her brother or the other two men, and she could only assume they had gone into the inner room.

Her mind was ablaze with unanswered questions concerning Raynor Warwicke. He was the most compelling man she had ever seen. Her lips tightened as she recalled the way he had barely acknowledged her presence. It simply would not do. Because of her own interest in him, Elizabeth felt a need for him to show some reaction to her.

Pensively she frowned. Not once in her life had Elizabeth been denied anything she wanted. And she did not mean to set a different precedent now.

She was not finished with Lord Warwicke yet.

The luxuriously appointed audience chamber left little impression on Lord Raynor Warwicke as he walked down the wide aisle at its center, leaving Stephen and Bronic waiting just inside the oaken door. He forced himself onward on legs that felt as stiff as tilting posts as he passed by the somberly dressed clergy and sumptuously dressed courtiers who stood at either side of him. All his attention was focused on his king, where he sat on a raised dais at the end of the audience chamber. Edward III was flanked by two of his knights, both members of the Order of the Garter. Roger Mortise and the earl of Caliber were men of exemplary character, and battle-hardened warriors loyal to the throne. Edward was a king who set such store by honor and chivalry that he had established the Order of the Garter in 1348 for the purpose of exalting those qualities.

The baron of Warwicke did his best to relax the rigid muscles in his face and shoulders. The king would not know that Raynor had come here fully prepared to forswear himself, nor that the very future of an innocent three-year-old child hinged upon his doing just that.

Raynor was totally aware of the tall, slim man who stood to the right of the dais. There was nothing in that one's outward appearance to tell the world that he was the most despicable of men. He was dressed as the other courtiers were, in rich fabrics and colors, and his face was strongly made, his Viking heritage firmly stamped upon it. Harrington's eyes were blue, the hair a deep golden-brown. Not one hint of the black heart that beat inside his chest was visible. But Raynor knew it was there. Nigel Harrington had caused more misery in twenty-four years than most would bring in several lifetimes. Raynor would not allow him to have custody of little Willow. After what the man had done to his own step-sister, he was not to be trusted with the care of any female.

But Raynor had no more time to think on that now. He came to a halt only a few feet from the seated monarch, squaring his shoulders, deliberately keeping his mind focused on what he had to do. Drawing the hatred down into the deepest part of himself.

King Edward shifted his long legs as he leaned back, studying the men before him, seeming to miss little. The baron of Warwicke forced himself to bear this scrutiny without flinching.

The forty-eight-year-old Edward's golden hair and beard were liberally streaked with gray, but he was still a vital and vibrant ruler. Over his chair was a shield that bore the arms he had taken for his own. Raynor knew it irritated the French greatly that Edward had chosen to place his own leopards on the first quarter of his shield, rather than the fleur-de-lis. Though of Norman descent, Edward had always been one to think of himself as an Englishman first and foremost.

The king caught and held Raynor's gaze for a long, tense moment. But Raynor kept himself erect, not giving away any hint of his inner anger.

Edward spoke, saying the words Raynor had feared he would. "And you are ready to swear on a relic of the one true cross, Lord Warwicke, that the child is yours?"

His back became arrow-straight. Even though he'd known all along that the situation would come to this, Raynor was surprised at the quick shaft of guilt that pierced him at the idea of forswearing himself. But the feeling was short-lived. He must carry through, for the sake of the little one. Raynor nodded, sharply, then raised his square chin. "I am."

He heard a quickly indrawn breath from his right, and looked toward Nigel Harrington with a quirked brow. If nothing else, Raynor was pleased at having shocked his adversary. Nigel had made the mistake of believing Raynor too honorable to play by his own tactics.

King Edward nodded to his cleric, then motioned toward Raynor. "Kneel down."

Raynor fell to his knees, his gaze locked on the front of the monk's black robe.

The cleric brought forth a small wooden box, which Raynor knew would contain a sliver of the Lord's cross. He held it toward Raynor. "Do you, on your honor as a knight, swear by this piece of the one true cross, and in the name of Edward III, king of England, that the child called Willow is of your own seed, without doubt?"

Forcing himself to take the box without hesitation, Raynor brought it to his lips. "I do swear this on my honor as a knight."

Nigel Harrington let out a growl of outrage. "He lies."

King Edward turned toward Nigel with an expression of forbearance. "My lord Harrington, in the days you have been at court you have shown no evidence that what you say is fact. Do you have some proof to offer us at this time?"

There was a silence as Nigel fumed, his blue eyes locked on Raynor's with fury. "No, my liege, I do not, but—"

Edward interrupted him. "Then there is nothing more to be said." He shrugged wide shoulders encased in purple velvet. "Unless you were present at the child's conception, you have nothing to add."

As the king spoke, Nigel cringed, but quickly recovered. Raynor felt a burning urge to run him through right there before them all, and his fingers passed fondly over the hilt of his sword. He and Raynor were the only two people on earth who knew the true circumstances of Willow's conception. The coward would not, could not, tell them that he had raped his own sister-by-marriage. Raynor had counted on this, but seeing the fear on the other man's face only made him all the more disgusted.

Nigel sputtered out, "But, King Ed—"

Edward looked toward him with a dark scowl. "Lord Harrington. We have listened to you, and done our utmost to bring this matter to a speedy conclusion. We have ordered Warwicke here in haste and put him to the test. In all things we have tried to do our duty by you." His lips thinned. "Warwicke has given his word, and as you have no proof that the child is not his, you may consider it done. We bear you no malice in this, Lord Harrington, feeling that your sister's death has clouded your thinking, and in your grief you simply try to retain some piece of her by wanting guardianship of her child. But 'tis most clear that the child is the natural offspring of Warwicke, and he has already assured us of his intent to see the little girl well done by. You may leave Windsor with those comforting thoughts to see you safe home.''

When Nigel opened his mouth as if to protest, the king raised an imperious hand. ''The matter is done.''

With that, Edward turned to Raynor. ''It is our hope that such a dispute will not again occur concerning you, my lord Warwicke. In future, should you dally, make most certain that the gentlewoman is your wife.''

Raynor lowered his eyes and nodded. ''King Edward, you have my assurance that I will do so.'' He did not add that he planned to stay as far away from that type of female as possible.

Edward motioned with a beringed hand. ''Arise, my lord Warwicke, and consider this dispute settled. I would have no more strife because of it.'' He stared at Nigel Harrington for a long moment.

Knowing that he had been chastened by the king, however politely, Nigel Harrington turned and hurried from the chamber.

Raynor felt a sweet relief ease the tight band of tension around his chest. Now Willow would be safe from that bastard who called himself her uncle.

King Edward waved a dismissive hand. ''We have many other matters to attend, Lord Warwicke, and thus I must bid you good-day.''

''My thanks to you, my liege.'' Raynor bowed himself from the room. He was more than glad to have this interview at an end. He forced himself to walk the length of the room with carefully measured steps.

Bronic and Stephen followed him as the great oaken door was opened, and they passed into the antechamber.

Bronic looked at Raynor, letting out his breath, as if he had been holding it for a very long time. He raked his hand through his shaggy blond hair. ''Praise God.''

Stephen was looking from one to the other with curiosity.

Raynor gave a mental shrug. He might as well tell Stephen the story he had decided upon. The day's events would be all over court in a matter of hours, anyway. And it might as well be Raynor's version of the tale as anyone else's.

He smiled at the auburn-haired man. They had fostered together as boys, with the earl of Norwich, but Raynor had left after only one year, when his father died. Though many things had passed in the thirteen years since, Raynor had always remembered Stephen with friendship and a sense of trust. He knew that Stephen would not embellish the story he was about to be told, but would relate it to others just as he had heard it.

Raynor said, "Harrington can go to the very devil, for aught I care. He has tried to make trouble for the last time. Edward has upheld my claim to guardianship of the little one. She will remain at Warwicke."

Stephen asked, "What is he about? Some weeks ago he came to court, whining to whoever would listen that his sister's child was stolen from him. Obviously the tale gained him today's audience, but nothing more, for Edward has upheld your claim. I had no idea you were the man who was supposed to have done the evil deed until just now. Why would Harrington accuse you of such a ridiculous crime? Who does *he* name as the father?"

Unable to stifle a rush of anger, Raynor looked at the floor. He didn't want Stephen to guess at his overwhelming hatred for Nigel Harrington. He must guard Willow's secret at all costs. He had promised her mother, Louisa. "He names none, because there is none besides myself. Harrington plays a game of greed. Willow is an heiress through her mother. The lands must pass through the female of the line if there are no direct male descendants, and there are none. Nigel is the son of Lord Harrington's first wife, and has no claim. Without the little one, he has no access to her wealth. That is why he has dragged me here to publicly humiliate both me and my child." Raynor's lean jaw flexed, and his lips twisted with derision. "King Edward could only take my word or Harrington's and he has no proof to discredit me."

"Well, it's hardly surprising that King Edward would believe you, when Harrington could not even name any other as the father. The man is hardly rational."

Even though his stomach was knotted with hatred and tension, Raynor nearly laughed aloud, albeit bitterly. To say Nigel was irrational was most surely a gross understatement. If Stephen only knew the truth of why Harrington kept the child's parentage to himself. "I fear," he said, "that there is no mystery here. Louisa's child is my own. I regret that I was not able to marry her before she died, because our child's parentage would not have been in question had I done so." His brown eyes darkened to walnut in sorrow as he remembered how he had tried to convince Louisa to marry him so that her stepbrother would no longer hold sway over her. But she had refused, saying Raynor had a right to some happiness of his own. Just taking Willow in and claiming her as his own had been more than Louisa had the right to ask. Raynor's voice was barely audible as he finished. "She died before I was able to convince her otherwise, shortly after the child was born."

Stephen laid a hand on his arm. "I am sorry, my friend. This trouble with Harrington must make it very difficult for you."

Bronic spoke up, his Nordic features hard, his blue eyes narrowed. "The man is crazed. Would that this were his throat." He clasped his large warrior's hands together tightly.

Raynor sent him a warning look. He did not wish anyone to suspect there was more to the story than they told.

If they displayed the depth of their hatred too openly, any reasoning person would begin to wonder at its cause.

And no one must ever find out the reason for Raynor's fear for Willow. Not even Bronic understood the true circumstances of Willow's parentage. His vehemence stemmed from loyalty to Raynor.

All Raynor said was "Harrington must follow his own course, as I must mine. Mayhap the king's decision today will set him on a more constructive path. Now he must realize that he cannot take Willow from me."

"You are a good and true father, to take the child though she be a bastard," Stephen told him. "Harrington has indeed tried to besmirch you there, as well. He lays it about that you are the one who would have the little girl for her inheritance."

Raynor stiffened. It was true that once he had been a poor man. His father had mismanaged and overspent in an effort to give his greedy mother all she wanted. After Raynor inherited the lands and title, she had tried to control and manipulate him in the same manner. But even at fourteen he had been too strong-willed for her to control him. No woman would destroy him as Mary Warwicke had his father.

The years since his father's death had seen him turn the properties around, and while he was not the wealthiest of the king's barons, neither was he the poorest. He knew that since Harrington had spread the lie, many would continue to believe he had taken on the responsibility of raising Willow because of her lands. But he didn't really care, not if it kept them from looking further.

Besides, Raynor controlled her lands only as her guardian and overseer. He took no payment of any kind for looking after her interests. Everything would go to her in the event of her marriage or her twenty-first birthday.

Stephen interrupted Raynor's thoughts with a clap on his back. "Enough of this, my friend. All has gone well for you today. Now you can be about some more pleasant sport. I have not seen you in years, and would hear what you have been about."

Bronic nodded, looking about the crowded antechamber with ill-concealed discomfort. "But we should find some more comfortable spot for the discussion to take place."

Raynor eyed his friend in agreement. He had no love of the court and its crowds. In fact, he would not be comfortable until they were well on their way back to Warwicke on the day after tomorrow. "I stand with Bronic. We are sharing a room with several other knights, but methinks they would not mind us bringing you along, Stephen. I'm sorry we cannot offer you better hospitality, but Windsor is full to overflowing, even with all the new building the king has had done in the past years."

Stephen laughed. "Do not apologize. I know the circumstances well. That is part of why I have a house in the village."

They started from the chamber with Raynor in the lead.

Raynor stopped as a woman moved between him and the entrance. He paused, his head tilted to one side as he looked at her. She was quite beautiful, with her creamy skin, high cheekbones and long-lashed sapphire eyes. And she seemed somehow familiar, though Raynor could not think why.

"Elizabeth," Stephen called out from behind him. His tone was sheepish. "I had forgotten you were here."

The woman did not deign even to glance Stephen's way. "Obviously."

Then he remembered. It was Clayburn's sister. He had been introduced on his way in to see the king, but he had been of little mind to take note of anything then. Even a woman as lovely as Elizabeth Clayburn.

His eyes met hers, and for a moment a strange sort of current passed between them, making his belly tighten pleasantly. But Raynor pushed it aside. This was his friend's sister, a noblewoman. And Raynor had no intention of dallying in that direction.

His lips twisted in a self-derisive grimace. Though he was guilty of nothing where Louisa was concerned, he had just admitted to being so. He had no intention of becoming entangled with Stephen's sister. Even if he did see a stirring of warm challenge in her lovely eyes when she looked at him. Long ago he'd decided no woman was to be trusted in his life. Raynor's father had loved his wife blindly, giving up every shred of self-respect to please her. And if that was love, Raynor wanted no part in it.

With that thought firmly in mind, Raynor stepped aside so that Stephen could speak with her.

He pretended not to notice how her gaze lingered on him as Stephen told her where they were going and made arrangements for her to be taken home.

Chapter Two

Late that night, Elizabeth waited in Stephen's bedchamber for him to come home.

She sat in his chair bedside the fire, a cup of warmed wine in one hand, drumming the fingers of the other in a steady rhythm against the seasoned wooden arm. She was still fuming over the way Stephen had sent her home, as if she were some child to be gotten out of the way. He had no right to treat her thus.

But truth made her admit, at least to herself, that Stephen was only a small part of her irritation. Most of it was directed at herself, because of her own reaction to Raynor Warwicke. Whatever had gotten into her?

Any number of men would fall upon their very knees to have her notice them. But she, fool that she was, looked to a man who acted as though he could not even see her.

But hadn't there, just for a moment, been a spark in his eyes, when she'd stood before him as the men were leaving the antechamber? Yes, she was sure there had been more than indifference in his gaze as it slid over her. He'd covered it so quickly that another woman might not have noticed. But Elizabeth was not another woman. She responded to even the slightest of reactions in the baron of Warwicke. When he'd looked at her that way, seeing her as a desirable woman, her body had answered in kind.

Elizabeth had been left achingly aware of him, the tanned flesh on the wide column of his throat, the very deep rhythm of his breathing. There was something about Lord Warwicke that made her feel alive as never before.

Why, she did not know. But Elizabeth was going to find out. She couldn't just let this feeling go, this strange singing in her veins that she had heard spoken of but had never thought to experience.

And she meant to enlist her brother's aid.

She simply had to see the baron again, speak to him, find out whence these stirrings came. What manner of man was he, to engender such feelings inside her? She knew he was handsome, with his dark eyes and unruly hair, but what of the person inside? Surely he must be a knight of great repute to awaken such amorous reactions in her so easily.

Then she forced herself to pause in her headlong thoughts. Mayhap he was not as he appeared. Her own girlish twitterings did not mean that Raynor of Warwicke was of good and noble character.

But Elizabeth could not make herself believe this. How could her own instincts be so badly askew as that? Surely, if she was to judge by her feelings, Raynor was truly a man among men. Else how could she explain how her heretofore-dormant emotions had been so suddenly awakened?

Just then she heard the sound of her brother's booted feet coming up the narrow wooden stairs that led from the large living chamber below. Olwyn must have let him in. Elizabeth felt a stab of guilt at thinking about the other woman. She'd managed to avoid speaking to her mistress since Elizabeth snapped at her upon coming home from Windsor. But she had given Elizabeth many long, disapproving looks to let her know how badly she had behaved.

Elizabeth knew that as soon as Olwyn was ready to listen, she would need to apologize to the woman who was more friend than aught else. After all, it was Stephen she was unhappy with. Olwyn had been her companion since the day Stephen brought her to court, after their parents died, seven years ago. At seventeen, four years Elizabeth's senior, Olwyn had just been widowed, and had needed a way to make her living. Her husband had been the youngest of six brothers and thus had left her with little but his horse and sword. Stephen had felt the older girl would be able to teach Elizabeth about the realities of living at court, and hopefully keep her out of trouble.

But Elizabeth didn't want to think about that now. She and Olwyn had had more serious disagreements over the years, and had settled them quickly enough. At the moment, she wanted to concentrate her attention on Stephen.

Stephen opened the door of his chamber, his face taking on a pained expression as his gaze swept the room. The chamber was not large, and in the cheery glow of the firelight he could see that it was immaculate. The wooden floor had been scrubbed clean, the hangings on the bed had been pulled back, so he could see that the linens were tucked so tightly he could have bounced a sword upon them and not made a wrinkle. Not one single item of a personal nature was visible. The lids of his two chests were shut tight upon their contents, which were usually spilled about in happy disarray. "Ah, Beth, you've been cleaning again."

She smiled with feigned politeness. "I thought your chambers in need of a good airing, dear brother. You would not have me neglect you."

He grimaced. Not so much as a speck of dust dared lend a hint of casual livability to the room. The only objects she had let remain unhidden were the pitcher and cup on the table beside his chair. And, judging from the mug she held in her hand, that had not been for his comfort. He shut the door behind him with a sigh. "It will be weeks before I am able to find everything again. What has come over you now, woman? I asked you last time to stay clear of my personal chamber."

Her chin tilted. "But think, dear brother, and you will have your answer. I was most laboriously occupied in helping you to fend off the attentions of your former mistress when I suddenly found myself banished for home." She shrugged, her blue eyes wide with feigned innocence. "I but looked about for some way to make myself useful."

"God's blood, Beth. Do you mean you hold that against me? I hadn't seen Warwicke for years."

She arched delicate black brows. "I do mean just that."

He sat down on the edge of the bed, shaking his head. "I do suppose I could have been more considerate of your feelings, but I didn't think you'd mind. After all, you had done nothing but complain about going up to the castle with me, as it was." He lifted an apologetic hand. "I can but say I am most sorry for having offended you."

Feeling that she had made him suffer quite enough, Elizabeth grinned. Stephen was really very good to her, and she did believe he had thought she would be happy to be gone from the castle. He could have no idea that she had become so easily enamored with his friend. She inclined her head. "You are forgiven. And if you like, I will go through your chests and throw everything about as it was before."

He chuckled wryly. "Nay, help me no more. I knew where things were then. You could not put them back where they belong, did you try."

She rose and poured him a cup of wine, then held it forth as a peace offering.

Stephen took the cup.

It was a long moment before Elizabeth got around to the next order of business. But get around to it she did. "Did you enjoy your evening?"

He grinned. "Aye, that I did."

"And Lord Warwicke? He enjoyed the evening, as well?"

Stephen frowned. "I suppose. We caught up on many years. I had not seen him since we were both boys of fourteen."

Ah, she thought. That might explain why Stephen had failed to mention the other man. "And has he changed a great deal from when you were younger? You recognized him readily enough, after so long a time. And he you."

"You are right. I did recognize him, but as I think on it, it is not really so very surprising. Even though he is a man now, rather than a boy, his eyes are the same. One doesn't forget those walnut-brown eyes so easily, they are most uncommon. And we were rather close as fosterlings. Both of us trained with the earl of Norwich, and shared a room for the year Raynor was there. He left upon his father's death, when he was but fourteen."

"He has been a baron since the age of fourteen. 'Tis a great responsibility," she remarked thoughtfully.

Stephen cast her an assessing glance before he went on. "What you say is true. But what have you, Beth? What concern is it of yours?"

She looked toward the fire, hardly feeling its heat on her already flaming cheeks. "I am but curious because you never mentioned him before now. Please go on. Tell me all you know of him."

Stephen's expression told her that he was not wholly content with her answer, but he did continue. "He spoke little of his family. I do believe that he loved his father, but I felt there was some bad blood between them. Of his mother I know nothing. He seemed reluctant to mention her at all. I do know that she died some few years after Raynor inherited."

'Tis most odd, Elizabeth thought as he took a sip of his wine. With a pang, she recalled the deaths of her own parents by plague. She and her brothers often spoke of them, even now. They had been a close-knit family. It had been hard to lose them both so quickly, but she felt her father would not have been happy without his beloved wife.

Perhaps Lord Warwicke was one who did not wish to share his personal life with others. That he was something of a mystery simply made him all the more interesting to Elizabeth. He only needed the right person to confide in. Not that Elizabeth would allow herself to think that she could be that someone. She refused to go that far in her imaginings.

"What is he like now?" she queried softly. "Is he noble and kind and true?"

Stephen watched her intently. "We spoke of general matters, Beth. Many years have passed since we knew each other well but if he is anything like he was as a boy, Raynor is a decent sort. Neither saint nor devil, just a man. He was more open as a boy, but then, life has a way of changing people, does it not?" Stephen stopped, obviously tired of pretending he didn't see her too-avid interest. "Have you taken a fancy to Raynor?" He laughed. "That's a tangle, when you could have half the men in England, did you but want them. You don't even know the man, in fact barely spoke to him."

"I..." She scowled, her delicate brows meeting over her slender nose. Then she shrugged, deciding to just come out with the truth. There was no sense in prevaricating with Stephen, he knew her too well. "He is quite fascinating, don't you think?"

"Well, I couldn't really comment from a woman's point of view, but I'll be content that you might think so. But hear me, Beth, you'd best set your sights elsewhere. From what he said tonight, I got the impression that Raynor is in no hurry to wed. He told me his personal life has been more than complicated of late. Raynor has a bastard child by a noblewoman, though that is a tragic story in itself."

He went on to tell her of why Raynor was at court and what he had told Stephen about his child, Willow. He concluded by saying, "Though I do like him, you will stay clear of Warwicke, Beth. It would not be right for you to set your sights upon him. Though he meant to wed the child's mother, the fact is, he did not."

Elizabeth listened to all this with complete fascination. Many men tarried with serving women as a matter of course, but to get a gentle woman with child and then not marry her? That was another matter.

Yet Stephen had said circumstances had kept them from marrying. And hadn't Lord Warwicke come to court to claim the child? Wasn't that the act of a truly honorable man?

Far from discouraging her, Stephen's remarks made her even more determined to know Raynor better. She had thought, simply by looking at him, that he was not a man to live by the rules of others. His long hair, his arrogant walk, the cool indifference in his eyes, set Lord Warwicke apart on first sight.

She smiled at her brother with not-inconsiderable charm. "I want you to invite him here to sup."

Stephen stared at her. "I have already done so. But had I known then what I do now, I would not have. As I said, you must set your sights elsewhere, Elizabeth. Mayhap I will send a note and cancel."

Sapphire eyes widened in horror. "You will not! When is he to come?"

Looking as if the reply were being forced from him, Stephen said, "On the morrow."

"On the morrow!" Elizabeth rose in flurry of velvet skirts. "How could you give me so little time to prepare?"

His expression relaxed in relief. "I will simply go to him and explain that he can't . . ."

She appeared not to hear him. "You must excuse me while I go speak with Olwyn. We will need every moment to prepare a proper meal. We will need fresh pastries and bread. And I shall certainly call in the butcher to kill a pig in the morning. We cannot feed Lord Warwicke salted pork."

She passed through the doorway with a gentle sway of her slender hips, leaving Stephen staring after her. He knew he should be concerned for his sister, but the only sympathy he felt within him was directed toward Raynor Warwicke. Stephen would himself be here to see to Elizabeth's well-being.

Raynor had no one to protect him from Elizabeth.

Besides Raynor had said he was returning to Warwicke on the day after the morrow. How much trouble could Elizabeth get herself into in one day?

The next afternoon found Elizabeth and Olwyn standing in Elizabeth's bedchamber, looking at the array of gowns they had laid out on the high, wide bed.

"I think the red," Olwyn said at last, tucking a stray lock of streaky blonde hair into her kerchief. Her gray eyes studied the scarlet cotehardie, with its embroidery of gold.

"Aye." Elizabeth nodded. "It is my favorite, but I just wondered if the blue . . . or the saffron . . ." She turned to run her gaze over the nearest of the three trunks that stood open, their colorful contents spilling over the sides. "I did wear the other red yesterday."

Tilting her head to one side, Olwyn frowned. "Nay, the red will do very nicely. Men never remember what you wore the previous day. Only that you looked well."

Elizabeth grinned. Red was her favorite color. "Then that's that. And I think I'll wear the new gold underdress."

Olwyn eyed her mistress with surprise, then uncertainty. "But, Elizabeth, I thought you were going to have me loosen it. You told me yourself that it was too tight for common decency." The slender blond woman went to the chest beneath the unshuttered window and took out a tunic of fine black samite. "I had thought you might want this one."

Elizabeth blushed, but tried to hide it as she picked up and began to fold the blue cotehardie. "I have rethought the matter. 'Tis not so very tight."

She would not have Olwyn know why she had changed her mind about the gown. The older woman seemed to think she must still look after Elizabeth as closely as when she had first come to them. But she was no longer thirteen, and would not be treated as such. Elizabeth hoped that if she made an attempt to be even slightly alluring, Lord Warwicke might find it harder to ignore her this night.

For the most part, her beauty meant little to her. It was not something she had earned or achieved by her own hand. It was something God had seen fit to gift her with, and until yesterday she accepted it as such.

But for this once she found herself thinking of her attributes in a different way. She would make Lord Warwicke take notice of her. He was a man, after all, and if all Stephen had said was true, Raynor was not completely immune to the fairer sex. Why couldn't he at least pause long enough to notice that Elizabeth was a woman? She didn't think that was so very much to ask.

When Olwyn continued to watch her with speculation, Elizabeth could not control the further rush of color in her creamy cheeks.

"What are you about, Elizabeth?"

Elizabeth gave up trying to dissemble. Olwyn knew her better than anyone, and there was no use trying to hide anything from her.

She put the blue gown back on the bed and turned to smooth back the heavy amber velvet bed hangings with a sigh. "I do not know. I can't explain what has come over me. I just saw this man for the first time yesterday, and I can't stop thinking about him. And the worst part of it is that he barely seemed to notice me." She dismissed that one moment of awareness, for it could have been nothing so much as wishful thinking on her part.

"Ah, Beth..." Olwyn put her hands to her slender hips as she sank down on the edge of the one chair in the room. "I should have known it would be this way. All these years the men have been after you like hounds after a bitch, and you don't even look at them. And now one comes along who ignores you, and you lose your foolish head."

The sound of booted feet on the stairs saved Elizabeth from making a reply. The footsteps came across the solar and halted outside her bedchamber. There was a scratching at the door. "Beth."

"Come," Elizabeth called out, recognizing her brother's voice.

Stephen entered, and she looked at him with curiosity, as he was dressed for traveling, in a dark woolen cloak that was held together at the shoulder by a heavy silver brooch that bore the Clayburn emblem of a griffin rampant. "You are going somewhere?" she asked.

He seemed less than eager to speak. "Yes," came the reply.

"You must needs hurry, as Warwicke will be here within hours."

"Well, you see, that is going to be a problem." Stephen looked at the floor. Then he raised his eyes and shrugged. "I am away to deliver a message for the king."

Elizabeth knew a growing unease. "How long will you be gone?"

"Several hours."

Disappointment flooded her. "Several hours. Stephen, how could you? You know how I have been planning this. Everything is in readiness."

"It cannot be helped. We will simply ask Lord Warwicke to come at some other time."

"When?"

He hesitated and Elizabeth frowned. "When, brother mine?"

"I know not. Raynor must return to his estates on the morrow." He wouldn't look at Elizabeth. Obviously he had hoped to avoid having to tell her they were leaving so soon.

She placed her hands on her hips, glaring her anger. "Do you mean that this is it? I shall not see him again?"

Stephen smiled encouragingly. "Mayhap he will come to London again in the future."

"You know he will not." She couldn't seem to breathe past the unexplainable ache in her chest. It was as if something dear to her had died aborning. "All these years you have not seen him because Warwicke only chose to come to court when he was summoned. What chance is there that he will return before another ten years has come and gone? I shall be an old woman."

He eyed her sternly. "Now, Beth, don't carry on so. I told you that Warwicke is not for you. I but live up to my responsibilities in protecting you. Besides, I have no choice in whether I stay or go. The king does require me to see to my duty."

She subsided then. What Stephen said was true. He must needs fulfill his duty to the crown. But she had wanted so badly to see Warwicke again. Not that she was under any illusions about what would happen between them. Elizabeth had hoped for no more than to make him take note of her as a desirable woman, nothing else. Stephen really had no need to warn her away again.

It seemed particularly unfair that Raynor could not come simply because Stephen would be late.

Then an idea came to her. She looked at her brother with an expression of cool reason. "Why can Warwicke not come here anyway? He has been invited. It would be rude to ask him to stay away now."

But Stephen began to shake his head before she had even finished. "Nay, Beth, 'twould not serve. The man cannot come here and spend the evening with you unchaperoned."

She faced him squarely. "It would not be the whole evening. I could simply entertain Lord Warwicke until your return. By your own mouth, he is friend to you. Can you not trust me to spend a few short hours in his presence?"

He scowled, his dark brows meeting over his straight nose. " 'Tis not so simple, madame, as well you know. I am not blind. You have an interest in him that goes beyond any I've seen you show before. You as much as admitted it last eve."

"But, Stephen—" She stamped her foot. "I am not a child to be ordered about. I am a woman full grown, with my own funds to support me. I have no need to be commanded by you."

He stopped her with a raised hand. "What you say is true." He looked into her eyes, and when he spoke again, his tone was reasoning. "But, Beth, I am your brother. In all conscience, I must not allow you to do anything that would be of harm to you. Please, I say again, the answer can only be nay. It is for your own good. You cannot be alone with him." He paused for a long moment, obviously torn. She knew it was very difficult for her brother to deny her anything. Finally he shrugged. "There is one way, and one way only."

"Yes?" she answered eagerly.

"We will ask Raynor to come at a later time. That way there can be no hint of impropriety. I'll write a note to explain the matter to him."

Elizabeth rushed to her chest and removed a piece of parchment and a quill, which she handed to her brother. Quickly Stephen scratched out his message. "You will send this around to him at Windsor, please." He held the missive toward his sister.

Elizabeth took the parchment between two fingers. She gave Stephen a sweet smile. "Thank you, brother."

"I will see you ere long." Stephen told her, with obvious relief at having the matter settled to both their benefits. "And now, I must be off. I go with two of the king's own guard, and they wait for me in the lane outside."

He put his hands on her shoulders and kissed her cheek, then turned and dashed from the house.

When he had gone, Elizabeth stood there, the note to Raynor Warwicke in her hand. This was not what she had hoped for. If Warwicke was leaving in the morning, he would as like not stay for long now. Elizabeth sighed, her gaze lingering on the sheet of parchment. As she looked at it, she began to experience thoughts of mutiny. Why should she do as Stephen told her? He was only her brother, not her master.

What harm would it do for Warwicke to spend an hour or two in her sole company?

He was a knight and a nobleman. Surely there could be no harm in serving him a meal and speaking with him. She looked toward her companion, who had said nothing during her conversation with her brother. Olwyn was watching her with a frown, as if she knew what Elizabeth was thinking and liked it not.

Elizabeth tilted her chin. "You will be close by."

"Nay," she answered. "As your brother said, it will not serve." Olwyn held out her hand. "I shall have that sent around to Lord Warwicke for you."

Putting the missive behind her back, Elizabeth smiled. "I think not," she said.

They argued for some time. But in the end, the message did not go out, though Olwyn never stopped frowning and muttering dire utterances about the consequences of behaving foolishly.

Chapter Three

Raynor rode his charger through the narrow tracks that passed for streets just as the sun was beginning to set. Its early-spring light gilded the castle walls above and behind him, as if to give testament to King Edward's belief that Windsor was somehow special. Having been born there, the king had a deep fondness for his home, and believed that King Arthur of old had once housed his knights of the Round Table on this very site. Looking back over his shoulder, Raynor studied the castle with appraising eyes. Four massive stone towers ran the length of the immense wall at equal intervals where it rested on the hill behind him. Nothing was visible of the magnificent round tower, begun by Henry II and finished by Edward, save the king's flag, which fluttered golden in the gentle breeze.

Edward's Windsor was awe-inspiring.

Raynor would certainly give him that. But it seemed as if a great deal had been spent on the castle to beautify it, as well as add to its strength. To Raynor's way of thinking, England had already been drained dry by the war in France. There had been no money for the luxuries apparent in the spacious and well-appointed rooms of the round tower.

At least with King John now ransomed, Edward would have a source of income besides the backs of his own subjects. Knowing his opinion of the sovereign was not held by most of his fellow noblemen didn't change Raynor's thinking. Necessities came before comforts. It was one of the things Raynor had learned watching his father squander everything he had for his mother's whims.

Lips tight, Raynor gripped the reins more securely in his hands and turned his thoughts to the present. Thinking of his father always brought on feelings of resentment and anger. But those emotions were also mixed with love and pity. If only Robert Warwicke had not been so weak. He shook his head to clear it. It would be best to center his mind on the coming meal with Stephen Clayburn and his sister.

Raynor didn't know why he had accepted the invitation to sup. Mayhap because seeing Stephen again had reminded him of what he was like at fourteen. Then it had seemed as if he had any number of bright possibilities before him. On being fostered to the earl of Norwich, he had suddenly discovered that there were men who lived by the rules set out in tales of chivalry. Raynor had believed that he, too, might become one of those men. He might someday meet some fair maiden who would return his love with all faith and honor. But his father's death had called him home to his mother and her daily attempts to control his every thought or action. He was determined to never put himself in the position of having to battle a woman for autonomy again.

As he rode into the heart of the village, Raynor slowed his mount with a pull on the reins. He studied his route, carefully following the directions Stephen had laid out for him.

The town was much like the village at home in Warwicke, only larger. Narrow daub-and-wattle houses sat at odd angles on irregular-size lots. On these bits of property, tenants kept their animals, which were mostly chickens, pigs and sheep. But there was an occasional cow, expensive to keep but producing a great deal of valuable manure. Plump children played in the doorways, barely glancing up at the passing knight. Living in Windsor, they saw many finer-dressed folk than Raynor, in his service-able brown tunic, russet cotehardie and dark hose.

Urging his charger around the last turn through the maze of hard-packed dirt tracks, Raynor looked up to see a two-story whitewashed house that stood out among the others because of its size and the cleanliness of its yard. There were no animals roaming about, and no pile of ma-nure graced the small strip of grass in front of the low, narrow door that stood open to admit the last of the sun-light.

Now that he was here, he knew a moment's hesitation. Mayhap it was a mistake to come. He didn't know Ste-phen anymore. He raked the heavy hair back from his forehead as he told himself that neither did Stephen know him. He had treated Raynor with warmth yesterday be-cause he remembered the boy. It wasn't likely that he would be so forthcoming, did he know the man.

And if that wasn't enough, there was one other reason he should turn and go back to the castle. Stephen's sister, Elizabeth. Though Raynor had barely allowed himself to even think of her, he did recall that one moment when he had looked at her with startling clarity.

Elizabeth Clayburn was most certainly the kind of woman he had learned to avoid—young, beautiful, and sure of her female power.

As he approached the structure, his gaze ran over the whitewashed walls as if, did he but look hard enough, he would be able to see inside. In that house, Elizabeth would be in her own element, where she was most comfortable and self-assured. Not that Raynor felt she was any real threat to him. He just preferred to avoid such as her. He knew her kind, wanting everything from a man, his life, his fortune, his heart, but unwilling to give anything of themselves in return.

Most assuredly it would have been wiser to decline this invitation. And he was still free to turn around and go. What matter if he offended folk he was not likely to see again?

But the moment to depart was taken from him. As Raynor came to a halt before the house, an older man in worn but clean and neatly patched clothing scuttled out to meet him. He looked up at the knight with a polite nod of his gray head. "Good day, my lord."

Raynor nodded in return. "I am seeking Stephen Clayburn."

"Aye, you have come to the right house. I can take your horse out back to the shed, my lord."

Dismounting and handing him the reins, Raynor said, "My thanks," and moved to enter the dwelling. Passing through the door, he had to stoop, but he stood to his full height once inside.

The living chamber was wide and long, with a fireplace in the center along the north wall. A trestle table was set up at one end, ready to receive the meal, but there was no one about. The rushes underfoot gave off the sweet scent of herbs as he took a few hesitant steps inside, wondering if he should call out.

Just then two women entered from the back of the chamber, one bearing a jug, the other a tray with cheese and meat. The older woman with the tray, obviously a servant, judging by her coarse clothing, moved to place her burden upon the trestle table.

The younger of the two women came forward, shifting the heavy jug she carried. "My lord Warwicke," she said, greeting him with deference. Her dress was of better quality than the other's, and he wondered who she could be. Her blue eyes smiled in her pretty face as she looked up at him. "I am Lady Elizabeth's companion, Olwyn. You are expected above. Will you please come with me."

She turned, and Raynor moved to follow her up a narrow set of stairs.

He took note of the golden hair that fell from her kerchief, and her trim waist and hips. Now here was the type of woman Raynor might be inclined to dally with. She would provide a release for his body and expect no commitment in return. Not that Raynor would force her. In his twenty-seven years, he'd had no need of that.

But the moment he stepped through the door of the solar, all thoughts of the blond woman fled his mind.

Elizabeth Clayburn came forward to great him, her cherry lips turned upward in a smile of welcome. "Lord Warwicke." When she spoke his name, a chill of awareness ran down his spine. Her eyes were the color of deepest sapphire and fringed with thick black lashes. But the way she looked at him was what gave him pause. The expression in her gaze was one of happiness and barely repressed excitement, and from the way she focused her whole attention upon him, Raynor could only feel that he was the cause of her pleasure. Unaccountably he felt himself basking in the glow, like a lynx soaking up the sun. Not once in the conscious years of his memory could he recall anyone looking at him with such uncomplicated approval. He marveled as the color in her cheeks went from palest cream to dusky rose. She looked down, and the sheer golden veil she wore over her tumbled mass of black curls fluttered forward to hide the delicate flush.

"Lady Elizabeth." He swallowed, managing to sound almost normal, though he did not know how. Fighting off an urge to wipe his sweaty palm against his tunic like some unschooled lad, Raynor briefly clasped her slender hand in his. Her fingers were smooth and cool, but she drew them back quickly to press her hand against her bosom.

She seemed to have some difficulty communicating herself, for she started, stopped, and began again. "My lord...I... You are most welcome."

"My thanks," he replied. He didn't know what had come over him. Raynor was well accustomed to women, had believed himself long over the nervousness that now assailed him. He could only tell himself that it was slightly unnerving to be greeted with such enthusiasm. Elizabeth Clayburn could not know what she was about. Though he hoped that she did not meet her other male visitors with such warmth. Not all men had learned self-discipline, as Raynor had. They might take her obvious pleasure in a way it was not meant.

For, judging by the innocence in her eyes, it was clear she had no idea of her effect on him.

Unaccountably he felt a moment's worry for her. But he quickly told himself not to be ridiculous. Stephen was her brother, and thus her rightful protector, not Raynor.

As Elizabeth turned to tell her woman to place the pitcher upon the table, he allowed his eyes to study her as he had not the day before. She wore a cotehardie of scarlet that was slashed wide at the sides to show off a gold velvet tunic that caressed the sweetly swelling curves of her breasts and hips. He felt a tightening in his loins and envied the fragile fabric its contact with her flesh.

Whatever had he been thinking yesterday, when he met this woman, not to notice how truly lovely she was? He knew he had been nervous about his coming audience with the king, but could any man worthy of the title have seen Elizabeth Clayburn and failed to take note of her uncommon beauty?

Thank God Stephen would be present this eve. The last thing Raynor needed was to be alone with this siren. Elizabeth was enough woman to give rise to the name.

Raking a hand through his hair, he forced his gaze away. Not in years had Raynor reacted to any woman this way. Gladly would he see the end of this visit.

He looked about the solar, saw the table, with its two chairs, set up as if for a meal. He took note of the warmth of the fire and the pillows that were piled on the carpet before it. He admired the rich tapestry that hung upon the outside wall, with its rich colors and fine detail. There were two doors besides the one through which he had entered. They must lead to sleeping chambers.

It was an appealing scene. But something appeared to be missing. Frowning, Raynor rubbed the side of his head as he glanced about, his gaze going back to the two chairs at either side of the table. Two chairs.

Stephen!

He cleared his throat as he turned to Elizabeth. The servant named Olwyn paused in the act of leaving and faced him. "Lady Elizabeth?" he asked.

She didn't look at him as she moved forward to pour a cup of wine. And if he wasn't seeing things, her hands were shaking. "Yes, my lord Warwicke?" she said.

Raynor frowned, surprised that she seemed as unsettled as he.

He reached out to take the cup from her, willing her to look at him. But she didn't. "Where is Stephen?" he asked bluntly.

She did glance up at him then, but only for a moment. With a bright smile, she waved a hand airily. "Oh, my brother. He was called away most unexpectedly, but he shall be returning ere long."

Raynor knew a prickling of unease. Stephen had told him that he and Elizabeth lived alone here, with only Elizabeth's companion and their servants. It seemed unlikely that Clayburn would want Raynor to be alone here with his beautiful sister. "He knows I am come in his absence?"

"Of a surety." Finally she looked at him, those bottomless sapphire eyes ingenuously wide. "Stephen felt so badly about having to go. You see—" she spread her hands "—he has his duty to the king. But he had no wish to appear rude, and thus asked me to attend you until his arrival. He felt it would be wrong to call off the meal, when he will not be so very long." She gave a nervous laugh as she moved to stand before the fire, her slender body bathed in its warm light. "Stephen mentioned that you were returning to Warwicke on the morrow and said he would not miss this chance to see you before you go. My brother is ever like this. His friends have always been of great importance to him. Is that not so, Olwyn?" Elizabeth looked to her companion.

The other woman cleared her throat, her gaze fixed on her mistress's face. "Oh, aye, my lord Warwicke. Sir Stephen spoke exactly thus." With that, she swung around and left the room.

Elizabeth turned back to him with another one of those sweet smiles. "You see. All is well."

Raynor watched her, mesmerized by the strand of hair that had fallen over her shoulder to end in a curl on her right breast. He tried to think clearly. Certainly Stephen had set great store in his friendships as boy. It could be so now. Mayhap Stephen did trust him to be alone with his sister.

Dragging his wayward gaze from that gently rounded breast, Raynor determined to be worthy of that trust.

Elizabeth Clayburn was trouble. More lovely and compelling than any woman he had ever met.

There was no way around the matter though. Raynor must fight this strange attraction. He could not, would not, become involved with her, or any other woman who would expect more than he was willing to give.

It was this that helped Raynor to come to his senses. He could eat this meal with her and go on his way, for her good, as well as his.

He turned to her then, his eyes refusing to see the lovely vision of her. With silent precision, he raised a wall between himself and the golden glow of her warmth. She was a woman, nothing more, nothing less.

Elizabeth felt the change in him immediately. It wasn't that he said or did anything that let her know, it was simply that he turned to stone. One moment his eyes were alive on her, the next there was nothing.

Confusion made her hesitate as she looked up at him, the words she had been going to say gone from her mind.

When Raynor first arrived, she hadn't been able to contain her happiness at seeing him again. It was just as before, that same crazed rush of awareness that made her blood sing and her heart pound. She'd been so afraid that she had imagined the way she felt when she looked at him.

And for a few moments, Raynor had seemed different, more open than the previous day. He'd looked at her as if seeing her for the very first time, and he hadn't seemed displeased.

Rot, but she couldn't think of what she might have said or done to make him change.

She was saved from having to say anything when the door opened to admit Olwyn carrying a heavily laden tray. With shaky legs, Elizabeth moved to the table as Olwyn set the tray down. "Thank you, Olwyn."

As the other woman left, Elizabeth realized that she could not allow Raynor to see that he had upset her. Obviously she was not to his liking. The best she could do now was to get through the evening without making a complete fool of herself. Keeping her voice and manner carefully polite, Elizabeth turned to Stephen. "We can begin now, if you like."

The first part of the meal passed in a blur as Elizabeth served them both, then used her eating knife to toy with her food. She barely tasted the bites of roast pork, eels and assorted pastries that she did take, though they had been painstakingly and well prepared.

But as the moments stretched onward, Elizabeth began to grow angry with herself. Whatever Lord Warwicke's annoyance might be, this silence was fair driving her mad. She would stand no more of it. She was a Clayburn, daughter of a proud and noble line. No man could be allowed to render her so self-conscious.

Elizabeth met his gaze directly as she lifted the pitcher from the table between them. "Would you care for more wine, my lord?"

He looked down at his plate, then nodded, passing her his cup. "My thanks, Lady Clayburn. It is the best I've tasted in some time. It is warm in here, and the wine is refreshing."

As she filled the vessel, Elizabeth thought about what he had said. The room seemed a trifle cool to her, rather than warm. March's recent arrival had brought no rise in temperatures. They had kept the window open most of the day to catch the light as they readied the room for the evening, and along with it the cold. Just before Raynor arrived, she'd had Albert light a fire in the hearth to take the chill from the room.

Feeling Raynor's gaze upon her, she looked up at him and paused. The intensity in his dark eyes rocked her. She felt she was being studied with appreciation, yes, but also with doubt. Her tunic suddenly felt too tight across her breasts, and she shifted restlessly on her cushioned chair.

He was right, the room was quite warm. Her tongue came out to lick at the perspiration that beaded on her upper lip, and his gaze followed. He swallowed, taking a ragged breath as he closed his eyes, releasing Elizabeth from their spell.

She turned away, trying to still her beating heart even as she felt a rush of elation. So he was not completely indifferent to her as he pretended.

That left the question, why was he making the pretense?

Elizabeth didn't know, but she was through with trying to fathom the answer. The anger that had been directed toward herself a few minutes before now shifted to him. If Raynor Warwicke wanted to keep to himself, that was fine with her, or so she told herself. And she was determined for him to see that it didn't matter. She would go on with the meal as if he were any other guest, then see him on his way.

But there was a nagging awareness in her that told Elizabeth it would not be so easy as she thought. Why, he had only to look at her and she melted like butter in sunshine.

Elizabeth picked up her own cup and took a long drink of the wine. He was right, it was cool to the tongue, even as it trickled a liquid courage into her veins. If need be, she could surely drink enough wine to get her through the hours in his presence. She had heard it could be of help. She poured herself another cup and drained it, as well, before deigning to speak to Raynor again.

Taking a deep breath, she began politely. "My brother tells me you are leaving tomorrow for Warwicke Castle."

He gave her one of those long, enigmatic looks. "Yes." Then he turned back to his plate.

Elizabeth took another sip of her wine. She was growing quite relaxed, her arms and legs pleasantly heavy. It was beginning to matter less and less that Raynor was rude and distant. In fact, she was feeling almost amused by the whole situation. What Raynor needed was to allow himself to loosen up just a bit. He might benefit from a few glasses of wine himself.

Arching a fine black brow, she lifted the pitcher in offering. "Would you care for more?"

He barely nodded, handing her the cup. Elizabeth filled it for him.

"My thanks," he told her, taking a long pull before setting it down next to his dish.

At least he was being polite now, she thought, settling back in her chair, her own cup in her hand. She sipped at the wine, no longer caring to make the pretense of eating.

He glanced over at her, frowning as if she had done something to irritate him in some way. "You aren't eating."

"Nay," she replied languidly. Her own gaze went to his plate, and she saw that for all his studied concentration, Raynor had managed to eat very little of his own dinner. She laughed huskily. "My lord Warwicke, it appears you are not hungry, either."

With an angry grunt, he pushed the dish aside. "I am not."

She drained her cup, then watched as Raynor did the same, her eyes never leaving his. This time it was he who leaned forward to refill the vessels, without speaking.

He took another drink of his own wine, his gaze fixing on the tapestry behind her. His lean profile was hard, but undeniably handsome in the glow of the fire, leaving her with a desire to run her hand over the strongly etched jaw. Despite his best efforts, there was an air of loneliness about him that even his confidence and self-possession could not disguise. From somewhere inside her came the thought that this strong man needed someone to share the weight of his troubles. And even though it was obvious that that someone was not her, she couldn't help wishing he had given her a chance to at least know him better.

Suddenly Elizabeth found herself speaking. It was as if she couldn't halt her wayward tongue. "You would not have come here tonight, knowing Stephen was gone?"

He turned to her, his brows knit in surprise at her frankness. He took a long pull of his wine before answering. "Nay, I would not have come."

Even though she had known the answer, Elizabeth felt an unbidden twinge of chagrin. She couldn't keep herself from replying with the first thing that popped into her mind. "I am really not so very wicked."

His grimace belied his polite answer. "Of that I am most certain, Lady Elizabeth."

She laughed. The words were so blatantly at odds with his expression. "Methinks you do not answer truthfully, my lord. What do you hold against me?" She raised her arms wide, then lowered them, feeling recklessly daring for talking so openly. "Am I not pleasing to you? Do I bring to mind some long-despised woman from your past?"

His gaze moved over her with slow deliberation, his eyes dark with some undefined emotion that made her pulse quicken. His voice was husky as he spoke. "You are most pleasing to me, Elizabeth Clayburn. And you remind me of no one I have known in my entire life. In fact, I find you too pleasing."

Elizabeth knew a moment's elation before he went on, his tone grown cool.

"But therein lies my problem. You are a noblewoman, and thus can be nothing to me. I want no complication in my life such as you would bring. I have troubles enough to keep me till the end of my days. Why would I willingly bring more upon myself? I know your type. You gently bred damsels think nothing of leading a man a merry chase until he is caught, then you show your true colors by taking all he can give you and more. Don't try to deny it." He raised a hand when she opened her mouth to argue. Raynor's gaze caught Elizabeth's, and would not let go. "When I take a woman, it is of necessity, a thing of the body, no more no less." He laughed harshly at her shocked gasp, then released her gaze and paused to fill his cup before draining it.

As if his anger were too much to contain, Raynor pushed back his chair and went to stand before the fire, unmindful of the cushions he scattered in his wake. "No woman will own me." He hit the wall above the hearth with a white-knuckled fist. Then he took a deep breath, turning back to her.

He came to stand beside the table, his face dark and unreadable with the fire low and behind him.

Elizabeth could only sit there, her wine-fuddled mind trying to make sense of what he had told her. "Obviously someone has betrayed you in some way, my lord Warwicke. But you cannot blame all noblewomen for the actions of one."

He didn't even try to answer her, simply shook his head. "You know naught of what you speak. I don't even know why I am telling you of this. Perhaps I have had too much wine, or mayhap I needed for you to understand that, though I find you more than comely to look upon, I cannot allow myself to see you as anything more than that, a well-favored thing."

That did not set well with Elizabeth. Obviously Raynor was not the man for her, if he felt thus. She was a woman who needed to be appreciated for all of herself, not just her face and form. Groggily she peered up at him. "I can see that we have completely opposite views on this most important matter," she told him, as soberly as she could, considering the way her head was swimming. "I need someone who will love me as my father did my mother, with his whole heart and mind. Aye, they fought, but then Father would pick her up and take her up into the tower. They would be gone for hours at times, but when they came back they would be smiling. Mother wasn't like the women you have known. She was my father's friend and helpmate. They discussed their problems and took care of each other. My oldest brother, Henry, is married, and he has found the same happiness with his wife Aileen, though they had their problems in the beginning. You are most wise to keep your distance from me, my lord Warwicke. What you are willing to give would not be enough for me. I am no well-favored thing.''

Even though Raynor knew she was simply reacting to what he had said to her, the words stung. Flung back at him that way, the statement sounded worse than he'd thought. But Raynor had no intention of retracting it.

He looked at Elizabeth and saw that her head had tipped forward and her eyes were closed. He looked more closely. The vixen was asleep. Surprise wiped his self-deprecating thoughts from his mind.

In his lifetime many things had happened in the presence of a beautiful woman. But rarely had one fallen asleep with so little warning, and then only after he had thoroughly made love to her.

Raynor looked about the room. First he would move her to the rug before the fire, and then he would be on his way. Enough had been said between them, far more than Raynor had ever told anyone or ever meant to.

He went to her chair and pulled it away from the table, then bent and scooped her up into his arms. Though she was tall, Elizabeth was delicately formed, and her weight was no strain for his hardened muscles.

When he reached the carpet, he used his foot to rearrange the cushions he had scattered about, then went down on one knee to lower her onto them. She stirred in his arms, and he looked down. The heavy fringe of her lashes lifted, and she gazed up at him, the expression in her eyes flirtatious and all woman. ''My lord Warwicke, am I to believe you have overcome your scruples concerning young noblewomen?'' She giggled, putting her hand over her mouth.

But not before Raynor had caught the heavy scent of wine on her breath. Of course, how could he have been so incredibly stupid? She'd gotten drunk before his very eyes, and he hadn't even noticed. Now that he thought back, Elizabeth had drunk a fair amount, but not nearly as much as he. Raynor wanted to absolve himself for not stopping her, on the grounds that he had been too occupied at first with his need to keep his distance, and then with his efforts to convince her he was not right for her, but it wouldn't suffice. Mayhap his lack of perception had partly to do with his having consumed a fair amount of the strong liquid, also. Raynor was feeling more than a little muddled himself.

The firelight was rosy on the delicate plains of her face as she turned toward the flames and began to speak. At first he was confused, but then he began to understand that she was continuing their conversation of a few minutes before. "I love my brothers dearly. All three of them are good, strong, but fair men, even Peter, who is only sixteen."

She cast a glance toward Raynor, her gaze holding his over the few inches that separated them. "I could only give my heart to one such as they." She gave a self-derisive laugh, and lifted her hand, only to have it fall back into her lap. "But for reasons I don't understand, it is you who draws me like a bee to a buttercup. There is something I would ask of you. And please know, if you choose to comply with my request, I will not take this a sign that you are interested in me." Her lashes fluttered. "You see, I have never been kissed, have not wanted anyone to do so, that is until yesterday, when I saw you." She looked up at him beseechingly. "I was wondering if you would kiss me just once, before you go. We will never see each other again, and so it seems a little thing to ask."

For a long time, Raynor just knelt there, looking into her eyes. What she had requested was completely beyond the realm of sanity, wasn't it? After all, he had already acknowledged, if only to himself, that Elizabeth was the most beautiful and desirable woman he had ever met. He would be stepping beyond the boundary he had set for himself by kissing her. Such an act might just release some of the passion she awakened in him.

But as he looked down at her, at the ingenuous hope in her blue eyes, he knew he could not hurt her by refusing. She seemed so utterly vulnerable at this moment, with her inhibitions stripped away by too much wine. What harm could there be in giving her one chaste kiss? He doubted that Elizabeth would even remember on the morrow.

Slowly, and with a tenderness that surprised even him, Raynor placed his lips on hers. Elizabeth's mouth was soft and warm, and her skin smelled sweetly of rose petals. Her softly rounded breasts pressed close to him as she opened herself to his embrace. There was not the least bit of resistance in her, only soft, giving female. Raynor felt the hot cramp of desire, there in his gut, threatening to burst free and consume him. But he held it at bay. He drew away from her with infinite care, fearing that if he moved too quickly he would lose control.

She opened her eyes and looked at him, sighing with contentment. "I shall never forget."

He raised a hand to brush a silken curl from her brow. His voice was softer than a whisper as he answered, "Neither shall I, Elizabeth Clayburn." And he knew it was true. Raynor didn't understand what had happened here between them, but he knew she had awakened tender feelings he'd thought long dead.

And that was exactly why he must go from here and never look back. Raynor had no place for such weakness in his life. He had to stay strong and in control of his own destiny. Willow, and many others, depended upon him.

He moved to lay her back.

Her eyes opened, and she looked at him with a drowsy frown. "Nay, my lord, hold me yet a while. It does feel good to be in your arms, and this is all I shall have of you."

His reply was unexpectedly regretful. "But I must go."

Her gaze cleared then, for a moment, and her expression was filled with a sympathy so deep it startled him. "Nay, Raynor. Abide here with me for a time. You will come to no harm. I wish you nothing but good. Rest, if only for a while. It will serve you well."

She reached up to run her soft hand over his cheek, and Raynor was lost. It was as if she gave him a modicum of peace simply by reaching out to him. Never in his life had he been touched with such tenderness.

It almost seemed that Elizabeth was absorbing some of his cares into the softness of her woman's flesh. She looked up at him, her eyes soft and languid. "Kiss me again, my lord."

His arms tightened, and he lowered his dark head, one of his hands slipping down to cup the delicate curve of her bottom, unable in that moment to deny her or himself.

Stephen led the other two men around the back of the house, to the shed where he kept his horse and Elizabeth's. The animals could feed and drink while the men were having their own meal.

Their mounts had been hard-ridden, but Edward had wanted the archbishop's reply to his letter without delay. He and the other two knights had made very good time to return so quickly. Once the message was delivered to the king's chamberlain, Stephen had suggested some refreshment at his home, and they had agreed most readily. His invitation had not been solely out of hospitality. He thought that with these two present there could be no question of Elizabeth being too forward in regard to Raynor and giving him the wrong impression.

Stephen dismounted and led his charger forward into the low building, with its two stalls. He stopped short. Dancer's stall was not empty as he had expected. A strange chestnut stallion reared and pawed at the air upon seeing Stephen approach. Obviously Raynor had already arrived. Though he could not have been here for long, as Stephen's note had specified one hour hence.

Stephen backed Dancer from the shed.

He tied the white stallion outside and helped the other two men do the same to their horses. After they were fed and watered, he hurried to the house.

It was only a moment before his pounding at the door was answered. He heard the heavy bolt drawn back, and Olwyn's pale face appeared in the opening.

But it wasn't until she opened the door all the way and Stephen saw the very real apprehension on her face that he felt the first twinges of unease. What had Elizabeth done? Drat his impulse in asking the other two men to join him!

He took a step into the room, trying to appear casual. "Lord Warwicke has arrived?"

She nodded, her eyes wide. "Yes, my lord."

"I see." He smiled. "We will go up, then." He refused to even contemplate the question of how long Raynor had been here.

She looked from him to the other two knights, biting her lower lip. Olwyn stared at the brooch on his cloak. "My lord, I think it best if I talk with you in private."

The other two men looked at each other, then at Stephen. They were members of the king's personal guard, and trained to be suspicious of anything unusual. Clearly they wondered what must be kept secret from them.

Having no wish to have to explain Olwyn's bizarre behavior to the king, Stephen gave a groan of impatience and strode across the room. Distantly he heard himself explaining, "She is a shy girl, much given to whispering and such. I find her a trial at times." He had no choice now but to take them up to the solar. Stephen could hear the men muttering in commiseration as they followed him. They had to hurry to keep up as he took the stairs to the upper floor, but he didn't care. He hoped to put at least a small distance between them, so that he might arrive first.

On opening the door of the solar, he stopped dead. There on the carpet where Elizabeth usually read before the fire were Raynor of Warwicke and his sister. And they were kissing, one of Raynor's hands resting possessively on his sister's backside. They started and looked up at Stephen, then each other, in dazed but abject horror. If it hadn't been for the fact that a nightmare was unfolding before his very eyes, Stephen would have laughed.

Though he moved to block their way, he heard one of the men behind him take in a sharp breath.

Elizabeth looked toward the door at the sound, her blue eyes going wide with misery when she saw the men with her brother. Her veil had come out of her hair, and the ebony mass tumbled about her in wild disarray. As she moved to her knees, she groaned and put a hand to her head.

Obviously Warwicke fared no better, for he looked as though he were not quite sure what was happening. Stephen watched while realization dawned and Raynor's lips thinned to a grim line as he rose to his feet facing the door.

Why could Elizabeth not have heeded him? And why had Raynor acted so foolishly himself? Now that the king's men had seen the two together, Stephen had little choice as to what must be done. Though both were clothed and gave no indication that they had been otherwise, Elizabeth's reputation was in question. Raynor was already the subject of much talk concerning his illegitimate child.

Damn her, but he'd tried to warn her. But Elizabeth had ever been one to make her own decisions, and usually proved right. The problem was that this one mistake might cost her more dearly than all the others in her life combined.

But there was nothing to be done now. Stephen addressed only Raynor. "I hope you are prepared to right the wrong you have done this night."

Raynor straightened his shoulders, his eyes direct on Stephen's, but giving no hint of his feelings. "I am."

"Nay!" Elizabeth cried, tossing her hair out of her eyes. "I will not."

Raynor went on as if he hadn't heard her, the expression on his handsome face cold as frozen marble. "I will marry your sister."

But even as Elizabeth opened her mouth to argue, one of the king's guards raised his hand and said, "I will bear witness to his promise."

She looked to Stephen, but he could offer no assistance. She had brought this upon herself. If the other men had not been here, things might have been different, but not now. Word would spread throughout the court by midday.

Stephen almost reached out to comfort her when Raynor would not even meet her gaze.

Elizabeth cried, "Stephen, surely you must see that a marriage between us is impossible. Nothing happened here. We had too much wine and shared a kiss. That is all."

Raynor addressed Stephen. "I can delay only one day. I have responsibilities awaiting me at Warwicke. It must be done by tomorrow."

Stephen nodded. "It will be so."

Chapter Four

Elizabeth's black palfrey stamped and snorted, expelling a cloud of breath into the chill morning air. It jerked restively, pulling at the reins she held in her gloved hands.

The weather had turned cold overnight, as cold as Raynor Warwicke's demeanor since he'd uttered his agreement that he would wed her two day ago. It was as if spring knew its warmth would find no welcome in his eyes.

Elizabeth's gaze went to her husband, where he sat atop his stallion at the front of the wagons. He never even glanced in her direction, but made his impatience to be gone known in the stiff line of back and shoulders.

The wagons were ready, had been since dawn. All that delayed them was Elizabeth's goodbye. She turned to Stephen, who stood stony-faced, only his dark green eyes betraying his sadness. That was until she reached up to put her arms around his neck. Then he broke down, holding her close as he said, "I am sorry, Beth. There was no other way."

She hugged him tightly, comforted by his embrace. Despite wanting desperately to retain this feeling of love and safety, she answered him bravely. "I know, brother. This trouble is of my own making, and I must live with the consequences."

He held her head close against his shoulder for a long moment before letting her go. There was nothing more to be said. In the hours since he had found her and Raynor together, they had been over it all.

As she swung around to mount her horse, still without a word from her new husband, Elizabeth raised her chin. She would not let him see how his coldness hurt her. If that was what he desired, they would be like two strangers. And that did seem to be the way he wanted things. Looking at the rigid line of his wide back, it was difficult for her to believe they were even wed.

Only the hollow ache in her chest told her the truth of it. This was not some horrible dream from which she would awake to find herself in her own bed.

The marriage had been accomplished without circumstance in the king's own chapel. Elizabeth had not garbed herself finely, nor had her bridegroom. When word came that the deed was to be done, they'd gone up to Windsor as they stood.

Not since the priest had declared them wed had Raynor so much as spoken to her.

He'd left her at Stephen's side without even a backward glance. It was only after her brother took her home that Elizabeth had received word to inform her that she and her belongings were to be ready to travel by the next morning.

Which brought her to this moment of leaving her home, with little thought of hope for her future.

Studying her husband's unyielding posture ahead of her, Elizabeth couldn't help wondering yet again if Raynor believed she had deliberately trapped him into the marriage. From the cold way he had behaved, she could not but think he did. If only there were some way of making him understand that nothing could be farther from the truth. But he had given her no opportunity to explain, and seemed unlikely to.

If only he could see that the idea of marrying a total stranger was as distasteful to her as it appeared to be to him.

As soon as that thought entered her mind, she tried to ignore the voice of doubt that rose in her heart. The one that reminded her of how often she had relived the hazy memory of Raynor's lips moving against hers. Even though the image was not clear, the tightening of desire in her lower belly was more than sufficient reminder that she did not find this man completely abhorrent.

Raynor swung around, probably to see if the small entourage was at last ready to leave. His gaze barely grazed Elizabeth, and her cheeks blazed as she stiffened in reaction. Her gaze followed the path of his as he took in the two loaded wagons. His tight lips told of his disapproval.

God's eyes, she thought angrily, straightening her slender shoulders. If he was going to treat her thus, she refused to let him see that it bothered her.

Elizabeth knew that Raynor was thinking the wagons would slow his progress home, but there was nothing for it. She would not leave her household goods behind. The idea was unthinkable. As her husband, Raynor could fairly demand that she go where he told her, but he could not make her leave her belongings. Two of the four soldiers who had traveled to Windsor with Raynor and Bronic were to act as drivers. Their horses were tied securely to the back of the wagons.

Raising his hand in a farewell to Stephen, Raynor urged his mount forward as a signal to the others.

They started off.

Elizabeth sent a last glance backward, waving to Stephen and the two servants who stood in the tiny yard before the whitewashed house that she would likely never see again. Her heart ached at the realization. For a long moment, Elizabeth did battle with feelings of uncertainty and fear of facing the future with a virtual stranger.

She could feel Olwyn watching her closely from her seat in the lead wagon. She knew her companion was concerned for her. Over the past two days, the woman had tried repeatedly to speak with her mistress about what was happening, but Elizabeth had refused to be drawn out. Raising her chin, she avoided meeting Olwyn's eyes. She needed all her strength to fight back the sting of tears, like shards of glass behind her eyes.

Even at the early hour, many people came out to watch the passing entourage. The folk of Windsor were more than accustomed to the comings and goings of nobility, but never seemed to lose interest in watching them.

More than once she saw fingers pointed at the rear wagon, where Elizabeth's great bed rode in splendor. The cloth that had been draped around it to protect the massive piece of furniture from the elements did nothing to disguise it. Such a bed was a symbol of both position and wealth. Many of the nobility took their beds with them as they moved from one holding to another.

As they rode along through the village, the streets grew busier. Their progress was slow, which, judging from the frown on his face each time they halted to let a group of travelers or a loaded wagon pass, clearly irritated Raynor.

It was only as they started down the more open road outside the town itself that Raynor appeared to relax a little. After a time, he began to converse quietly with Bronic, who rode beside him.

Elizabeth didn't want to admit it, but Raynor's improved attitude caused her own stiff muscles to release some of their tension. Her buttocks, which had been aching with the tension of her body, relaxed in the saddle. She began to look around with some semblance of interest.

It was a fine, clear April day, despite the unseasonable morning chill. After the first couple of hours, their breath could no longer be seen as they went along. As the sun climbed higher in the blue sky, Elizabeth's sable-lined cloak began to grow overwarm, and she let it slip down from her shoulders to lie over the horse's white rump in a splash of scarlet color.

Now they saw few other travelers, only an occasional cart filled with produce. No words were exchanged with the drivers, who moved aside with meekly bowed heads and allowed the nobleman and his party to pass.

The fields beside the road were covered with the short green sprouts of new grain, which strained toward the sun. Oak, alder, ash and birch trees crowded the edges of the fields, offering up their own bright and tender buds in anticipation of the fullness of foliage to come. It was as if God were trying to tell her something with this joyous display of new beginnings. But Elizabeth could not be moved. Her own new life held no such promise of bounty.

The few cottages they saw sat far back from the road; thus, the occasional bark of a dog or the sound of a raised voice seemed distant and disconnected to Elizabeth and her life.

No one knew or cared that she rode north toward a life she knew nothing about and had not asked for.

But here she stopped herself with a jolt of self-examination. Had she not asked for what had happened? If not for her insistence on dining alone with Raynor, she would not now be married to a man who had no use for her.

No wonder Raynor resented her.

He'd made his attitude toward women abundantly clear at the outset. In no way was he responsible for what had befallen them. But, though honesty forced Elizabeth to admit her own guilt in the matter, there was little else she could do at this juncture.

If only in name, they were well and truly wed.

What she could do was try to heal the breach between them. Raynor was her husband, and she did not wish to spend her future years bemoaning her fate. All her life

Elizabeth had been a doer, a fixer. It was not like her to just accept defeat. And she could not do so now.

With the example of her parents' joyous marriage to lead her, Elizabeth knew she did not wish to settle for what existed between her and Raynor now. It was up to her to try and make things better. Mayhap if she tried, Raynor would unbend and see that they must make the best of their lot.

And she knew this was the most she could hope for. Not for a moment did she believe that Raynor would ever love her as her father had her mother, or even as her brother Henry loved his beloved wife, Aileen.

Firmly she stifled any hint of loneliness at the thought.

Such was not for her. The best she could achieve was a truce. Looking to Raynor's unyieldingly broad back, she had no idea how that was to come about. Yet try she must.

She was a Clayburn, and thus would show no sign of giving up, despite the adversity. Elizabeth straightened her spine, determined to present a brave front, no matter the sadness that tightened her throat.

Looking up to see Olwyn studying her with that worried expression again, Elizabeth moved to the side of the wagon.

She had made the decision to go forward with courage. Now she must begin to act upon it. No more would she avoid conversing with Olwyn, though she would draw the line at anything concerning her relationship with Raynor. What was between them was between them.

But Olwyn was an important part of her life, and Elizabeth would not forgo her friendship with her woman out of her own ridiculous ill humor.

From the front of the little troop, where Raynor rode beside Bronic, he was not able to look back at Elizabeth without being obvious. But he made much of keeping an eye on the wagons. Surreptitiously his gaze sought his wife.

Raynor watched as she moved up beside the first wagon and began talking to her woman. She laughed at something the other said, the sound pleasant and throaty, unwittingly drawing several pairs of male eyes. He frowned, feeling even more irritated with her.

Quickly he turned away.

How could she appear so unconcerned, when his own stomach was a coil of knotted frustration due to the events of the past two days?

He didn't want to believe she had deliberately set out to force him into a marriage. But the evidence was there. Why else would she have arranged for them to be alone, shown such pleasure in his company, convinced him to stay when he discovered Stephen was not there? Even at the time, he'd wondered about her overt interest in him. He cursed himself for being fool enough to disregard his misgivings, even as he remembered how her regard had warmed him. As Raynor's mother had been, Elizabeth was adept at getting what she desired without thought of the cost to others.

He'd seen his mother completely destroy his father with her manipulations. When Raynor was only an infant, Robert Warwicke had been called to serve his king in France. He had returned home two years later to discover that his wife had not only betrayed him with another man, but had bore that other a son, as well. Too much in love with her to cast his faithless spouse aside, Robert had forgiven her. Yet his compassion had not moved his wife to display any measure of gratitude or loyalty. She had seemed to see his kindness as a sign of weakness and disdain him for it. Completely in love with her, he had outwardly taken her manipulations with little or no demur. But over the years, Raynor had seen how deep the hurt had cut.

Elizabeth was obviously of the same manipulative bent, and had acted accordingly when she wanted a husband.

Though why she had chosen him, Raynor had still to discern. The most logical explanation was that she was too accustomed to having her way, and he had denied her. Thus becoming a challenge. 'Twas the only thing that made any sense.

Yet even as these thoughts ran through his mind, he knew doubt. She had seemed as displeased as he at Stephen's decision that they must wed, had gone through with the wedding white-faced and silent as snow. And her sorrow at parting with her brother this morning had appeared unfeigned.

An act, he told himself angrily.

Else why was she laughing and smiling unconcernedly with her maid, when he could think of nothing but the quagmire his life had become? The complication of a wife was one he had not needed at this point. Worry over what new devilment Harrington might get up to was already piled atop his usual concerns about the running of his lands and Willow's. He had enough problems to occupy his every waking hour without Elizabeth to plague him.

And plague him she did.

Every time he was near her, including the few moments they had spent together becoming man and wife, he had relived over and over that kiss. That dratted moment when he had abandoned all rational thought and taken her in his arms. That cursed moment when he felt his gentler feelings stir for the first time in years.

Repeatedly he told himself the event could not have been the way he recalled. No single kiss could be so moving. But every time he looked at her, his heart remembered, and a warm, liquid feeling suffused his chest.

He glanced behind him, his gaze flicking from his wife to the second wagon, where that enormous bed reposed under a protective covering. Elizabeth's bed. Raynor nearly gasped aloud as an image of Elizabeth naked, her blue eyes heavy with desire, sprang unbidden to his mind.

By the true cross, what was wrong with him?

He became aware of Bronic asking him a question. "What say you, Raynor?"

"Say?" he asked hurriedly, puzzled and trying to cover the fact that he had not been attending.

Bronic's blue eyes studied him. "As to Harrington? Think you he will leave well enough alone, now that King Edward has upheld your claim to the child?"

Raynor ran a hand through his already tousled dark hair. Guilt stabbed at him for worrying over Elizabeth when he had other, more pressing matters to attend. "Nay." His voice was hard. "He will not. The man's greed is too big to let go. He will not stop here. Harrington has already bled his tenants dry to fund his extravagant ways. He can get no more from that quarter. With Willow in his control, he would have access to her fortune."

A frown crossed Bronic's strongly handsome face. "You do not think he would try to reach Warwicke and take her before we can return?"

Raynor felt a moment of painful unease, then stifled it. He shook his head. "Nay, methinks not. Harrington is not a man to discommode himself by sleeping in tents, as we will. He will stay at every hostelry and monastery along the route north. Besides," he added as much to reassure himself as much as Bronic, "you know I have left word that Harrington is to be killed on sight if he tries to so much as approach Warwicke in my absence. And he would not have time to gather an army to lay siege before we can return."

Raynor turned to survey the two wagons behind them, his gaze going once more to Elizabeth. She laughed again, seemingly oblivious of him, and a black scowl darkened his brow. He turned back to the other man. "I had no concern before of beating Harrington back to Warwicke, but with these wagons, our progress will be slowed greatly. You, myself and the other four men could have been happily returned to Warwicke in half the time it will now take.''

Bronic swung around to look at the two women, Elizabeth on her white palfrey, Olwyn in the wagon. His tone was thoughtful as he answered, "We have made surprisingly good time thus far. The women have been of little trouble. Though we have been traveling for hours, neither has so much as offered a word of complaint."

"Thus far," Raynor reminded him.

"Soon we must begin to think about stopping for the meal." Bronic looked at him with long-suffering patience. "The women are likely tired, despite their lack of complaint."

Raynor colored. Inexplicably he had the feeling Bronic knew how upset he was about his marriage to Elizabeth. This displeased him not a little. He refused to allow his being wed to alter his life any more than necessary. "We have many leagues to go," he replied woodenly.

With an expression of surprise and disapproval, Bronic replied, "Raynor, I myself am growing hungry, though I could ride on without stopping, and have done so under more discomfort. But there is no need to go on until the women drop. You said yourself that as long as we make reasonable haste, all should be well. It is only right to treat your lady wife with some deference."

Raynor sat looking at him, Elizabeth's husky laughter ringing in his ears. He didn't care about her, and didn't want anyone else to mistake that fact. But neither did he want to be deliberately cruel. She probably was exhausted. It was true they had ridden on well past midday, and she'd uttered not a word of complaint.

But even though such stamina was new in his experience with women, Raynor was not yet ready to completely unbend. "Aye," he replied stiffly. "We will stop."

As Bronic dropped back to tell the others, Raynor halted him with a raised hand. "But tell my wife that it will only be for a short time. She is not to dawdle. We have far to travel before making camp for the night. I must needs return to Warwicke ere many more days have passed.''

With raised brows, Bronic gave him a long look. ''You may deliver that message yourself, Raynor. I will not. After all, you have not even spoken to the woman the whole morning. I know not what happened between you. I only know that Sir Stephen and the king's men found you together. Surely you cannot hold her solely responsible and absolve yourself, Raynor. 'Tis not like you. Furthermore, if you wish to be unpleasant with your lady after first ignoring her, you may do so with your own tongue.'' That said, Bronic moved off without waiting for a reply.

Raynor could think of no suitable answer, anyway. He knew he would have to speak to Elizabeth eventually, but he didn't know what to say. As to the subject of his own culpability in the marriage, Bronic did not know what Raynor suspected Elizabeth had done. Somehow she must understand that he did not mean for theirs to be a true marriage. Raynor wanted nothing between himself and Elizabeth, not companionship, not friendship, and definitely not love.

Naught good had ever come of closeness between a man and woman, and Elizabeth was not the kind who could easily be used and discarded without thought. Those few moments when he held her in his arms had assured him of that.

He had no intention of allowing himself to care for her, or any other woman. Not now, not ever.

Louisa had been the one exception to that rule, and they had met as children. Early on, she had told him of the cruelty of her stepfather. Though he was nothing but a boy, Raynor had responded with kindness. And even then she had chosen Raynor over the older Nigel, following him about with sisterly devotion. How could he fail to respond in kind?

But there was no connection between that and what had passed between himself and Elizabeth. She was a woman in every sense of the word, clearly willing to use her mind and body as silken threads to bind a man to her.

Staying where he was, ahead of the others, Raynor looked back and saw Bronic speak to the man who drove the lead wagon. He pulled to the side of the road. The other driver followed his lead.

They were right next to a small clearing near the road, where the trees rested back a bit. The short grass grew thick and inviting. It was a suitable spot to rest and eat.

Lips tight, Raynor watched as Bronic helped Elizabeth's woman from the lead wagon. The serving woman reached into the back and drew out a large woven basket. One of the other four men spread a blanket on the ground as another helped Elizabeth from her white mare. Bronic took the basket and carried it to the blanket where the two women took over and began passing out its contents.

Soon the small group was chatting amiably.

None of them so much as made a pretense of paying attention to Raynor. The five men seemed bent on seeing to the two women's comforts, to the exclusion of all else.

If he'd thought his stomach was in knots before, he now had to make a conscious effort not to put a hand over the cramp in his guts. He sat up straighter, determined to conquer the feeling.

But the longer Raynor sat there atop his stallion, watching the others eat and talk as if this were some outing planned solely for the entertainment of his wife and her companion, the angrier he became.

How dare she insinuate herself into his life in this manner? These were his men, bound to him and no other. Yet here she was, making him feel unwelcome in his own camp.

It was more than he was willing to accept.

Without stopping to think about how ridiculous he might appear, Raynor rode up to the group, his horse nearly treading on the blanket. "It is time to go. We have dallied here long enough."

Elizabeth swung around from her place on the blanket. She faced him with regally arched brows, but her tone was pleasant enough when she spoke. "It will be as you say, my lord. But first I must beg your indulgence for a slight delay. I need a few moments to myself."

He scowled, his horse prancing dangerously close to the blanket, sensing his master's foul humor. "We will leave now. I will brook no delays, madame." He turned to Olwyn. "You there. Get these things cleared away and get back in the wagon."

Though he first looked to Raynor with a frown of consternation, Bronic quickly turned to assist Olwyn as she began to repack the basket. Clearly the blond man felt it would serve no purpose to comment, and Raynor was glad of that. He had no wish to argue with Bronic before his wife.

The other men said nothing as they moved to get under way, obeying their lord without question.

Elizabeth stood slowly and gracefully, only her hands, which were clenched tightly around the edges of her skirts, giving any hint of her agitation. She made no move toward her horse.

Clearly she meant to defy him. Anger seethed in his belly. Raynor leaned close to her, not sure where his rage was coming from, but unable to stem it. "My lady, you have already made me two days late in returning to Warwicke. I will not have you playing games with me to prove you can have your way."

She shrugged, unaffected by his offensive manner. When she answered him, her voice was as pleasant as if she were discussing the weather. "If you are in such dread haste, my lord, please feel free to go on without me. I will catch up to you in a short time."

Her aplomb only served to enrage him further. No one, save Bronic, ever openly defied him. She was too certain of herself, and totally confident of gaining her own way.

Just as his mother had always been.

His lips thinned. This woman who had made herself his wife was not going to manipulate him further. "You will come with me, and now!" he roared.

Before Elizabeth could react, Raynor reached down and dragged her up before him. Turning his mount, he thundered down the road at a gallop, trusting in the others to follow.

To his surprise, Elizabeth made no move to fight or argue. For a time, they simply rode along in silence. She kept her back so straight there was only a bare minimum of physical contact between them, just the occasional brush of her back against his chest.

Gradually Raynor began to calm down and realize that, though he had shown them all, including Elizabeth, that he would not tolerate insolence, he had perhaps overreacted. He had allowed his men—and, even worse, Elizabeth—to see how much she had provoked him.

That had been a mistake. Raynor had no desire for Elizabeth to think she could have any power over him, even that of angering him. He would control himself better in the future, no matter how difficult that proved to be.

Mayhap sensing his changing mood, Elizabeth took that moment to speak, her voice stiff, as if the words cost her dearly in effort. "My lord husband, I really must ask that you stop. I must needs answer nature's call, and without much more delay."

As she spoke, Raynor felt a hot flush creep up the back of his neck. He had little experience traveling with women, and had thus thought nothing of such matters. Yet the truth was there for him to see, did he but wish. They had been riding for hours, and he had not seen her go off to the forest after they stopped. Raynor had been forced to do so himself once during the morning. It had been easy for him to ride off for a moment, then return to the others.

For a woman, things were more complicated.

Why had she not told him?

His embarrassment deepened as he thought back to those moments before he had taken her up on his horse. He had to admit, at least to himself, that mayhap she had tried. He had simply misconstrued her words for arrogance, when she must have been trying for tact.

He pulled hard on the reins, halting his mount with unexpected swiftness and bringing her rigid back into contact with his chest. But the contact was brief as she hurriedly slipped down from the horse without his aid.

Something, some inner impulse, compelled him to reach out and grasp her hand, where it lay on the stallion's broad back. She looked up at him, her sapphire eyes steady on his, her composure unwavering. Even in the bright light of day, her skin was fine as the petals of a white rose, her lips cherry red and sweetly formed. Only the dusky flush along the perfect curve of her cheek gave any hint of agitation.

God, but she's lovely, he thought before he could stop himself.

He felt a tightness in his chest.

"My lord?" she queried when he continued to hold her.

Quickly Raynor gathered his scattered wits. What was he about? He did not wish to feel anything for her, and he would not. Mayhap in this case he had wronged her, but the truth remained that he was wed, and against his will, through this woman's fault.

And yet he felt compelled to apologize for what he had done. "I... Forgive me for not understanding your need."

She gave no verbal answer, only inclined her head with regal elegance, then strolled into the woods that grew a few feet from the road side. She had removed the scarlet cloak she'd worn earlier, and her slender hips swayed enticingly in dark blue velvet.

For some reason, this irritated him immensely. He had no wish to see anything noble in Elizabeth, and even less to be attracted to her. He must remember what he suspected, that she was a scheming woman who would do whatever she must to attain her goal.

At the same time, Raynor could acknowledge that he had behaved badly. Although he did not suffer disobedience or foolishness lightly, he was generally slow to anger, able to mete out justice with calm deliberation. He had not done so today, and for that he was truly sorry. In all fairness, he must treat Elizabeth with at least a modicum of decency, if only to live up to his own standards of behavior.

Elizabeth came out of the forest and approached Raynor with some trepidation, though she gave no outward sign of this. She was striving desperately to hold on to her resolve to try to make a marriage with Raynor, though that was proving difficult. He was indeed a prickly one, this man she called husband. But she would not allow him to intimidate her. That was not part of her plan to bring them together. He must learn to see that she was a woman deserving of his honor and respect.

As she approached Raynor, where he sat atop his stallion, waiting for her, Elizabeth looked back the way they had come. To her immense relief, she could see Bronic and the wagons only a short way back. Now she would not have to ride with Raynor any longer. She could see her own mare tied to the back of the wagon, beside the driver's.

Elizabeth had no desire to sit before Raynor on his horse. Despite the fact that he acted like a brute and a spoiled child in one incarnation, she could not control her response to him. She had been unable to quiet the tingle of awareness that raced up her spine every time the horse's movement caused her to brush against Raynor. Heavens above, she wished he did not affect her so.

Nay, she would not go before him. If she waited here for only a few moments, she could then mount and ride her own horse.

Biting her lip, Elizabeth glanced at Raynor, who had followed the direction of her gaze. If he knew what she was thinking, he said nothing.

What could he have been thinking, she asked herself, to carry her off that way? Why did he have to behave so, when she was trying so very hard to learn to tolerate him? It was especially irritating as Raynor seemed disinclined to make any overtures of peace toward her.

She thought of his apology, then dismissed it as insignificant. It was only decent that he had done so, and nothing to recommend his good nature.

As the wagon came toward her, Elizabeth stepped into the road, forcing the driver to stop. It was Bronic and not Raynor who helped her to mount her palfrey.

To her surprise, Raynor stayed with them as the party started off again, instead of riding on ahead.

They traveled on in silence for a time and that was fine with her. She had no more goodwill to offer her husband this day. Mayhap by the morrow she could think of trying to come to terms with him.

But Bronic seemed unaware of her need for solitude, and spoke cheerily. "My lady Elizabeth, your companion tells me that you are quite a horsewoman."

Elizabeth nodded modestly. "I have some skill." The truth was that her father had first set her on horseback at the age of two. None of her brother's save the youngest, Peter, had beaten her in a race for years. They all said that no horse was immune to Elizabeth's ability to manage everything and everyone to suit herself.

"That is not what I am told," Bronic insisted. "Is it true that you once dressed as a boy and won a race at one of the king's own tourneys?"

Elizabeth could not help smiling at the memory. "I did, though now I realize how very foolish I was." She shrugged. "But I was only sixteen, and newly come to court. And Lord Hastings did lay it about that no one could beat him. How could I resist?"

Glancing toward her husband, Elizabeth saw that he was looking from her to Bronic with a frown of displeasure. Her own smile disappeared.

Why did he have to be so very unpleasant?

Bronic seemed to sense Raynor's disapproval, but, unlike Elizabeth, he was clearly amused by it. "Raynor is ever a one for a race. I have given up trying to outdo him. Mayhap you would care to try, my lady?"

Elizabeth turned to look into her husband's walnut-dark eyes. Raynor gazed over at her with a mocking smile. When he spoke, his tone was slightly condescending. "Though beautiful and intelligent, Elizabeth is still a woman, and not likely to be able to best me on horseback. I am a knight, trained in such matters."

Bronic smiled slowly. "I suggest a race."

Raynor laughed then, though Elizabeth found nothing pleasant in the sardonic sound. "Surely you jest, Bronic. Race Elizabeth? 'Tis preposterous."

Suddenly she wanted to race him, to wipe that superior grin from his lips. She held her head high and said with a barely disguised challenge in her voice, "Are you afraid you will be outdone by a woman, my lord Warwicke?

Raynor's dark eyes narrowed, and his lean jaw flexed as he slanted her a glance of disdain. "I am afraid of nothing and no one. Make no mistake of that, madame."

He turned to Bronic with cool intent. "As you suggest, I will race against my wife." Then he swung to Elizabeth and inclined his proud head. "That is unless you would prefer not, my lady. If 'twas a jest on your part, I will accept your withdrawal."

Elizabeth's hands tightened on the reins. Withdrawal? Did he really think she would turn coward, that she would run from the thought of contesting him? Not while there was breath in her body. "I accept, my lord husband, and with pleasure," she answered, taking up the proffered gauntlet.

His eyes flashed with barely disguised excitement when he heard her reply, and she felt an unbidden thrill within herself.

Now that the thing had been decided, Raynor seemed bent on the game. "If I don't mistake myself," he told her, pointing down the road before them, "there is a bridge some two leagues hence. The first one to the opposite side shall be declared the winner.

Originally Elizabeth had only been needling Raynor. But now she found herself wanting to best him, to show him what she was made of.

Raynor was too sure of himself, and his abilities.

He looked at her. "Whenever you are ready, damsel."

Elizabeth gazed back at him for a long moment. Everything around them seemed to still. She could feel his excitement, his wildness, beating her own blood to a pulse of exhilaration. This was what had drawn her to Raynor in the beginning. This was what she had sensed in him that first day at Windsor. No matter how he tried to cloak it, inside this man was a core of passion that would not be denied.

Without breaking eye contact, Elizabeth shouted, "Now!" and prodded her horse forward. But he was right beside her, having reacted with her, as if he knew what she would do as it was done.

Elizabeth leaned low over her horse's back. She was at one with the rhythm of the animal beneath her as they galloped over the the hard-packed track. Her hair came loose from the knot Olwyn had pinned atop her head, to tumble down her back.

For the first time since the night Stephen had found her with Raynor, she felt free. Free as the wind that whipped her tangled black curls about her.

On they rode, the sound of the horses' hooves no louder than the erratic beating of her heart. Before long, she knew she was gaining on Raynor, only in the smallest of increments, but gaining. First it was by a nose, and then by a head.

When she was a whole length in front, Elizabeth knew the lord of Warwicke was beaten. He'd said the bridge was only two leagues ahead. Surely they were nearly there.

She had won.

But as she rounded a bend and the bridge came into sight, Elizabeth knew something was dreadfully wrong.

Where the center of the span should be, there was nothing.

With only seconds to consider, she knew she had to make a decision. There was danger no matter what she decided. They were thundering along at an incredible rate. If she halted too quickly, she would risk the horse taking a fall, and if not quickly enough, they could go careering over the edge. On the other hand, should she risk making the jump with no time to judge the distance? Never would Elizabeth willingly put her mount in such unwarranted jeopardy.

At that thought, the decision was made.

She must trust in Minerva to respond to her signals correctly.

The edge was very near now.

Calling upon all her skills as a horsewoman, Elizabeth drew back on the reins while gripping tightly with her legs. She closed her eyes, willing the mare to react as she must if their lives were to be spared.

Responding almost as if she and Elizabeth were of the same mind, the horse came to a delicate but precarious halt on the very edge of the missing bridge.

With a whoop of exhilaration, Raynor sailed past her and over the gaping span.

Her heart in her throat, Elizabeth watched as horse and rider hung in the void between sky and land for what seemed an eternity. Then they landed, still at a gallop, safely on the other side.

A deep laugh rang out as Raynor wheeled his stallion and galloped back. To her complete amazement, he didn't even pause, leaping back to her side of the river with reckless abandon.

His horse reared and pawed the air as they landed near her, and once more she heard Raynor laughing.

Anger burned in her chest like a hot iron. But at the same time, she could not deny the rush of excitement brought on by the wild sound of his laughter. It was as if it called up some desire within herself to abandon all caution and fly over the chasm herself. To feel the rush in her blood the danger would bring.

All this she could imagine for herself, but not for Minerva. She had no right to take such chances with her beloved animal.

And how dare Raynor take such chances with his mount? With hers? Surely he'd known all along that the bridge was out. She could have been hurt, or even killed.

Raynor was coming back to her now, the smile of triumph on his handsome face making her even more furious.

He came to a stop and leapt from his horse, restless with excitement. He reached up before she could stop him and lifted her from Minerva's back. "I have won."

It was then that Elizabeth found her voice. "Lackwitted madman," she cried, balling her fist struck him full on the hard wall of his chest.

He reacted with unadulterated surprise. "What have you, damsel? Are you so angry at having lost the race?"

"Lost the race?" she sputtered. "You nearly killed me! You knew the bridge was out, and wished to be rid of me!"

He dropped her on her feet, backing away as if stung. "I knew nothing of the bridge, woman. When last we came here, some days ago, it was fully intact, if a trifle rickety."

His surprise at her accusation was so great that Elizabeth could not but believe him.

But Raynor wasn't finished, her words having cut deep. "How dare you accuse me of deceit? It is you who have proved to be the less honorable of we two. It was not I who tricked you into marriage. You but judge me by your own mode of thought and deed."

"My own?" she yelled, then closed her eyes. So now it was said. He did think she'd purposely entrapped him, just as she'd suspected. Elizabeth took several long breaths. She would not, could not, allow him to rile her this way. With every ounce of her will, she collected her scattered emotions. Not for all the stars in the heavens would she willingly have Raynor see her behaving hysterically. It was completely unlike her to allow herself to become so overwrought.

Her anger eased as she willed it out the tips of her fingers, just as she'd learned to do as a child, when her brothers enraged her. She'd discovered long ago that the way to best handle a male was to stay rational, in spite of his irrationality.

She opened her eyes, her gaze searching out and locking on his with determination. She would make him listen to her. When Elizabeth continued, she was pleased to hear the evenness of her tone. "I did not behave dishonorably. Foolishly, yes, but not dishonorably. How can you think I would willingly tie myself to a man who had made clear that he did not want me?" She gestured to herself with an open hand. "Do you find me so displeasing yourself that you can believe no other man would desire me, or have me to wife?"

He watched her for a long moment, then broke the contact of their eyes. Slowly he shook his head, his attention on some distant object in the sky. "Nay, Elizabeth, I do not believe such a thing. I am most certain that you have been desired by many." Then his jaw tightened in anger as he turned back to her. "Therein lies my dilemma. Why, then, did you allow me to dine with you, when you knew Stephen would not approve, that he had ordered you not to?"

Not now or ever would she willingly have him know how attracted to him she had been. He would only use that knowledge against her. "I... He should not have ordered me. I do as I will, not as others choose."

Ah, this Raynor could well believe. Elizabeth did seem to cherish her own wishes all too well. "And thus here we are, trapped," he said, putting his hands to lean hips. "Because of a fit of pique."

An unexpected needle of pain pierced her throat at the word *trapped*. She told herself not to be foolish. Raynor had never made any secret of his feelings about their marriage.

But then he continued, his dark eyes studying her carefully. "Is that all there was, Elizabeth? Were you simply angry with Stephen for telling you nay? At the time, I thought you might... You seemed to..." He stopped, as if uncertain of how to go on.

As what Raynor was trying to say hit home, Elizabeth flushed. Dear heavens. She put her hand to her burning cheek. He had guessed at her attraction to him. 'Twas what she had most feared.

Then, doing her utmost to hide her embarrassment, Elizabeth raised her head high. It really mattered very little that he knew. What did matter was how she reacted to that knowledge. She spoke coolly, hastily. "My lord Warwicke, there is no point in denying that I was, shall I say, interested in you."

He opened his mouth to reply, and she raised her hand to forestall him. "But I must tell you that your behavior toward me has changed my feelings greatly. You are rude, overbearing, and disdainful of women. What meager attraction I felt for you has certainly been laid low. You may rest assured that I have no designs on you."

She stood there looking up at him, her regal bearing an open challenge.

Raynor knew he should be pleased by what she had said but he was not. He felt an unexpected rush of irritation. Which was completely ridiculous, because he wanted nothing between himself and Elizabeth.

Unbidden, he knew a flashing memory of the kiss they had shared. But it wasn't the passion of the moment that haunted him so relentlessly. It was the tenderness, the protective instincts that had risen up to claim him.

In frustration, he reached for her. He would show her and himself that she was nothing to him. He would wipe those softer emotions from his memory, prove that he felt nothing for her beyond the physical, no more than he would for any beautiful woman.

As Raynor pulled her to him, Elizabeth guessed his intent, and resisted, but only briefly.

The moment his mouth touched hers, she sighed and melted against him like warm honey. His body reacted with alacrity. His pulse quickened, and a fierce river of pleasure rushed through him, making him deepen the kiss.

His mouth left hers, and he pressed hot kisses to her long, delicate throat. Elizabeth gasped, holding him to her. And he felt his own passion heightened by hers—what pleasured her, pleasured him.

The knowledge hit him like the dead-on blow of a lance.

He stiffened, drawing away from her. Elizabeth's lips were swollen from his kisses, and her eyes were heavy with desire. Even now, as her expression began to change to one of surprise and bewilderment, Raynor wanted to kiss her again, to draw her further into that state of longing.

With an incredible force of will, Raynor took his hands away from her back. This was not what he'd wanted. He was trying to show himself that Elizabeth was insignificant, just another woman, a body to take.

Then why was the thought of giving her joy more compelling than that of taking his own?

Somehow, somewhere, things had gone dreadfully awry, and Raynor had proved nothing of what he meant to.

Confusion made him awkward. He stepped away from her. "We..." he started, then cleared his throat when his voice emerged rough and husky. "We had best get back to the others. With the bridge out, we must needs find another or try to ford the river with the oxen and wagons."

Elizabeth stood looking at him in obvious agitation. "Raynor, what is going on? Have you lost your wits?"

Truth to tell, Raynor felt as if he had. But right now he did not know what to do about it. There was no answer he could find that she would understand, so he remained silent. He was out of his depth with this woman, and knew it.

She tried to meet his gaze, but he avoided her as he went to his horse. Seeing that he would not reply, Elizabeth stamped her foot and mounted her own mare, starting down the road ahead of him at a gallop.

He made no effort to catch her. Raynor knew there was nothing he could say to pacify her.

All he did know was that this could not happen again.

Chapter Five

On the second morning of waking in a tent, Elizabeth emerged to discover that they were only a few miles east of a village called Westcott. She knew that if they kept traveling in this same direction they would pass within a very few leagues of her brother Henry's main holding of Claymoore before nightfall.

She had not spoken to Raynor at all since that first afternoon when he had kissed her. And though it galled her to approach her husband with even the smallest request, she wanted to see her brother and his family. It wasn't an unreasonable query, as they would be so very close, and who knew when she would have an opportunity to visit them again?

Yet it was not easy to think of asking Raynor for anything at this point.

She flushed with shame as she remembered what had happened the day they raced. Raynor had kissed her, then turned on her as if she had somehow wronged him.

But what really made her want to stay away from him was the way she had reacted. Elizabeth could not have explained it even to herself. Every time Raynor touched her, it was as if she lost all sense of self. He had only to put his hands on her, his lips on hers, and all thought of anything else dissolved. It was as if there were some magical spell on her body, and Raynor were the magician who could conjure it.

Well, Elizabeth was not going to let that rule her. If she could do nothing about her reactions to him, she would simply have to learn to conceal them.

Her husband need not think she would be embarrassed into hiding from him.

With her head held high, Elizabeth walked through the camp. There were four tents erected around a central fire. The wagons were drawn up close behind the tents to make them easier to guard against thieves. She knew Raynor kept a watch posted every night for just this purpose, even though it was unlikely that anyone would be foolish enough to attack the armed party of a nobleman.

The fire had not been lit this morning, so she could only assume they would be eating dried meat and old bread—again. The one good thing was that the weather had turned milder again, so she had slept reasonably warmly.

On asking Noland, who was attending the horses, of her husband's whereabouts, Elizabeth was told he was in his tent.

She looked toward it where it lay, directly across from hers. Elizabeth would have laughed, were she not so irritated with Raynor. For clearly he had placed it as far from her own as possible.

Unexpectedly, this gave her some insight into Raynor; he was not so very sure of himself as he seemed.

Squaring her shoulders, Elizabeth strode directly to the tent and then stopped. She could hear Raynor's and what sounded like Bronic's voices coming from inside. What halted her was that she wasn't at all sure of the protocol for entering.

One could hardly knock.

Did she simply lift the flap and go inside? It seemed unlikely.

Shrugging, Elizabeth decided to take a direct approach. Loudly she spoke her husband's name. "My lord Warwicke."

Silence ensued. Then the tent flap was pulled back and a dark head appeared. Raynor's eyes fixed on her with chagrin. "Lady Elizabeth? How may I assist you?"

She smiled politely. "I have a boon to ask of you, my lord."

His tone was wary when he answered, "A boon? What might that be?"

She looked around. Some of the others had come out, and were gazing at them with open curiosity. It was no secret that lord and lady had not so much as spoken for days.

Turning to Raynor again, she smiled and addressed him most cordially. "Might we not be more comfortable inside, my lord?"

Seeming surprised at her pleasant demeanor, but still with an expression of reluctance, Raynor stepped back, holding the flap open for her to follow him. "Aye, come in then, if you desire."

It was not an enthusiastic invitation, but Elizabeth supposed it was the most she could hope for. She went in, being careful not to touch Raynor as she moved by him. If he was aware of her action, he made no sign.

Inside the tent was the same dim interior as in hers. Two bedrolls lay on the ground. But here both Raynor and Bronic's weapons rested on a cloak that had been placed beside the doorway.

Bronic stood to the side. He nodded politely as she looked at him. "Good day, Lady Elizabeth."

She returned the greeting. "Sir Bronic. I hope I have not interrupted something important." She glanced from one man to the other.

Raynor shrugged. "We were discussing today's route. After fording the river the other day, we must be certain to take a course that will not force us to do so again, if we can avoid it."

As he mentioned the fording, Elizabeth could have sworn the color deepened in Raynor's cheeks. But it was hard to be sure. His face was deeply tanned, and the light in the tent was not good.

She looked to Bronic. It did no good to try to fathom Raynor and his reactions to anything. "That is why I have come to speak with you. My brother lives some few hours from here, and I was hoping we could abide there for a night. I trust it is not out of our path."

"Where does your brother live?" Raynor asked.

When Elizabeth turned to him, she saw he was frowning. "Claymoore," she answered. "It is his seat. I do not mean to inconvenience you, but we are so close, and..." Elizabeth stopped and took a deep breath as her voice broke. "I know not when I might see them again." Her gaze captured Raynor's.

For a long time, he said nothing, and Elizabeth glanced toward Bronic in appeal. Raynor seemed to listen to him, if no one else.

But no help came from that quarter. Bronic's expression was intent but noncommittal as he watched the other man.

Finally Raynor answered. "Aye, we will go to your brother. But make note, madame." His gaze held hers. "We can stay no longer than one night. I have pressing matters to attend at Warwicke, and have already been delayed."

At his words, Elizabeth's heart soared. Though she could not fully understand why, it moved her beyond reason that Raynor would do this for her. But she made no outward show, knowing he would not thank her for making much of his kindness.

She simply inclined her head, offering him a smile of genuine warmth. "You have my thanks, my lord."

* * *

Raynor frowned, his hands tightening on the reins. He did not want to spend the night at Claymoore.

But Elizabeth had asked so politely and reasonably. And Bronic had looked on with such avid interest that he felt churlish for even thinking of refusing. After the scene between them two days ago, when he had made such a fool of himself by catching her up and riding off with her, Raynor felt compelled to be scrupulously fair in his dealings with his wife. It was true he needed to get back to Warwicke, but they would be stopping for the night anyway. It would as well be with her family.

And more than that, if he was honest with himself, he knew he was doing what she asked for another reason. Raynor felt guilt at the way he had treated her when he kissed her. Elizabeth had not deserved that. It was his own lack of control that had upset him.

Raynor now knew that he had best not touch Elizabeth at all, if he meant to keep his autonomy. He had no intention of giving that up for a woman.

And Elizabeth was more threat to his self-control than any woman he'd ever known. She spoke and behaved in ways that were completely foreign and amazing to him. Even that day when he came out and accused her of being attracted to him, she had surprised Raynor. Elizabeth had not become coy, nor postured and denied, she'd admitted the truth and stood proudly before him.

Raynor also felt that it would be well to be in company, if only to give himself something to think about other than the deep blue of Elizabeth's eyes, or the way her black hair fell in ebony curls down her back.

But when they arrived at Claymoore castle, the party learned that the baron and his family were not in residence. They were at Landview, his wife's keep, which was several hours away.

Irritated at the further delay, Raynor nonetheless said nothing. He had agreed to visit his wife's family, and would follow through. He indicated that Elizabeth should show them the way.

As the single tower at Landview came into sight some hours later, Raynor found his annoyance dissolving at the unadulterated happiness on Elizabeth's face. He pushed the feeling down, telling himself he hadn't brought her here for any reason other than to be scrupulously fair. He did not care what pleased or displeased his wife. But he couldn't deny that for a moment the sensation he felt at seeing her joy had been pleasant. And that left him feeling strangely unsettled.

He didn't want to care about Elizabeth, or what made her happy.

On gaining the inner courtyard, they were met by Henry, baron of Clayburn. He had obviously been practicing at arms, for he wore mail and carried his sword in one hand and a helm in the other. His black hair was matted to his head, and sweat beaded his strong, handsome face, but his startlingly golden eyes were lit with both surprise and pleasure.

Henry dropped the items as he rushed toward Elizabeth, plucking his sister from her horse and swinging her about.

A gay laugh rang out, the sound vibrating sweetly along the back of Raynor's neck. At first he didn't understand whence the sound had come. And then he knew. It was Elizabeth, and this was the first time he had heard her laugh with such joy.

Henry Clayburn set Elizabeth on her feet, and she threw her arms around his neck to hug him. Then Raynor watched as his wife swung around upon hearing a woman's voice calling out to her.

Raynor, too, turned at the hail and saw a tall woman, her wheat-gold hair pulled back in a braid. She came down the stone steps of the keep slowly, carefully leading a little boy of perhaps two by one hand. The little fellow's hair was a cap of black, and his large eyes were a vivid gold, like his father's. Her other hand rested on the gentle swell of her stomach. She was a beautiful woman, with direct gray eyes and strikingly sculptured features, pleasingly round at hip and breast, despite her pregnancy. A woman to make any man look twice.

But as Elizabeth ran toward her, enfolding the newcomer in her arms, Raynor realized he found her slighter more delicate frame more to his taste.

Unaware of her husband's thoughts, Elizabeth cried out cheerily, "Aileen, you sent no word! When is the babe to come?"

The other woman smiled ruefully, looking to her husband. "Not for some three months. Henry was to send word to you ere long."

Releasing the woman, Elizabeth bent to take the little boy up in her arms. "It matters not, except you'd best let Stephen know soon. And how is little Henry?" she greeted, kissing the little one's fair cheek.

He giggled and planted a wet kiss on her own cheek.

Henry turned to Raynor, his visage pleasant, but confused. "By the way, where is our brother? And who is this come with you, Beth?"

Looking to her husband, as if just remembering his presence, Elizabeth simply stood there for a long moment. Then, with an unaccustomed shyness Raynor had never seen her exhibit heretofore, she went to his side. Standing stiffly beside him, she smiled and said, "This is my husband, Raynor, baron of Warwicke."

The next silence stretched on for what seemed like hours.

Elizabeth knew that Henry was more than a little shocked. As head of the family, Henry had a right to be consulted as to her marriage. Not that he would ever try to make that decision for her. He would simply expect the formalities to be observed as a gesture to his position. Henry was a stickler for such things.

Besides, he was her brother and loved her greatly. That she would marry without even telling him must hurt a little, at the very least. But for the life of her, Elizabeth knew not what to say.

Besides, the unexpected news must be doubly hard to digest, as she knew her brothers had almost despaired of her taking a husband.

It was Aileen who recovered first. She moved forward to hug Elizabeth, despite little Henry, who squirmed between them. "You have my congratulations," she said, then turned to Raynor. "Elizabeth's husband is most welcome, is he not, Henry?"

The baron of Clayburn was a still a little slow to react, but at last he moved forward to hold Elizabeth close. Then he drew back when Henry complained at his father's fervor. "Beth, why didn't you send word? We would have come to attend the wedding. You are my only sister."

She shrugged out of his arms, turning to her husband. She hoped Raynor would not tell them the circumstances of their marriage. She did not want to face any recriminations from Henry. He could be quite overpowering at times, even though he meant well. Elizabeth knew she had made a mistake in dining alone with Raynor and was responsible for everything that had occurred because of it. She did not need her brother to tell her that.

Obviously Raynor decided to heed the pleading in her eyes, for he turned to Henry, holding out a hand as if asking for understanding. "I am most sorry for not inviting you, my lord Clayburn. But we came to a decision in the matter in haste, and your brother Stephen was inclined to agree with us."

Henry frowned, and Elizabeth could tell he would have much to say to his younger brother on the subject when next they met.

Of course, Stephen would tell Henry what had happened, and Elizabeth knew that was the right thing to do. She also knew that she should tell Henry right now. But she was feeling vulnerable and unsure as never in her life, and did not wish to discuss her marital problems with anyone. Least of all her volatile older brother.

When Henry continued to scowl but said nothing, Elizabeth breathed a sigh of relief. By the time Henry was able to question Stephen, she would be gone to Warwicke, and thus spared any recrimination about her foolishness.

Elizabeth cast Raynor a quick smile of gratitude. She didn't know why her husband had protected her, but she felt a small glimmer of warmth near her heart. Mayhap he did feel at least some small bit of allegiance toward her.

But Elizabeth could not allow herself to dwell on that now. She dared not hope for too much.

What she needed most was to find her equilibrium and keep it, if she was going to be able to deal with the unpredictable Raynor. Their relationship was complicated at best, and could turn disastrous at any time. As she had seen the day he kissed her.

It would be best not to press him too hard.

With that in mind, she turned to Aileen, thinking that if they went into the keep it might relieve some of the tension between them. There was nothing to be gained in standing about the courtyard, feeling self-conscious. The more active they were, the less likely it was that Henry would ask a question she did not wish to answer. Elizabeth said, "Now that that is all settled, I would love nothing so much as a hot bath."

Aileen laughed, taking her sister-by-marriage's arm to lead her into the keep. "Forgive me for forgetting how tired you must be." She looked over at Raynor, including him in the comment.

"Aye," Elizabeth answered. "A warm bed will be most welcome, after two days of sleeping in tents."

She was aware of Henry gesturing for Raynor to follow them. Henry chuckled huskily. "I would wager your lord husband will be glad of a warm bed, as well."

Hot color stained Elizabeth's cheeks as she strained to hear Raynor's reply. But if he made one, it was too low for her to catch.

She made a show of listening to little Henry as he pattered on in his baby language. Distracted as she was, Elizabeth understood no more than two words in ten. It gave her something to attend to besides Raynor, whom she was completely aware of as he followed them into the great hall.

Aileen went to the end of the hall, where a fire burned in the large hearth, and spoke to a woman who was turning a roasting pig on a spit over its heat. She nodded and rose. Then Aileen came back to Elizabeth.

Leaving the men to their talk, Aileen led Elizabeth to the same room she had stayed in in the past. It was a comfortable chamber and contained an X-shaped chair, a table and a high, wide bed.

"Your bath is being brought," the golden-haired woman said, taking her chattering son.

Elizabeth sighed, sinking down on the side of the bed as Aileen seated herself on the chair. "It will be good to be clean again." She reached up and pulled her sheer wimple from her head, her hair tumbling down in a tangle of ebony. Without thinking, she began to tick off a list of things that needed doing. "I will need my companion, Olwyn. She is with the wagons outside the gate. She will know to bring clean garments for me. Raynor has no squire with him, so she might ask his man for a change of clothing for him. Also, I doubt that you need worry about housing

Raynor's men. No doubt he will want them to stay with the wagons. But he may want his knight, Bronic, to sleep in the keep. They are more friends than lord and vassal. I trust you will find accommodations for Olwyn, as well." She paused as Aileen began to laugh.

Accustomed to Elizabeth's managing ways, Aileen took no offense. She knew there was no ill in the younger woman, she simply liked to have things run smoothly. "Of course. I will see to it. Is there aught else?"

Elizabeth grinned at the other woman. "Nay, not that I can think of at this moment, but if anything does occur to me, I will certainly let you know."

Aileen laughed again, as she was meant to. Then she grew noticeably more serious. "Now tell me of your marriage." It was obvious that she was unable to contain her curiosity a moment longer.

Elizabeth looked down at the gray stone floor, suddenly feeling awkward. "I..." she began hesitantly, then straightened her shoulders, unwilling to let her uncertainty about the marriage show. "There is really very little to tell. We met when he came to court."

"Why did you not write and tell us of the wedding?"

Elizabeth's reply was airy. "As Raynor said, there was really not time to write. It all happened so quickly."

There was some degree of censure in Aileen's next question. "Why not wait, at least long enough to send word to us? We do love you very much."

Standing, Elizabeth moved about the room restlessly. She had not meant to hurt them. Nor did she wish to lie, but neither could she bring herself to talk about the circumstances surrounding her marriage to Raynor.

Not with Aileen, whose relationship with Henry was nigh on perfect. Elizabeth did know that they had had problems. But Aileen and Henry had been in love. Raynor did not love her—nor she him.

Telling Aileen everything would not improve her situation.

Smiling with what she hoped was enthusiasm, Elizabeth said, "Stephen was the one who insisted on the marriage taking place so quickly. You see, Raynor must needs return to Warwicke, and Stephen felt we should definitely be married before he left."

That much was the truth.

Elizabeth turned away. "That is really all there is to tell. I have nothing to say beyond that." She knew Aileen, knew she was a very private person herself, and hoped that would be explanation enough to prevent her from prying further.

At that moment, the door opened and two serfs came in, bearing a large wooden tub.

Aileen stood, her eyes telling Elizabeth that she understood and would prod her no more. "I will go now and see that the meal is coming along. I wish you had sent word ahead that you were coming. I would have prepared something special."

"There is no need." Elizabeth smiled with relief and genuine warmth on seeing that there would be no more questions. She was fond of her sister-by-marriage, and glad she had found Henry. "I am happy to be here with you. That is special enough."

Seeming slightly embarrassed by the other woman's overt show of affection, Aileen flushed. Elizabeth knew some of the circumstances behind Aileen's reserve, and had nothing but sympathy for her. Not until Henry came into her life had she been able to conquer her fear of giving and receiving love.

But it was still difficult for her to show her feelings at times, and Elizabeth understood this. So she took no offense when Aileen changed the subject.

"I will have Lord Warwicke's belongings sent here, as well. Surely he, too, would benefit from a hot bath and a change of clothes.

Elizabeth's eyes rounded with horror. Raynor's belongings in her room? She opened her mouth to say it was not possible, then shut it again. She had led both her brother and his wife to believe her marriage was a desired one. She could not refuse to share a room with her husband of three days.

But what on God's earth was her husband going to say?

Elizabeth sat nervously beside her husband at the high table.

Aileen had insisted they take her and Henry's usual places, in honor of their recent marriage.

Raynor hadn't even looked at her. He sat eating little, seemingly lost in his own thoughts. The only evidence that he was aware of her at all was the fact that he had set the choicest pieces of meat on her plate.

She picked at these with her eating knife.

Raynor had not come to their room before the meal. He and Henry had gone off somewhere about the demesne. They had returned just before the meal, both of them with wet hair, acting as though they had known each other for years.

Elizabeth could only assume Henry had taken her husband swimming.

Raynor was acutely aware of Elizabeth beside him. She wore her lovely hair loose, and the glossy mass of curls had been brushed and draped over her shoulder to fall unbound to her lap.

Out of the corner of his eye, he saw the way she toyed with her food. A sigh escaped her as she wriggled beside him, and he wondered at her restlessness.

Mayhap pretending their marriage was a normal one was pressing upon her, as well. He felt guilty for allowing her brother to believe all was well between them.

Though he had just met him, Raynor sensed that Henry was a man of honor and forthrightness.

When they had first arrived and Elizabeth had sent him that beseeching look, he could not have denied the appeal to save his own soul. He did not know why she wished to keep the true circumstances of the relationship a secret from her brother and his family, but he could not betray her.

Raynor refused to allow himself to wonder why he would feel any sense of loyalty to the woman who had ruined his life on a whim. He simply tried to convince himself it would be easier to go along with her than to explain everything to these strangers.

Though in the past he had never been one to spare himself trouble by way of telling a falsehood.

Thinking to take his mind from his troubles with Elizabeth, Raynor turned to Henry, who was seated on his other side, engaged in a conversation with his wife.

Henry sounded none too pleased as he said, "The child will be born at Claymoore, Aileen. Our four months at Landview will be well over by then."

Raynor could hear the irritation in her voice when his wife answered, "But Henry was born at Claymoore, and I would have the next one birthed here, in my own keep. It is not too much to ask that one of them be born here."

He looked to Henry with surprise. Would the baron of Clayburn, who had a reputation for fierceness and arrogance, allow his wife to rule him? And what did she mean by her own keep? A woman's property became her husband's on their marriage.

Though Aileen continued with calm reason, Raynor could not help thinking he would allow no woman to tell him where his child would be born. It was only right that the offspring of a baron should be born at his own seat, should he desire it.

But as the conversation between the two continued, Raynor could see that Henry was weakening in his stance. Raynor was dismayed.

Never would he allow a woman to dictate to him. Aileen's attitude only served to further prove that no woman was to be trusted. Since their arrival Raynor had seen the baron treat his wife with nothing but affection and deference. Obviously Henry Clayburn had shown his wife too much regard and honor. And what did that good dame do, but use his devotion against him?

It was just as with his father and mother. She had used his all-too-obvious affection to bind and manipulate her husband.

Raynor would not accept such treatment from Elizabeth. She must not have reason to think she could use her obvious beauty and intelligence to control him. She would never be allowed to meddle in his affairs as Aileen did Henry's.

As if noticing that his guest was unduly interested in his conversation with his wife, Henry turned to Raynor with a dark frown.

Seeing her brother's ill humor, Elizabeth sought to interrupt. She, too, had overheard the argument between Henry and Aileen. Knowing them as she did, she was not the least bit concerned. Both of them were strong individuals and well liked having their own way. But that never stopped them from settling things in the end.

Yet, though they loved each other beyond reason, Aileen and Henry's relationship was a somewhat volatile one. And when he was arguing with his wife, Henry was more likely to be confrontational with others. It was just in his nature and not of much concern to those who knew him well.

Raynor did not know him well.

Elizabeth bit her lip. The evening was not going as it should. She should not have brought Raynor to Landview when things between them were so strained. She did not feel close enough to Raynor to try to explain the situation to him, and there was no reason to believe he would listen even if she tried.

"Henry," she said with a smile, trying to distract him instead.

Her brother looked at her, but continued to scowl.

"Henry," she repeated, the smile still fixed on her red lips. "Why don't you tell us what it was like in France?"

At his surprised expression, Elizabeth almost laughed aloud. In the past she had shown a marked disinterest in what he had done during the war. Her newfound curiosity concerning the subject must indeed have startled him.

It also seemed to have made him realize he was discussing something that might best be considered in private.

Henry turned to Raynor, obviously thinking she had asked for her husband's benefit. "Did you serve with the king's army in France?"

Raynor shook his head, chewing slowly, then swallowing. "Nay, I was but fourteen when my father died, and I was called home to take over our lands. Though I do feel I have contributed to that effort in knight's fees and gold. More's the pity, as it leaves me less protection from others who might want to do harm to my own lands and people."

Elizabeth looked at him in surprise. This she had not known. Then she realized that there was much about Raynor she did not know. She had just assumed that he must have been in France, as most of the men she knew had been. Stephen had not, but he served the king as messenger here in England.

She looked at her husband with interest. Mayhap Henry could get him to speak more of himself.

Velvet Bond

She also wondered what Henry would reply to his remarks. All knew him as a staunch supporter and friend to King Edward. There had been implied criticism of the war in what Raynor said. Not many would have the courage to speak thus before King Edward's own friend.

Leaning forward, she listened with avid attention.

Henry looked to Raynor with something like suspicion in his golden eyes. "King Edward rules by right. Do you think to question your responsibilities to him and the realm? Are your own interests of more import than those of the kingdom?"

Raynor became very still. He laid down his knife, folding his hands before him as he met Henry's gaze. "I, too, love my king and England. I but believe he should see to our own country first and worry about holdings on the Continent last. Our people have been bled dry in supporting this war to institute Edward as king of France. No man would give more than I to protect king or kingdom in the event of an attack upon our shores. I but state my opinion of what has thus far been a wasted effort to gain land in France."

For a long moment, Henry said nothing. Then he nodded. "I see your point, though I will beg to disagree. As I see it, Edward must show strength in order to make the French understand that they cannot push him further. If he had simply accepted France's invasion of Aquitaine, we might now have them to fight on our own shore."

As the two men continued to talk of the matter, Elizabeth breathed a sigh of relief. The two seemed to have agreed to disagree. The only possible solution to the problem. And after all, did they but realize it, their views were really not so opposed. Both of them loved their king and their country.

And as she thought about this, Elizabeth knew a growing respect for her husband. He had been brave to state his opinion so openly before Henry, knowing how he felt about the king. Besides, she tended to agree with her husband.

She interrupted the two men to say so. "Raynor is right. Declaring himself king of France has done Edward little good thus far. In fact, it has been to the country's detriment. There are problems with the Welsh and Scots along our borders that he must needs attend to."

She blushed as Raynor turned to study her thoughtfully. He seemed surprised and pleased by her support of his beliefs, though he said nothing of it.

As she watched him, his eyes took on a hint of uncertainty and his gaze moved over her face with unconscious vulnerability.

Suddenly it was hard for her to breath past the rising heat in her chest, and she was unable to break the contact of their eyes.

Raynor, too, seemed in the grip of some overwhelming emotion, for he reached out and placed his hand over hers on the table. A shaft of sweet sensation rose up the inside of her wrist, and she found herself leaning toward him.

A husky laugh interrupted her thoughts.

It was Henry, and he spoke with amusement. "Methinks, Aileen, that we'd best see these newlyweds to bed soon."

Flushing, Elizabeth jerked her hand back, leaning away from Raynor. How could she have given so much of herself away? It seemed he had only to touch her and she lost all thought of what she was about. Even now her heartbeat had not slowed to its usual pace.

Elizabeth looked at Raynor and saw by the taut set of his jaw that he was angry. She felt a jab of irritation in the pit of her stomach. It seemed he was forever perturbed and blaming her for what was between them.

It was her fault no more than his. Elizabeth might not feel so much guilt over the way she reacted to him if Raynor stopped fighting it. Why could he not even try to become friends with her?

Even as the thought entered her mind, Elizabeth knew she wanted so much more. What she felt toward Raynor had little to do with friendship and much to do with the mysteries that drew a woman to a man.

She recalled the way he had looked at her a moment ago, his eyes soft and unguarded. That one moment when he lowered his defenses, however briefly, had been more intense than any communication she had ever experienced.

Despite the bawdy remark Henry had made at dinner, it was sometime after Elizabeth left before Raynor sought his bed.

Aileen had directed him to the chamber just off the far end of the hall. As he opened the door, he sighed. Mayhap it would be good to lay his head upon a real bed instead of the hard ground this night. He'd had little sleep over the past few days.

But the thought was overshadowed by the knowledge that his lack of sleep had had little to do with sleeping on the ground. He was not unused to hardship.

It was thoughts of Elizabeth that haunted his nights.

Immediately he knew the room wasn't empty.

A fire had been lit in the hearth, and it cast a warm, rosy glow on the chamber and its occupant.

Elizabeth sat on a chair before the hearth. On hearing Raynor enter, she stood, turning slowly to face him. She was dressed in a long, filmy garment of white, and her black hair hung in a mass of curls about her. Raynor swallowed. It was a sight to fair take his breath away, but he gained immediate control of his reactions.

"Your pardon," Raynor said, making to back through the door. "I have obviously come into the wrong room."

Elizabeth held up her hand. "Nay, wait. 'Tis no mistake. Aileen has placed us here together. We are man and wife. It was only natural for her to assume we would be sharing a chamber.''

Raynor could not stop the rush of heat that ran up his neck. ''I see. Well, I will simply sleep outside the gates with my men.'' Raynor reached for the door. He would be glad of Bronic's familiar company. He had refused the offer of a room in the keep, saying he would leave Raynor to get acquainted with his new in-laws.

But Elizabeth stopped her husband with a shake of her head. She moved toward him slowly, and the fire was a yellow-and-red glow behind her, haloing her long, slender legs, her delicately curved figure. He felt a tightness in his loins.

Elizabeth spoke softly. ''There is no need for that, Raynor. As man and wife, we have the right to share this room.''

She stopped a mere arm's length from him. She watched him, her eyes dark, magnetic pools, but with her back to the light he could not read their expression.

''Nay,'' he whispered as he felt his resistance to her spiraling downward.

She inched closer, so close he could feel the heat from her fire-warmed skin. ''Why, Raynor? Why must it be this way? Can we not try to make a start?''

With Elizabeth standing here, asking him these questions, he found it hard to remember why he must keep his distance. He remembered the way she had looked at him over dinner, how she had voiced her agreement with his opinions, even though they differed from her brother's. He could not recall having been so warmed by such a small thing ever before.

Almost as if from outside himself, Raynor reached for her. And she came into his arms completely unresisting, offering her lips without demur.

He dragged her closer, so close their bodies seemed to meld. Raynor could feel his manhood growing against her belly, and could not keep himself from arching against her.

She groaned, wrapping her arms around his neck as he deepened their kiss. When he opened his mouth to give her his tongue, he found her open and willing. Her own tongue danced with his.

He shaped her back and hips with his palms, molding her to the hard length of him, marveling at the pliant weight of her in his arms. She sighed against his lips, undulating sensuously beneath his questing hands.

She drew back from him, her eyes locking on his as she took his large hand in her soft one. "Raynor, come to me. Come." She backed slowly toward the bed.

And he moved with her, lost in a sea of need that had been building since the first day he saw her. But as he looked at her, marveled at her beauty and the knowledge that she should want him so openly, Raynor's ardor cooled.

Why did she want him? He had given her no reason for such.

Raynor knew that, as Bronic kept saying, he was little short of cruel at times. There was no reason for Elizabeth to harbor any romantic emotions where he was concerned. Thus, this show of desire must be some trick on her part. With her beauty and woman's charms she wanted to bind him to her, take away his ability to reason for himself.

Just as his mother had done to his father.

He stopped still, forcing her to halt with him.

She turned as if sensing his withdrawal, her tone husky with confusion. "Raynor?"

He pulled his hand from hers. "Nay, witch. Say nothing. You have nearly succeeded in your scheme."

Elizabeth looked up at him. Now that they were closer to the hearth, he could see that her sapphire eyes were large and luminous. "I know not what you mean," she said.

His voice was hard with determination. "I will not be bound to you. I will not be controlled by you."

If he hadn't known better he would have thought her words sincere when she answered, for her voice shook with emotion. "I do not seek to bind you. Only to be your wife. We must at least try to begin a life together. It is our only hope of a future."

"Nay." He backed away from the temptation she offered. "There is no hope for me in what you suggest. I heard the way your brother's wife rules him. I will not be tamed like a pet hound."

With that, he turned and strode from the room, forcing down the impulse to look back. In that direction was ruin.

Elizabeth had just shown him how much power she did have over him. For a time, he had lost all concept of himself and what he wanted. Losing himself in her would be far too easy.

She contained the ability to completely swallow all that he was in the pleasure of having her.

And, worst of all, he could barely convince himself that rejecting her and that promise of pleasure was what he wanted.

Chapter Six

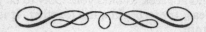

Elizabeth's fingers tightened on the reins as she caught herself staring once again at Raynor's back. It seemed she was ever doing so.

She turned away, forcing herself to focus on the beauty of the forest around them. The sharpness of spruce and fragrant cedar and the dry mustiness of fallen leaves mingled to produce a pungent, rich scent. At the roadsides and beneath the trees, trailing myrtle, violets and daisies bloomed in delicate clusters.

In other circumstances, she might have enjoyed this trip across England to a new place. But Raynor's resentment of her made that impossible.

Sweet Jesu, the man was near driving her mad. He'd barely spoken to her since the night she'd offered herself to him at Landview. Her cheeks became warm when she remembered how he'd run from her as if she might infect him with plague.

Their party had left the next morning, and though Raynor was polite and gracious with her brother and Aileen, he'd not spoken to his wife more than was absolutely necessary.

Although she'd said nothing, Elizabeth felt her sister-by-marriage knew something was wrong between the newlyweds. Aileen had watched Elizabeth and Raynor with speculation.

Elizabeth knew there weren't any traces of the tears she'd shed after Raynor left, for she had been careful to wash them away. When she left her solitary chamber, the mirror had shown no outward evidence of her unhappiness, save that her face seemed slightly paler than usual.

Her gaze drifted back to her husband.

Why was he being so difficult? It seemed the more she tried to know Raynor the more determined he was to keep her at arm's length. Couldn't he see that it was in both their best interests to try to get along?

She'd only been trying to break though the barriers that separated them.

Elizabeth tried to quell the thoughts that gave lie to that reasoning. But they would not be quelled. The truth was that she desired her husband. Had since the first moment she'd seen him. And nothing he'd done had changed that fact. There was just something about him, a freeness of spirit that told her he lived by his own rules and no others.

Elizabeth could not help admiring this strength of spirit, even as it maddened her.

Her face flamed anew as she recalled the way she reacted to his kisses. Raynor must be aware she desired him. Elizabeth could not hide it, even did she have a desire to do so. Every time he touched her, she came alive as never before.

Could that be what troubled Raynor? Was he repulsed by her open desire for him? She bit her lip in confusion.

Women at court attested to the fact that a man wanted a willing woman in his bed. And Elizabeth's brothers certainly appeared to desire this willingness in a woman.

But mayhap Raynor was different.

He had behaved unexpectedly in other ways. Did he expect her to remain unmoved by his lovemaking?

The way her body had turned to fire at his very touch, Elizabeth knew that pretending indifference would prove nigh on impossible. And what right had Raynor to think it should be so? she asked herself indignantly.

She had been able to feel the all-too-obvious evidence of his response. Just the memory of his rigid need pressed to her belly made her clench her thighs in reaction.

Elizabeth shifted restlessly in the saddle. She must needs drag her mind from that path. Thinking on the matter would gain her nothing. For whatever reason, Raynor seemed bent on denying the passion he felt toward her, and that was something she would have to acknowledge. Even so, it was very hard to accept the fact that not only would she never know love, she must also be denied the physical desire that was all Raynor seemed to be able to feel for her.

Angry with herself for allowing thoughts of Raynor to cloud her mind yet again, Elizabeth decided she would be best served by some companionship.

She slowed Minerva, dropping back to the wagon where Olwyn sat. Knowing how Raynor reacted to any delay, Elizabeth studied the situation carefully.

Seeing what Elizabeth was up to, Olwyn slid over to the middle of the seat, her brows arched in an unspoken question.

That settled it. Elizabeth leaned over and gripped the rough wooden side with both hands.

The driver of the wagon reacted with horror, but Elizabeth quelled him with a look as he made to slow down. "Keep moving," she said regally. "You know how Lord Warwicke mislikes having to halt this entourage. I know what I am about, and am in no danger."

After one pained look toward his master, where he rode ahead of them, the driver did as she said.

Agilely she climbed inside. The pace was slow, and the maneuver proved simple.

Catherine Archer 113

Once settled, Elizabeth called out to one of Raynor's mounted men to take the reins of her horse. He did so, then tied Minerva to the back of the moving wagon.

Obviously they felt it would be well to leave her to her husband, did he take issue with her. It was clear they had already realized that Elizabeth acted by her will and no other's. She was pleased, for it was best if they understood her from the outset in this situation.

Olwyn reacted to this performance without the least bit of surprise, being accustomed to Elizabeth's ways. And she felt no real concern, for she knew her mistress would do nothing to cause herself harm.

Happily distracted from the sewing in her lap, Olwyn smiled in welcome.

Elizabeth sighed, and returned her smile. "I am grown weary of my own company."

Olwyn laughed. "I will be glad of yours." She held up the needle and cloth with a rueful expression. "I fear I am making a muddle of this mending, what with all this swaying and rolling."

Elizabeth eyed the tangle dubiously. "Why do you make the effort?"

Shrugging, Olwyn placed the sewing in the basket behind her. "Sheer boredom." She looked ahead of them to where Raynor and Bronic rode at the front of the group. "Think you we will stop ere long? I am sore tired of traveling."

Elizabeth shrugged, her gaze following her woman's. "I know not. My lord husband keeps his plans close to him."

As if sensing that she was speaking of him, Raynor glanced back over his shoulder. Then he frowned with surprise and displeasure as his eyes came to rest on Elizabeth in the wagon. Raynor said something to Bronic, who nodded and dropped back.

Bronic approached, his admiring gaze was trained on Olwyn.

Elizabeth looked to her woman with a considering expression. Olwyn's cheeks were stained with delicate pink color, and she studied her hands in her lap with obvious determination.

Oho, Elizabeth thought. Could there be something brewing between these two? Elizabeth was not sure how she felt about the idea of Olwyn and Bronic together. Olwyn had been with her for many years, and the thought of being without her, especially when so many things were changing in her life, was completely unsettling.

Elizabeth stopped herself. What she need not do was dwell on the matter. If the moment came for Olwyn to leave her, Elizabeth would send her off with love. Until that time, she would simply watch to see how things developed.

She had enough on her trencher with Raynor as mate.

When the wagon came level with Bronic, the blond man fell in beside them.

"Lady Elizabeth," he said.

"Yes?" she replied politely. It was obvious that he was uncomfortable with what he was about to say, for his face became flushed as he met her eyes for a brief moment.

"Your husband requests that you ask the wagons to halt next time you wish to change places."

Elizabeth's lips tightened. "I see." She smiled then, almost too sweetly. "Clearly I fail to please my lord Warwicke at every turn. Hoping to avoid conflict with him, I sought only to save a delay in our progress to Warwicke. As it seems to make him angry no matter what I do, would you be so good as to tell my husband that I will do as I please in this respect? And should he have more instructions regarding my actions, he should have the courage to face me himself."

To Elizabeth's complete surprise, Bronic let out a burst of unrestrained laughter. "I have done so, my lady, be assured of that. The only reason I agreed to speak with you this time was that I had had enough of his ill-tempered company. He has been as a wounded wolf these past days."

So Raynor was not himself... If Bronic was surprised by Raynor's ill nature, then she must assume he was not always thus. The news came as a great relief. Elizabeth had begun to wonder if she had married a man who was capable only of anger.

Nay, Elizabeth reminded herself. Not only anger. He was certainly capable of passion, though he seemed to take little joy even in that.

But Raynor's faults were not Bronic's, and she did not wish to embroil him in her conflict with her husband. "On second thought, methinks I would be well pleased to deliver my own message to Raynor when next we speak. I have no need to send another in my stead."

Bronic laughed again. "In that case, my lady, may I ride with you awhile? Your fair company would be more welcome to me than that of one who shall remain nameless."

"Of course," Elizabeth replied. But she could see that as he spoke, Bronic's admiring gaze was on Olwyn's profile. And that fair dame was blushing like a sunset. When the companion glanced at the knight from the corner of her eye, those orbs were dark with uncertainty and longing.

Elizabeth frowned pensively. She could see that her woman did indeed return Bronic's regard, and more than a little. Elizabeth only hoped that Bronic understood that Olwyn was not to be used lightly. She felt a certain protectiveness toward the other woman even though Olwyn was older.

Of a certainty there would be no trifling with Olwyn. If Bronic desired Elizabeth's companion, he must be prepared to marry her. And, though things had not progressed so far at this time, Elizabeth could see that her notion of not worrying about the situation might not be the correct one.

This would certainly bear watching. Bronic seemed a good man, and he was definitely handsome, with his blond hair, blue eyes and Nordic features. But those qualities alone were not enough to recommend him. He must prove to be kind and loving, as well. Nothing less would do for Olwyn. She realized it was her duty to discover if Bronic was indeed a good enough match for her beloved Olwyn.

With half an ear, Elizabeth listened as the generally straightforward Olwyn answered Bronic's attempts to draw her out with uncharacteristic shyness.

Nay, there would be no harm in making sure Bronic was a good man. Elizabeth did so love order, and she sought to do all she could to make things around her go smoothly. It would not serve to leave Olwyn's future to chance.

Realizing that Raynor would likely know more about Bronic than any other, as the two seemed so close, Elizabeth determined that she would first go there for information. She had no intention of telling Raynor why she asked of his man. She had no doubt her husband would try to interfere with the budding romance, feeling as he obviously did about women, in some misguided attempt to protect Bronic.

Indeed, the very idea of Olwyn being the aggressor was quite amusing. In the years they'd been together, she'd not so much as looked at a man. That was a large part of the reason Elizabeth took her interest in Bronic so to heart.

Elizabeth knew she would have to go carefully with Raynor or he'd surely become suspicious of her motives. He'd not be able to understand that she was only trying to look after Olwyn, as she was duty bound to do.

Elizabeth's opportunity to speak with Raynor came several hours later, after they stopped to make camp for the night.

Olwyn and Elizabeth roasted several hares that Raynor brought to camp, while Bronic and the other men set up the four tents.

As this was going on, Raynor made himself busy with feeding and watering the horses, only coming close to the fire when the meal was ready. As was his wont, he quickly separated himself from the rest of the group, taking his roast meat to a large flat stump some distance away.

When Bronic sat down to chat with a shy but smiling Olwyn, Elizabeth rose and went to sit by her husband.

Raynor had obviously been deep in his own thoughts, for he seemed not to even notice her until she had settled herself beside him. For a long time, he said nothing, but his discomfort was evident in the start he gave, though she tried to hide it with a too-casual shrug.

When she saw this, Elizabeth knew a moment of puzzlement. What had she done to startle the indomitable Raynor? Then she nearly laughed aloud as understanding dawned. She had done the unthinkable and come to him. Always before, it had seemed as if Raynor had the upper hand between them. Now it was she who had made a move toward him.

Oh, but it was good to see him rattled. He did work so very hard at pretending to be indifferent to her.

Feeling wonderfully confident, Elizabeth simply sat beside her husband, taking small bites of her own well-cooked rabbit. Olwyn had stuffed the animals with the wild onions she'd gathered, and they were really quite delicious.

Finally Raynor spoke, trying too hard to keep the strain from his voice. "Elizabeth."

"Raynor," she returned politely.

"Might I do you some service?"

She turned and smiled at him, feeling quite amused. "Did you have some specific service in mind, my lord?"

His dark brows met over a strongly masculine nose. He seemed to be trying to understand why she was being so pleasant. "I did not, madame. I but refer to your presence. I must assume you desire something from me. Else why would you be here?" He indicated her place on the tree stump. Clearly he wished to get it done and see her off.

Some imp of mischief made her want to tease him but a moment longer, though she had to admit her motive was not entirely for fun. It did plague her that Raynor was so very eager to be rid of her. He was, after all, her husband, and he had neglected her terribly, even sending his man to tell her when he was not happy with her behavior. That galled her no small amount.

As Elizabeth became aware of his rising agitation, she decided she had best get that matter settled and out of the way first. "My lord husband—" she began. Elizabeth had to then bite back the retort that sprang to her mind as he grimaced at the word *husband*. She would not allow him to rile her. Like it or nay, he was wed to her.

Taking a deep breath, Elizabeth began again. "My lord husband, it has come to my attention that you have some concern for my safety."

For moment he looked perplexed. Then his face cleared, and he nodded. "Aye, you will not be climbing back and forth from horse to wagon in the future. 'Tis not safe for you to do so. You will ask the driver to stop and assist you."

His dark eyes held all the condemnation of a reprimanding father, and his lean jaw flexed with irritation. He was so very sure of himself that she longed to wipe that condescending expression from his handsome face.

But what bothered her most was that even though her stomach churned with aggravation, Elizabeth could not deny that she still found him attractive. Almost against her will, she watched that pulsing muscle and wondered what it would feel like beneath her fingers. Was the dark stubble along his cheek rough, as it appeared, or would it be soft against her palm? What would she do if at this very moment he turned to her and took her in a passionate embrace?

Why, enjoy it, of course. She had no will to do otherwise.

Rot, but that was definitely a problem. One for which she had no answer. Especially when Raynor had proved himself completely adept at resisting her.

Determinedly Elizabeth pulled her scattered thoughts to her. All that aside, what she could do was let Raynor know that he must treat her with at least a modicum of respect, if nothing else.

Regaining her former smile, Elizabeth turned to him, not speaking until he looked directly into her eyes. Her tone was oh-so-reasonable as she began, and for a moment he did not seem to understand that she was defying him. "My dear lord, I must assure you that I do appreciate your concern for me. Especially as I have not seen any evidence of such until this very day. In other circumstances, I would be most gratified by your care." She paused. "But as things are, I must assure you that I can, and will, do as I please in this matter. As I told you the day we raced, my father first set me upon a horse at the age of two, and I have been riding since. I make no false claim when I say that I can outride any man I know, including my brothers, who are no unskilled horsemen. Any one of them will uphold this claim, do you but ask them. And lastly, after the way you treated your own mount the other day, jumping him over that fallen bridge, I feel you have little right to lesson me on such a point."

As she spoke, Raynor's scowl returned full measure and more. His chest expanded until she thought the material of his brown tunic would surely burst. With a flick of his wrist, he threw the rest of his uneaten meat away and rose to stand before her. "Of course, madame, you must do as you will. As you did the night you had me to dine and Stephen came in upon us together. Your will has certainly proved to be best thus far. Why would you change your ways at this point in time?''

Elizabeth gasped as the remarks stung sharply. She stood before him, her voice rising to match his. "We have already discussed that matter, sir. I have already told you I was not trying to trap you, and my word should suffice. Why, I wouldn't have you on a wager."

A loud laugh rang out, and Elizabeth looked over to the other occupants of the camp, who were watching them with unabashed curiosity. It was Bronic who was laughing, and when her gaze met his, he winked.

Seeing they were being studied with such openness, Raynor called out, "Have none of you anything to do? If I try, I may surely find things to occupy you."

But even as the men turned away with sheepish grins, Raynor took her by the elbow and led her into the forest away from their prying eyes.

Immediately he came back with a scathing reply to her last comment. "Oh, I do believe you, Elizabeth. You've made your dissatisfaction with our union quite clear." He leaned over her. "I just make the point of indicating how capable you are of deciding what is best for yourself."

She put her hands to her slender hips. "You know nothing of me. What has gone between us is no indicator of my character or ability to make judgments."

"And thus I must go by what I see with my own eyes." His tone was rife with scorn.

She was getting very angry now, though she tried to hide it. Not for anything on God's green earth would she let him see how much he had hurt her. The worst part of it, what made tears sting behind her eyes, was that he was too near the mark. Since meeting Raynor, she had not been herself, and had made several irretrievable mistakes. The worst of which had led to their unwanted marriage.

He went on, seemingly oblivious of her attempts to stay reasonably calm, beside himself with outrage. "You women, you think of nothing beyond your own desires. My mother was one such as you. She lead my father a merry dance, thither and yon. He was as a puppet in her hands. She had only to flutter her eye lashes and sway her hips and he would come running like a studhorse. Even when she became pregnant by a man she refused to name, then gave birth to Bronic while he was in France, he had no strength to turn her away. And was she thankful for his love and forgiveness? Nay, on the contrary. She never forgave him for his weakness, using his care for her to ever gain her own way."

Elizabeth's eyes grew wider as he spoke. There was too much to take in, not the least of which was hearing that Raynor and Bronic were brothers. But she had to first focus on the revelation about his mother. Finally she was able to understand some of her husband's strange attitude toward women. She reached out to him. "Raynor."

But he brushed her hand aside, turning his back to her. "Nay, I need no gestures of sympathy from you."

She tried again. "Raynor, please. I want to understand. I had no idea . . ."

"And if I had been in my right mind, you would not even now. I am a fool for telling you all this." He pounded his fist against his open palm. "I know not how you do it. How you slither beneath my skin. But I won't allow you to keep manipulating me thus. I left that all behind me years ago, when my mother died. And even she, try as she would, could not needle me as you do. I won't have it just because some overindulged damsel can't see there are consequences to her words and actions."

He swung around to face her. "You will try to think about how your behavior might influence others in the future. It is not a request, but a demand."

She clenched her teeth, stamping her foot. He had gone too far. "How dare you! How dare you! You insufferable knave! I will not be ordered by you!"

Raynor simply stood staring down at her, his nostrils flared, as he fought for control.

Even as her mind blazed red with outrage, Elizabeth tried to regain her equilibrium. She knew there was something she must think of, something more important than the fact that Raynor had given orders he had no power to uphold. Not in her deepest nightmares would she ever take such ridiculous talk seriously. And she knew that in the rational part of his mind Raynor was aware of that fact.

What was bothering him most, what had made him speak so harshly, was what he had just told her. He had given her a glimpse, no matter how small, of the man inside.

After what she'd just learned about his past, Elizabeth realized that Raynor must be completely unnerved to think she might use what she'd just heard against him.

Battling hard with her own anger and hurt pride, Elizabeth took deep, calming breaths. If they were to have any hope for even civility between them in the future, she must go carefully now.

Elizabeth didn't know how to react. She needed time to think about what he had said, but that was a luxury she did not possess.

All she could do was try to make him see that she would treat these personal revelations gently.

It was most important for him to understand that she would not use this confidence to gain some kind of power over him. Elizabeth hesitated, began to reach out again, then pulled her hand back. "Raynor, about what you just told me . . ."

He held himself very still, his gaze directed over her head. "Do not put too much importance on what I said. It means nothing." Clearly he wished for nothing so much as for her to stop talking of the matter, to stop trying to further worm her way into his confidence.

But she could see by the pain in his eyes that the words were not true, and her heart ached at the loneliness of this man. She remembered the first time she had seen him, and how she had likened him to a wolf.

She became aware of the darkening shadows of the forest around them, the soft rusting of the spruce, pine and oak trees as they welcomed the approaching coolness of night. The dense green growth of underbrush offered cover for all manner of creatures, from deer to mouse. Over all lay a sense of restlessness, the same restlessness she sensed in Raynor. Here he was in his element. Dressed in forest colors, with his hair tousled and that faraway expression in his walnut eyes, the lupine image was very strong. Raynor was the lone beast who roamed the forest for sustenance, rest and, mayhap, solace in another of his kind.

Was it possible that she could be that one?

Elizabeth dismissed the notion as soon as it formed in her mind. And yet that ready denial was strangely distressing.

Almost as if she had no control of her tongue, Elizabeth spoke from the depths of her, knowing that she risked calling up his fury anew. ''I...I don't know what to say, Raynor. I find I know so very little of you. I cannot imagine what it must have been like to grow up that way. And yet you have gone beyond it. I am most moved that you would treat Bronic with the love you do, considering the circumstances of his birth.''

Raynor looked surprised that she had focused on this, of all the things he had said. He took several deep breaths, his gaze trained on the thick humus on the forest floor. Then, to her complete amazement, he raised his head, raking a hand through his thick hair, and replied, ''I cannot hold the sins of my mother against my brother. Bronic had no more say in his begetting than any other child.''

"Nonetheless I must tell you that I am honored to call such a man husband," she told him, with clear blue eyes open wide. "Not many would be able to accept such a thing with such kindness."

He only stared at her for a long time, his gaze confused and a little thoughtful. She went on cautiously, knowing she would be treading on treacherous ground with her next comment. But Elizabeth had wondered about his daughter since hearing of her. She would now be the three-year-old's mother. "It must also be thus with your child, else why would you go to such lengths to claim her? I admire your determination to proclaim her yours." Even as she spoke, his expression changed, became guarded and remote, as usual.

Elizabeth felt like stamping her foot, but she knew it would serve no purpose to let him see how frustrated she was. Was it because she had referred to him as husband again? Or was it because he didn't wish her to speak of his daughter?

"What you think of me, ill or good, has no bearing," he said in a monotone.

"But why must it be this way?" she asked. "We have to try to get to know each other. To make a marriage."

His hands clenched and unclenched at his sides, and he refused to look at her. "We do not." Without another word, he walked away, deeper into the forest. The stiff set of his back told her clearly that she was not to follow. He would have none of her.

No longer could she contain herself. She stamped her foot in utter frustration as she watched him go.

No man had ever been more difficult than Raynor Warwicke. Though at least now she had some notion of why he seemed to resent not only her, but all women, so much. He'd watched his mother destroy his father.

Why could he not see that she was not like his mother? She would not try to control any man to further her own ends. It was completely repugnant to her even to think of such a thing, when she knew that if the situation was reversed such a life would destroy her.

And if he could come to see that, why could they not have a marriage? They were wed, like it or nay. It could only serve them both to try to come to accept that. Even a marriage without love could know some peace, or even friendship.

Elizabeth did not ask for love. She knew better. But surely Raynor could be made to see that she was herself, and unlike any other. Now that she knew the root of the problem, Elizabeth was even more determined to work toward something more amicable than the combative state they currently knew.

Raynor did not look back as he went unheeding into the depths of the wood. He would not allow himself to do so. He needed to put some distance between himself and the witch he called wife.

What was happening to him? It was as if he lost his mind when he looked into those wide blue eyes. She seemed to be able to make him say things he'd never thought to tell a living soul. It was as if she managed to somehow get past the barriers he kept between himself and other people.

Not even Bronic knew how much his mother's manipulative nature had affected him.

Why had Elizabeth come to disrupt the life he had made?

He was proud of himself and the things he had accomplished. His father had run the lands to ruin in order to provide all the things his mother demanded. Through wise management, Raynor had renewed their prosperity. And not on the backs of his villeins.

He was a fair and conscientious manager of his lands and people. He was skilled at warfare and confident of his ability to protect what was his.

And as far as women were concerned, Raynor did not hate them, he only knew what was truth. The women he did take to his bed were infinitely more loving and passionate when he purchased them some bauble, or gave them a piece of silver.

He simply would not allow himself to become close to one. Though when he did take a woman into his bed, he was thoughtful of her pleasure, as well as his own.

In all save being able to freely give his heart and trust, Raynor felt confident and in control. And he would not risk that control, that autonomy, for a woman.

Not even one as beautiful and strangely compelling as Elizabeth. A woman who had seen his love and friendship for his illegitimate brother for what it was, and not thought him weak for caring.

For one mad moment, that had given him pause, made him wonder if Elizabeth was indeed different.

But then he'd recovered himself, when she asked about Willow. He was certain his wife would feel differently about that situation. Though she professed interest in the child, her concern was surely an act. Even the most tolerant of gentlewomen had little sympathy for their husbands' illegitimate offspring.

Surely she was simply playing to his obvious sensitivity in this area. She was intelligent enough to do so, of that he'd seen much evidence.

Elizabeth sought only to sway him with her soft words. Then, when he cared for her, when his will was no longer his own, she would use his love to get what she desired.

Else why would she make the effort to get to know him better? There was no other explanation.

It could not be because she held any regard for him. She'd made her distaste abundantly clear when she told him she had not tried to trap him into marriage.

Aye, he told himself as he let the mystery of the wood surround him with its familiar sights and sounds. Elizabeth was like all the others, seeking only to get what she wanted.

She was most clever, and must needs be resisted all the more diligently, no matter how difficult that might prove.

Chapter Seven

Elizabeth didn't know what she had expected, but Warwicke came as a surprise. Though, on thinking about it Elizabeth could not understand why. It was the home of a man who wished to keep and protect what was his, a man who gave very little of himself away.

The castle and grounds were surrounded by a high, wide wall with a walkway all around it. Over the drawbridge stood an immense thirty-foot tower. As they approached, a man leaned out over one of the merlons to watch them with apparent suspicion.

As soon as Raynor called to him, he cried out a greeting. He then turned and bellowed for someone to open the drawbridge.

Elizabeth tightened her grip on the reins. Nervous perspiration trickled down her backbone as she sat up straighter in the saddle. Although she was happy to have the journey ended, she was uncertain as to the welcome she might receive from Raynor's people. Of a surety, they had not expected him to return to Warwicke with a bride.

There was no telling what to expect.

Many times Elizabeth had wondered what the castle and its folk were like, but there had been no opportunity to inquire of her husband. Since the incident when he had told her of Bronic and his mother, some three days gone by,

Raynor had gone back to treating her as if she did not exist, for the most part. Though he had been careful to address her personally when he did have something to say, he had been no more than icily polite. And even those occasions had been few, as he had limited communication to only the most necessary of exchanges.

Elizabeth still knew nothing of his child, Willow, and the time had come for them to meet. How would the little one react to her father's marriage? Even when forewarned of such an event, children often took to a stepparent badly.

It wasn't that Elizabeth doubted her ability to mother the little one. She generally had a good rapport with children. She was simply worried that Willow might take her attitude toward Elizabeth from her father. Anyone with eyes could see that Raynor had no liking for his wife.

But the time for concern in these matters had passed. The reckoning was at hand, and she would simply have to make the best of things, as was her wont.

Elizabeth held her head high. She had garbed herself carefully this morn, in a gown of rich ivory samite and a tunic of emerald green. Olwyn had brushed her hair and covered the mass of ebony curls with a sheer ivory veil held in place with a circlet of gold. Whether Raynor wanted her or no, Elizabeth meant to show her new people honor by looking her best for her first meeting with them.

If Raynor had taken note of his wife's pains with her appearance, he'd certainly given no sign of it. After a brief, penetrating glance when she emerged from her tent that morning, he'd ignored Elizabeth as steadfastly as always.

Though his dismissal had stung, Elizabeth refused to let it daunt her. It was the goodwill of the people of Warwicke she sought. It was toward this end that Elizabeth set her sights now.

Raynor had already made it all too apparent that his could not be won.

It was his dependents with whom she must develop a rapport. Castle living was a close and intimate proposition. In order to expect any kind of harmony, she would need to gain the respect and trust of those she commanded.

In a very short time, Elizabeth was riding across the drawbridge, which spanned a moat that was relatively free of debris. As it was April, and the weather still fairly cool, there was no foul stench emanating from the water. What smell was present at the moment was more like the richness of a still meadow pond. But she had the feeling that it would not be very bad even in high summer, if the moat was kept so clean as now.

The castlefolk ran to greet them as they entered the bailey, with Raynor and Bronic in the lead. Elizabeth rode behind them on her white palfrey, and no one seemed to pay her more than cursory attention. But they smiled and called out in welcome to their lord, clearly heartened to see him safe returned to them.

Elizabeth felt her sagging spirits begin to rise just a little. Obviously Raynor's people were fond of him, and not afraid to show it.

This, in her estimation, was a good sign. And Elizabeth was eager to look for good where she could find it.

But then, as the wagons full of Elizabeth's household items followed them into the courtyard, the lively chatter died down, and the people looked to their lord and then Elizabeth with curiosity.

Raynor swung around in the saddle, staring back at his wife with a frown of displeasure on his handsome face. With slow deliberation, he dismounted from his stallion and handed the reins to a waiting groom. Still, he said nothing as he drew off his gauntlets, then ran a hand though his hair, which had been lightened by a film of dust. He did not look at her again as he tucked the gloves under his arm with studied indifference. To Elizabeth, it appeared he would rather do most anything than tell them who she was.

Beside him, Elizabeth could see Bronic grinning, as if he knew of his brother's discomfort and was completely amused by it.

Elizabeth wished she were free to enjoy Raynor's discomfort as much as Bronic appeared to. But she could not, for she was most assuredly the cause of such.

The longer Raynor remained silent, the quieter it became.

Finally, as if he could contain himself no longer, Bronic spoke up, calling their attention to him. "Good people, I fear your lord has trouble finding the words to tell you of his joyous news. As he is too overcome to speak, I will do so in his stead. My brother, Lord Raynor, has taken a bride."

All eyes went back to Raynor, as a collective murmur of shock was given. Just as Elizabeth had foreseen, it was clear from the surprise on their faces that none would have expected this.

Silence came again as they waited for Raynor to speak.

But he simply stood there, looking frustrated and uncomfortable.

Irritation made Elizabeth shift upon her palfrey. Whatever was Raynor thinking? Did he mean for them all to know how unhappy he was with his lot?

Well, Elizabeth had no intention of starting her new life under such a cloud. What was wrong between her and her husband was their business and theirs alone. She would not bear the stigma of everyone knowing she was an unwanted wife.

And it was clear she could not count on her husband for any assistance, so she must manage for herself.

Lightly she slipped from her horse and went to stand beside Raynor. With an unfaltering smile, she said, "My most dear lord and husband, do you not wish to introduce me to your folk? I fear this eager welcome has made you shy to speak of us.''

Giving himself a mental shake, Raynor looked at Elizabeth, seeing the determination in her eyes. He did not know what had come over him. He could only plead not being prepared. Ridiculous as it might seem, not until they had ridden into the keep had he even considered that he would have to introduce her to his people.

Before that, he'd been too caught up in his own anger over being saddled with her.

But he had no wish to shame Elizabeth before them all. She was his wife, and she deserved the people's honor, if for that alone.

Raynor also had no wish for anyone to know how easily he had fallen into this trap. Thus, he must put a good face on it, at least for the moment. What was between them in private was another affair.

"Aye," he said aloud, "I only search for the right words to begin." Turning to Elizabeth with a warm smile, he took her hand with courtly grace. "Let me present you to my wife, Lady Elizabeth of Warwicke. I hope you will welcome her as you do me."

There was a cheer of enthusiasm.

Elizabeth gave an unintentional start as her eyes met Raynor's. Not since that first night had he looked upon her with such an expression. The sweetness in his dark gaze near took her breath away, and her fingers involuntarily tightened on his. His hand was strong and comforting around hers, and a strange tingling raced up her arm and into her chest, making her heart throb erratically.

Then, as she glanced at him out of the corner of her eye, Elizabeth noted the lines of tension around his mouth and knew this act for what it was.

Disappointment rose to block her throat. And only the fact that he held her so securely kept her from jerking her hand away.

What a fool she was to have believed his performance for even a moment! By now she knew Raynor better than to think he would really demonstrate such open affection for her without some reason.

But, deep within herself, Elizabeth wished that things could really be so. Angrily she chastened herself, knowing she should be grateful that he had been willing to put on this act to save her dignity. More than that she could not expect, and she'd best remember that.

So thinking, Elizabeth leaned close to her husband and whispered, "You have my thanks, my lord."

Raynor was surprised at the warmth and gratitude in her eyes. He'd felt her fingers tighten in his, and for a moment he'd thought...

No, it was his own physical reaction to her that made him believe she felt the same. Just the touch of her slender fingers in his was enough to force Raynor to fight off images of those delicate hands on his skin.

As he looked into her eyes, she seemed so young and uncertain. It was a new side of the confident and assured Elizabeth. One that drew him as the night did the moon.

Before he could stop himself, Raynor gave her hand a reassuring squeeze, then released it when he realized what he had done. He should not fall into the trap of believing Elizabeth was vulnerable. No matter how she appeared at this moment, he'd well experienced how this woman was able to look after her own interests.

With that, Raynor moved away from her. "We will go into the hall. My lady wife is tired after our long journey, and would rest before she greets you each in turn. I hope you will take no offense at this and understand that I wish to keep her in good spirit." The last was said with a lascivious wink that brought a laugh from the crowd.

Elizabeth felt a deep blush steal over her cheeks as she glanced to Raynor and away. She'd had no idea he had a sense of humor of any kind, and now, suddenly, she found he did. And a bawdy one at that. The castle folk seemed not the least surprised by the remark, and she was reminded anew of how little she knew him.

As she peered around at the smiling faces, Elizabeth wondered what they would think if they knew the truth of it.

It was obvious to her that Raynor had done his utmost in presenting her at all. It would tax him beyond measure to keep up this charade for much longer. By saying he wished to conserve her strength, Raynor but sought an excuse to put his trial to an end.

And the people seemed only slightly disappointed by Raynor's pronouncement, as the reason he had given was one they could understand and sympathize with. To Elizabeth's immense relief, they began to disperse.

The hall was a long, wide chamber with a high, open-beamed ceiling. It encompassed the entire first floor of the three-story keep. A few of the castlefolk had followed them inside, but they went about their chores with only an occasional glance toward their lord and his new lady.

As Raynor led his wife across the floor, an attractive and lushly rounded young woman came from the other end of the hall, leading a small child by the hand.

She drew her up to Raynor and Elizabeth, then stood nervously before them. The fair-haired woman addressed only Raynor. "She wanted to go out into the courtyard, my lord, but I told her she mightn't, for fear of her getting trampled by the horses." To Elizabeth's eyes, her smile was obviously ingratiating.

When the woman glanced in Elizabeth's direction, her blue eyes were filled with resentment. Apparently the servant had heard of Raynor's marriage and was not pleased. Elizabeth looked away from the pretty woman with a mental shrug. She could not expect all to accept her with open arms. Understandably, it would take time to gain their true loyalty.

For his part, Raynor seemed oblivious of his woman's demeanor. "You did rightly, Hyla. She is far too reckless around the horses."

Turning to Elizabeth, Raynor cleared his throat. "My daughter, Willow."

Elizabeth looked at the child with rueful amazement.

She was dressed as a peasant, in a garment of undetermined shape made of threadbare gray wool. Smudges of dirt obscured her tiny features, and Elizabeth could not tell if she was a pretty child or not. Her brown curls were a tangle of snarls and even held some strands of straw. "What is this?" Elizabeth asked the woman, reaching to extract a piece.

"She's been sleeping in the rushes, my lady," the serving woman answered sullenly.

"On the floor?" Elizabeth queried with a scowl. The baron's daughter, sleeping in the rushes? It was appalling. Surely, she thought, Raynor will upbraid this Hyla for not looking after the child more fittingly.

He did not. It was all too obvious that her husband did not see anything amiss in this.

Elizabeth's frown deepened, but she bit back the words of censure that sprang to her tongue. As a new arrival here, she felt it was not her place to criticize what had gone before her. What she was resolved to do, though, was make sure such did not happen in future.

Now that she was lady of Warwicke, neglect of the child, even out of ignorance, would not be tolerated.

Going down on her knees, Elizabeth held out her arms to the little one. Her expression changed to one of gentleness. "Good day, Willow."

The child stood staring at Elizabeth, her limpid brown eyes wide, her fingers worrying her full bottom lip.

Elizabeth realized that the girl was terribly shy. She ran a hand over the tangled mass of curls. "I am Elizabeth, but you may call me Beth." She smiled with gentle encouragement.

Willow glanced to her father, and Raynor nodded.

She looked at the floor. "Beth," the child whispered, so softly that Elizabeth could barely hear her.

"Well," Raynor said, patting the little one on the head awkwardly. "I will leave you with Lady Elizabeth now. I have been gone for some time, and there is surely much that needs my attention."

Elizabeth's lips thinned, and she stood to face him. "Raynor, is this your only greeting for your daughter?" Despite her fierce expression, she spoke evenly, keeping her voice low, so as not to frighten the girl.

He stiffened at the censure implied in the words. "I have a bauble for her in my pack, but I must attend to some business before I can take the time to give it her."

Obviously he had no idea that his behavior was in the least bit odd, for he was looking at Elizabeth as if she had sprouted an extra head. No wonder the little girl was so shy with them, she thought. It looked as though Raynor had need of some lessons in being a father. Her own father had taken an active interest in her from her earliest memories, and she had loved him dearly.

But now, on her first day at Warwicke, with a servant looking on, was not the proper time to mention this. Besides, Elizabeth knew when tact would best serve. This was for the child's benefit, not for hers. Raynor must be made to see the proper way of treating his daughter, rather than be told.

All she said to her husband was "How very kind of you. I'm sure Willow will be most grateful for your thoughtfulness."

She took Willow's hand. "Come, dear, we shall get acquainted while your papa takes care of his business. I'm sure he'll have a big hug and a kiss for his girl later."

As she said the last words, Raynor's eyes widened in surprise. Clearly he had not so much as thought of embracing the little girl.

At Raynor's startled look, she said, "I trust your women will show me to my chambers."

He watched her, eyes narrowed, as if considering her previous remarks carefully, even as he answered her. "Of course. I will tell them where to put your belongings."

Elizabeth stopped him with a haughty look. "I would not dream of keeping you, my lord. I can attend my own affairs. If you will just point me in the right direction, I will trouble you no further."

Elizabeth started off with purpose. Already she knew she could be of some use here, no matter that her husband did not want her. Despite what he believed to the contrary, he did, at least in this one area, have some need of her.

For all that he seemed so sure of himself and all he ruled, Raynor had no notion of how to raise a child. But she meant for him to learn.

Wearily Raynor dismounted and handed his horse to a stable boy.

Since their arrival at Warwicke the previous day, he'd barely had time for thought, let alone rest. Last eve he had been called upon to settle a dispute among the men in the barracks that had lasted long into the night. There had been no opportunity for him to see Willow again.

Then, first thing this morning, the village council had sent a message begging his attendance.

Now he meant to find his daughter and give her the gift he'd brought. Much as he hated to take anything Elizabeth said as being significant, Raynor could not help thinking of what she'd said about his coming back to give the child a hug and a kiss. In all the time she'd lived with him, Raynor had not considered that the little one might be desirous of his affection. He provided food, clothing, caretakers, and protection from harm. Raynor had simply trusted to his women to see to her other needs.

The thought that he might show her affection was new, and somehow appealing. After all, he did feel a sense of love for the child. How could he not? She was an innocent pawn in what had been done to her mother.

Raynor was most eager to see how his attempts at demonstrating his caring might be met by the child. He quickened his pace, meaning to go to his chamber and retrieve the comb and the small mirror of polished silver he'd purchased for her in Windsor.

Surely even such a tiny female would not be unmoved by such treasures.

But as Raynor left the stable and approached the steps to the keep, he heard a commotion coming from around the east side. Curious, he looked in the direction of the noise.

The sight that met his eyes made Raynor stop dead in his tracks, his mouth agape in shock.

A group of his serfs and soldiers stood at the base of the keep. Above them dangled a bed, an enormous creation of dark seasoned wood with a high back and heavy posts. But what was even worse was that it was suspended on ropes that led from a gaping hole in the top floor of the keep. A hole where windows had been that very morning.

Without being told, Raynor knew whose hand was at work in this disaster.

Elizabeth.

As if thoughts of her had conjured her up, his wife's face appeared in the opening above him. "Do be careful," she was instructing, so bent on her task that she took no note of him below her. "I will not have it scratched."

How dare she go so far? To remove the windows without even asking him for his leave to do so?

With a growl of anger, Raynor made for his adversary, barely conscious of his route as he went.

It wasn't until he was in her chambers, which had previously been his mother's, that Raynor became aware of his surroundings again. He took in the group of workmen who held the ropes, his wife, still half dangling out the opening, and Bronic, who stood to one side with Olwyn. And then the pile of stones that lay against the wall to his right. His rage flashed anew, dimming his view for a moment. Not only had the vixen removed the windows, she had taken out a goodly portion of the wall itself.

His voice emerged in a bellow of rage. "Elizabeth!"

She gave a start at the sound, then took an exasperated breath before turning to him with an expression of irritation. "Yes, my lord. Can you not see that we are busy? I will attend you presently."

"You will attend me now," he commanded. "Who gave you permission to demolish my keep?"

She looked at him, her eyes narrowing to slits of displeasure. "I have demolished nothing. The bed was too large to bring up the stairs. Even with the windows out, it would not fit." She shrugged, as if any fool should be able to see that. "There was little choice but to remove a section of the wall. It will be easily repaired once we are through here. And as far as permission, I asked for none, thus could receive none." Her slender nose rose arrogantly.

Raynor gestured toward Bronic, who stood with his arms folded over his chest as he watched this exchange with amusement. "And you, you gaping fool! Why did you not stop her?"

"Stop me?" Elizabeth said, interrupting. "He could not, did he try." She strode to her husband, her hands on her slim hips. "That bed is mine, left to me by my grandmother on my mother's side. It was brought to England from Normandy with my ancestor, when he came with the

Conqueror. Think you that I mean to sleep on any other bed, my lord?''

Raynor's chest burned with anger, but for this he had no answer. Such a bed was not just a possession. It was a symbol of her station and position, as well as a family heirloom. In truth, Elizabeth did have a right to expect to sleep in it.

But to take out the very wall! Sweet Jesu, but the woman would surely drive him mad!

He looked down at her as she faced him defiantly, her blue eyes flashing with outrage. A flush colored her creamy cheeks, and her breasts rose and fell with each heaving breath she took. In spite of his fury, Raynor found himself thinking of how beautiful she was in her anger. He longed to reach out and pull her into his arms, to turn that heat of anger to passion.

Then he halted himself. Was he indeed completely mad? Here one day, and already she had thoroughly disrupted his life.

With a growl of frustration, Raynor spun around and left the room.

He was halfway down the steps to the hall when Bronic hailed him from behind. "Raynor."

The lord of Warwicke stopped, turning to his brother with a black frown drawing his brows together. "Aye!"

The blond man looked to his brother with a puzzled expression. "Raynor, you must see that she has the right of this. The wall can be repaired by the same masons who installed the windows for your father. It will not be such a great feat."

Without meeting his eyes, Raynor answered stiffly, "I was not consulted. That woman has no right to do as she pleases in my keep."

Bronic's tone was coolly reasoning. "She is your wife."

"Not by my choice, as you well know."

Shaking his head, Bronic moved to pass his brother on the stairs. Then he stopped, throwing one last remark over his shoulder. "Methinks you make a hell out of heaven, brother dear. If I had a woman like that and a bed such as that one to take her in, I would not be bemoaning my fate. Of that you may be sure."

Raynor stayed there, looking after his brother with no small amount of confusion.

He could not help remembering how restless had been his sleep on the journey here as he thought of Elizabeth's bed beneath its cloth covering. How often had he thought of his wife, naked and willing, in that very bed, though at the time he had not so much as seen it. Was that why his anger had risen so quickly?

Was the bed a symbol of his unwanted desire for Elizabeth?

And what had Bronic meant when he said he would be glad of having a woman like Elizabeth? Had Bronic fallen victim to her feminine wiles?

For a moment, he knew a fierce rush of resentment toward his brother. No matter that Raynor did not want her, Elizabeth was his.

At this Raynor stopped himself, his hands going to his head, as if he could squeeze the thoughts from his mind. Nay, he would not let her make him doubt his brother. Never would Bronic betray him, in thought or deed.

Raynor was certain of that.

A fortnight later, Raynor strode purposefully into the hall, then nearly backed out again. All the rushes had been removed from the floor, and several women were working with buckets of water and brooms to clean the stone of grime.

But he resisted the urge to leave. This was his hall, and he was not going to be driven from it.

This time Elizabeth had gone too far, and he meant for her to know it.

At the far end of the hall, near the hearth, was a trestle table. A woman was bent over it, her gently curved backside in the air as she scrubbed it with a hard brush.

Elizabeth. He felt an unexpected surge of approval toward his wife, however grudging. Not many fine ladies would demean themselves with physical labor.

But Raynor soon found himself distracted from the thought as he stood there, unable to look away while the taut line of her bottom swayed back and forth before him. He felt a tightening in his loins as he wondered what it would be like to reach out and run his hand over that sweet curve. To lift her gown and bare the creamy flesh to his view.

Sweat beaded on his brow, despite the coolness of the room.

Then, as if sensing his presence, Elizabeth turned and straightened, a look of uncertainty clouding her eyes as soon as she saw him. She wore an old wimple over her dark hair, but an ebony curl lay upon her forehead, and she pushed it back with trembling fingers. "Raynor."

He licked his lips, wiping his own hand over his face. Thank the Lord, she had no way of divining his thoughts. What was wrong with him? Mayhap it had simply been too long since he'd lain with a woman.

"Elizabeth," he answered lamely. For a moment, it was difficult to remember why he had sought her out. Ah, yes, the blankets.

In the time Elizabeth had been at Warwicke, she had turned the castle upside down. She had begun with her chambers at the top of the keep, having them cleaned, aired and set up with her own belongings.

Since the day he'd come home to find the bed being hauled up the side of the keep, Raynor had not ventured anywhere near her. He'd even forsaken his own chamber, on the top floor with hers, to bide with Bronic on the second floor.

He had refused to answer any of his brother's open gibes about the arrangement. Gladly would he deal with Bronic's sarcasm, rather than the temptation offered by his wife.

He clenched his teeth, then began, "Madame, I wish a moment of your time...."

"Of course." She called out to one of the women working nearby, "Jean, please bring wine and cheese to my solar." Elizabeth set the scrub brush on the table and turned back to Raynor. "Please, my lord." She motioned him toward the stairs at the end of the room. "We can speak more freely in my chambers."

Raynor hesitated for a moment, reluctant to venture into her sanctuary. Then he righted himself. This was his keep, every stone and beam of it. He was free to go where he would. He followed her.

At the top of the stairs, she went through the door that led to the solar. As Raynor went after her, he realized that previous to the other day, when he'd confronted Elizabeth about the bed, he had not entered these chambers since the night of his mother's death.

He braced himself to endure the unpleasant memories of returning. But his eyes widened in surprise when he looked about. The room was completely changed, from the tapestry on the wall to the cushions on the window seat.

The chamber seemed draped in rich color, the dark greens, golds, reds and blues of the tapestry's forest scene reflected in the deep carpet, draperies and cushions. He watched as Elizabeth went to the door of the bedchamber, looked inside, then closed it again. Raynor wondered if the pastels his mother had preferred were gone from there, as well.

Almost unwillingly, he realized the change was good.

Elizabeth motioned toward the chair before the empty hearth, then settled herself on the window seat.

He seated himself, feeling somewhat out of his element in such elegant surroundings. He'd never had much use for luxuries. Which reminded him of why he had come here with her in the first place.

He cleared his throat. "Elizabeth, I must speak with you."

She smiled. "So you said, my lord. I am listening."

"There is a man unloading a wagon of blankets into the storage shed. Can you tell me something of this?"

"Oh." Her brow cleared. "Of course, the blankets. Is it not a wonderful circumstance? The old rags your people are using as coverings have quite outworn their usefulness. The peddler who brought them claims they are the work of Thomas Blanket himself, and come all the way from Bristol."

Raynor stood to give weight to what he was about to say. "That is all well and good, Elizabeth, but I cannot allow—"

At that moment, there was a scratching at the door, and then Jean entered, bearing a tray of wine and cheese.

"Just one moment, my lord." Elizabeth stood and moved toward the table. "Please just put it here."

Jean set down the laden try. "Would you like me to look in on Willow?" she asked, nodding toward the closed bedchamber door. Obviously Willow was sleeping inside, Raynor thought.

"There is no need. I did so only a moment ago," Elizabeth answered as she poured out a cup of wine.

"She has been sleeping for a long time."

Both women listened for a moment, and Raynor wondered that they were making such a fuss about the child taking a nap. Before Elizabeth came, no one had seemed to make such a to-do. His women simply saw that Willow was dressed and fed as she should be.

Raynor recalled the gifts he had gotten for his daughter. The problem lay in the fact that the child was ever with his wife. In trying to avoid close contact with Elizabeth, he had not found an opportunity to give them to her. Guilt stabbed at him.

Determinedly Raynor resolved to do so this day. He would not allow Elizabeth to control his actions.

Seemingly unaware of Raynor's thoughts, Elizabeth smiled fondly. "The little one plays and sleeps with equal vehemence." She looked at the maid. "That will be all for the moment."

Jean nodded and left.

Elizabeth turned to Raynor, offering the cup of wine. "You have thirst, my lord?"

"Aye," he answered, realizing that his throat was indeed dry. He took a long pull of wine as Elizabeth sliced cheese and laid it on a thick piece of fresh bread.

"Would you care for some, my lord?" she asked sweetly.

His stomach rumbled, and he held out his hand. He had missed the midday meal. "I...thank you, Elizabeth." He sat down in his chair and bit into the delicious food.

He watched as she took a piece of cheese to nibble on, seating herself behind him at the window once more. But she did not speak as he ate his meal, waiting patiently for him to decide when he wished to continue.

Raynor sat up straighter, swallowing his food in two more quick bites. He wanted to have done with this and get on with his work. "About the blankets," he began.

"Well, sweeting," Elizabeth said, startling him so badly his mouth dropped open and he swiveled around to face her. Then he saw that she was not speaking to him at all, but to his daughter, who stood in the now open doorway between solar and bedchamber.

Raynor watched as Willow came forward shyly, her chubby fist against her rounded cheek. She looked warm and sweet and clean, in a white tunic over which she wore a cote of spring green. He'd never seen the garments before. "Willow has new clothing?"

Elizabeth didn't look at him as she moved forward to scoop the little girl up in her arms and kiss her rosy cheek. "I found several chests full of garments in these chambers when I cleaned them. The fabrics are of good quality, and should not be wasted. The best of them are being made into garments for your daughter, the others I am giving to the servants. The gowns were made for someone much shorter than myself, and thus can be of no use to me."

Raynor knew the clothing had been his mother's, and wondered that Elizabeth would simply take it upon herself to use them as she thought fit, without asking him. "Did you not think to ask me before doing this?

She glanced at him then, her eyes filled with genuine surprise. When she spoke again, though her tone remained even, there was no mistaking the irony in it. "Nay, I did not. I am not accustomed to gaining permission to act on what is only reasonable. The cloth would have moldered eventually. Why should it lie there wasting, when your daughter had no decent garments to call her own?"

Smiling down at the child, Elizabeth hugged her tightly with encouragement. "Can you say hello to your papa?" she asked, turning Willow to face Raynor.

"Hello," Willow whispered, then buried her face against Elizabeth's delicately rounded bosom.

For a crazed moment, Raynor wished that he, too, could place his face there and breathe in his wife's warmth.

But sanity returned in a rush. It was ever so when he was with Elizabeth, wishing for things he refused to allow himself. And knowing he would be a madman to wish circumstances were any different.

He stood. "Really, Elizabeth, I beg your attention for a moment." He strove to keep the irritation from his voice, but could not completely. He had no wish to argue with his wife before the child, though she tested him sorely.

She turned to him, her cheek against Willow's hair.

They made a sweet scene, with the light from the window behind them, the tall, slender beauty and the delicate child.

Why did she have to appear to be something she was not? He knew the truth only too well. She cared for nothing save her own will.

Forcefully he turned the conversation to suit himself. "My lady, I do not wish to purchase blankets. And will not do so. You should have consulted me before making such a decision."

She looked at him in surprise and growing agitation. "Should have consulted you..." she began.

Willow fidgeted, as if sensing Elizabeth's unhappiness. "Sweeting," his wife said in carefully controlled tones, setting the little girl gently on her feet. "Why do you not go and ask Jean for a cup of milk and a sweet?"

Elizabeth took her to the door of the solar and saw her on her way. "Be careful on the stairs," she added as the child scampered off.

"My dear lord." She spoke evenly, closing the door carefully and turning to Raynor again. "I must have you understand that I could not have consulted you on this matter, had I desired to do so. I see you not at all. You have not so much as eaten a meal in my presence, let alone presented yourself for discussion."

He blanched, knowing there was some truth in what she said. But that did not give her the right to keep making decisions without his permission. "I am a busy man," he reminded her. "I was gone longer than I had planned to be. My lands do not run themselves."

She smiled, but there was not the least hint of warmth or humor in her eyes. "I can and will see to the running of this keep. That much you will not deny me, my lord husband. It is my right.''

''It is not your right to make purchases.''

She spoke slowly, as if to a half-wit. ''It is, if I use my own moneys.'' She stood, her hands clenched at her sides.

He stared down at Elizabeth, feeling completely frustrated in the face of her refusal to listen to him. Words burst from Raynor, all his frustration emerging in anger. ''What gives you the right to supersede me, to come into my home and order everything to suit yourself? You change what you will, cleaning and decorating, removing windows, as if you had some right.'' He waved a wild hand. ''You have even taken over my child.''

All thoughts of staying calm and rational flew from Elizabeth's mind. She knew he had been hurt in his past and did not trust himself to love a woman. But that did not give him the right to sentence her to an existence of utter uselessness. She would order this keep as its lady should. It was her only hope of having any kind of life. Raynor couldn't possibly think she could sit in her room doing nothing for the rest of her years on this earth.

She stood tall, not giving an inch. ''My lord husband, I will not languish in this tower like some maiden in a fable. You may not want me, but I can do some good here, and I will. This castle was in a disgraceful state. Not that I blame your women. They are not the lady of the keep, and thus have no authority to set things right. But I do, and I will. And as far as Willow is concerned, you hardly have a right to the term *father*. The child was running wild about the demesne, like a serf. Do you have no thought to her future? What man would have her without a proper upbringing? She is your heir, sir, barring the birth of a son, and you give no more thought to her than if she were a pet.''

He growled deep in his throat. ''How dare you!''

She raised her chin. "I dare much, my lord. You have no concept of living with a real woman, and think to judge me by your mother. This will not serve for me."

Elizabeth glared up at him defiantly. The time had come for Raynor to begin to face some truths. She spun on her heel and stalked out, leaving him standing in her solar alone.

To her complete surprise, Raynor was in the seat of honor at the high table when she came down for dinner. He was speaking to Jean, the head serving woman.

It was the first time he'd dined with them since they had arrived, and Elizabeth seemed to be the only one to notice. Apparently Raynor always had come and gone as he would.

Of course, who here would say him nay? Bronic was the only one who might do so, and he seemed no more interested in the finer rules of daily living than his brother.

Mayhap her conversation with him earlier had made some imprint on Raynor's thinking.

She halted the thought immediately. Elizabeth knew better than to really think that might be the case. It was most likely no more than coincidence that her husband had decided to make an appearance at last.

As she came within a few feet of them, Elizabeth could hear him asking, "Why is the meal not begun?"

It was Elizabeth who replied, with studied blandness. "Because I have instructed them to await my arrival." Unhurriedly she took her own place next to him.

To her surprise, Raynor accepted this without retort. Neither did he comment on the fact that the table had been set for them with her own pewter cutlery and plate.

As soon as Elizabeth gave the signal, the servants brought out huge trays of meat, stew, bread and fish, the best of the portions going to the high table and so on down the room. The first night she dined at Warwicke, Elizabeth had been appalled to find the people already eating when she came down. In patient but firm tones, she had called the head woman aside and told her that this was not to happen again. The rules of polite society would be observed as long as she was mistress of the keep.

Raynor did not make small talk, as men were taught to do in mixed company. But he did serve her the tenderest potions of the roast deer, as would any man versed in the arts of entertaining a lady. Elizabeth had to admit that he had gone farther in attempting to be civil than she had thought he would. And he had bathed and clothed himself in a well-made tunic of forest-green velvet.

Elizabeth had just taken her first bite of the succulent stew, flavored with dill and thyme, when one of Raynor's soldiers, dressed in watch colors, entered through the wide oak door that led outside. He approached the head table with deliberate haste. "My lord," he said as he halted before the lord of Warwicke. "A man is without the castle walls, begging entrance."

"Yes?" Raynor replied with raised brows.

"'Tis a messenger from Lord Nigel Harrington."

Elizabeth felt Raynor stiffen beside her, even though they were not touching. It was as if every muscle in his body had become tight with tension.

Through clenched teeth, Raynor replied, "Tell him that he has no more than the count of ten to leave my gates, or he will be shot."

"Very good, my lord." The soldier bowed and left the hall.

Into the stillness that lingered after him, Elizabeth asked, "Who, pray tell, is Nigel Harrington?"

Raynor did not look at her. "He is Willow's uncle."

"Her uncle? But why have you sent his messenger away without even hearing why he came?"

Raynor did face her then, his eyes were dark brown pools of hatred. Though she could tell it was not directed toward her, she shivered. "Lady Elizabeth, I have accepted your interference in much of my life, even in the aspect of raising my child. But in this you will have no say. What your opinion is in this matter is of no concern to me. I will not be questioned or moved in the case of Nigel Harrington. And I will thank you to never speak that name in my keep again."

With that, he rose and strode from the hall.

Elizabeth was stung. Whatever had she done? The man was a lackwitted imbecile. Every time she thought they were making some headway in getting along, he had to prove what he was really made of.

Elizabeth looked up to see a garden of staring faces at the other tables. But every time she tried to meet someone's eyes, that person looked down.

Slowly she stood, pushed back her chair and walked from the hall.

Not only had Raynor been unfair, but he had done so before the whole of the castlefolk.

Late that night, Raynor came into the hall and saw the serfs settling down for the night in the hall.

He went to Jean, who as head woman had a place close to the fire. He watched as she shook out her bed cover over her pallet and realized that Elizabeth had been right. The cloth was worn very thin.

The woman looked up at him, her gaze unreadable in the dim light. "My lord?"

He hesitated before asking, "Has Lady Elizabeth gone to her bed?"

Jean replied with a trace of never-before-heard disapproval. "And where else would she be, my lord?"

Raynor drew back, ready to reprimand the woman, then thought better of it. Jean had known him since he was a child, having had more care of him than his own mother. And never had she spoken an unpleasant word to him.

Something was wrong with her. He had a sneaking suspicion as to what it might be.

Elizabeth.

Though she had been at Warwicke only a short time, the castlefolk seemed to have developed an uncommon fondness for her. He knew she worked alongside them, and they respected her for that. But it was more. Elizabeth cared. She wanted to make the castle a home, a place for all of them to take pride and comfort in.

"I . . ." he began, then halted. "I fear I behaved badly this eve, and for that I am sorry."

"Aye, you did, my lord Raynor." Her tone had softened. "But 'tis not me you should be saying the words to, but your lady. She knows nothing of what lies between you and Lord Harrington. As none of us do," she added. "We are simply accustomed to this feud, and as your subjects have no right to question you on it. But Lady Elizabeth, she is your wedded wife. Though you treat her as if she is not."

"It isn't fitting," she went on, as if forgetting who she was speaking to, "her sleeping alone in that big bed night after night."

Raynor sucked in his breath in shock.

Jean had gone too far, and the hand she placed over her mouth told him she knew as much.

He stepped away from her, his jaw tight. "I will thank you not to meddle in things that are beyond your understanding."

She dipped a curtsy. "Forgive me, my lord. I had no right. All I know is that Lady Elizabeth is a kind and lovely woman. Any man would be fortunate to call her wife, unlike another who has been lady here in the past."

It hung between them, the knowledge that she spoke of his mother, but not even Jean would dare to continue with that subject with Raynor. She knew the pain his mother's selfishness had inflicted upon them all.

Almost against his will, Elizabeth's face came into his mind. Her blue eyes, which could flash with anger one moment and with compassion the next.

Deep inside himself, he longed for someone to share his life, but the ghosts of the past would not quit him.

Raynor turned and left the keep.

Chapter Eight

As the weeks wore on, the one thing Raynor could not fail to credit Elizabeth for was her care of Willow. Though his wife knew nothing of the child's inheritance, she was right in training her in the duties of a landed noblewoman.

He could readily see the difference in Willow since she had been under his wife's gentle tutelage. The golden-brown curls were most often tied with ribbons to match the array of tiny cotes and tunics her new mother had made for Willow. No longer did she sleep where she happened to lie down. She did not wander about the hall with bits of bread or cheese when she grew hungry, but sat at table like a miniature lady.

Elizabeth was unfailingly patient and kind, while at the same time getting the little one to do what she wanted.

Somehow Elizabeth had been able to give the child's life structure and order. And far from resenting this, as one might think, Willow seemed to adore her, following her about the keep.

Though endearing, this circumstance did give Raynor some cause for consternation. While he had resolved within himself to try to develop a closer relationship with his daughter, he did not want to do so under Elizabeth's jaundiced eye. Because for some reason he, who controlled and was responsible for the lives and safety of hundreds of people, was nervous with the idea of openly offering his heart to a tiny little girl.

As the days passed, he began to despair of an opportunity to put his intentions into effect.

Then, one afternoon, Raynor was returning to the keep from the barracks when he came upon Willow unexpectedly. She was sitting on the ground, playing with a small, rounded stone, but she looked up at Raynor as he approached.

"Good day, my lord," she said, very politely. He nearly chuckled aloud as he realized she was perfectly imitating Elizabeth's tone and manner of addressing him.

"Hello, little Willow," he answered with a gentle smile. He looked about, wondering where Elizabeth might be. There were several serfs working in the courtyard, a woman churning, a man shoeing a horse, another woman carding wool, and various others, but there was no sign of his wife. "Are you alone?" he asked.

"Beth is making cheese," she told him She wrinkled her small, turned-up nose. "It smells bad."

This time Raynor did laugh. He had to agree. He liked cheese as well as the next man, but the sharp richness of hundreds of rounds was a bit overpowering in the cool storage chamber beneath the castle.

He gave his daughter a long appraising look, which she returned, unblinking. It was as if she, too, were taking his measure. All this time he'd thought of her as a babe, but she had become an individual who had her own thoughts and attitudes.

Now he found that having a dislike of lingering in the cold cellar linked them in some basic human way. Raynor realized that he did not know this child he'd claimed as his daughter, had not thought of her as someone to know.

But that could be changed. And Raynor would start by doing what he'd meant to for over a week. He hunkered down close to her. "Do you recall that when I first came home with Lady Elizabeth I told you I had brought you a present?"

She nodded.

"Well, let's see about that, shall we?" On an impulse that he didn't even try to resist, Raynor held out his arms. With an ever-widening smile, Willow came into them.

Standing, he cradled her small, warm body against his chest as he had seen Elizabeth do. Her soft curls smelled of rose-scented soap and he breathed deeply of its sweetness. Willow sighed and settled back against him. With that, a bridge was built between them. He knew it was just a beginning, but one had to start somewhere.

It was then that Willow smiled at him, her soft brown eyes luminous with unwavering trust.

Unexpectedly he felt a wave of such love and tenderness tighten his chest and throat that it near sent him to his knees. This was someone he could love without reservation, who might love him equally in return. What a fool he had been not to see it.

Tears stung his eyes and he had to blink them back as he carried her to the east side of the keep. Never again would anything come between them, including himself.

By the time Raynor reached the practice yard, he was in control of his emotions once more, but they were not lessened, only dampened down. It might frighten the little one to see him cry.

Looking out across the field, which held targets, tilting posts, a list, and all manner of other devices necessary to practice the art of war, Raynor called to his squire. "Arthur."

The boy laid down his bow and hurried toward Raynor. If he was surprised to see his intractable master holding his daughter, his green eyes offered no hint of it. A sturdy lad of twelve, Arthur was dressed like Raynor. He was as alike the powerful knight in all things as possible.

"I would have you go to my chambers and fetch the small pouch that sits atop my chest," Raynor told him. "And bring it to me in the orchard."

Arthur nodded and rushed off to do as he was bidden.

Raynor started across the grounds, as Willow squirmed excitedly against him. "What are we doing?" she asked, her brown eyes alight with curiosity.

He pressed a finger to the end of her button nose. "That is for you to see, minx," he answered teasingly.

In the back of Raynor's mind was one of the few happy memories he retained from childhood. One day when he was about six, his father had happened upon him trying to make a swing from a length of knotted rope. To Raynor's surprise, his father had volunteered to help, and the two of them had spent an hour without tension, or interruption from his mother. The vision of that day, and his father's relaxed smile, still lived in his heart.

Though Willow was somewhat younger, he felt a need to share some of that past happiness with her. He leaned close to her soft pink ear. "Willow, do you know what a swing is?"

She nodded, her eyes enormous. "I seed one in the village."

"Would you like to help me make one here on the castle grounds? One that you could play with yourself?"

She laughed and clapped her chubby hands together. "Oh, yes! I would Papa! I would like that!"

First Raynor went to the stables and obtained a length of sturdy rope. Then he took Willow to the orchard at the rear of the castle behind the keep. There they found several rows of neatly trimmed apple and pear trees. It was to one of the small but sturdy apple trees that Raynor went.

There was a thick limb that ran parallel to the ground, some ten feet up. It was perfect for Willow's swing.

He was just setting her down when he heard Elizabeth's voice call out the child's name.

Feeling somewhat dismayed at the idea of Elizabeth finding him playing with his child, Raynor answered hesitantly. "She is here." He told himself not to be foolish. He had every right to spend time with Willow. But the discomfort remained.

He wondered if the feeling had anything to do with the fact that Elizabeth had been the one to point out his failings as a father. He had no desire to bear the brunt of her smugly approving attitude. It would simply add to his guilt that he had not done better in the past.

As Elizabeth came toward them, Willow ran to her. "Papa is making a swing! It is for me."

Elizabeth took her hand. "Did he?" To Raynor's surprise, there was not the least hint of condescension in her manner, only a quiet curiosity. "I met Arthur on his way here," she said softly. "He told me he was bringing this to you." She opened her free hand to expose a small black velvet bag.

Raynor took it from her, then turned to Willow. He handed the pouch to her, and she began to tug at the lacing at the top. Raynor leaned forward to offer his assistance, but Elizabeth halted him with a gentle hand on his arm. "Half of the pleasure is in the opening," she told him confidingly. And, to his surprise, Raynor felt no rise of resentment toward her for offering him instruction.

At last Willow got the bag open, spilling the contents into her hand. The tiny mirror and comb were just perfect for one so small. She rushed toward him, throwing her arms around his leg. "Now I can be pretty like Beth!"

Raynor bent down and hugged her close, tears smarting in his eyes for the second time that day. "You are that already, love."

The child moved off to play with her new treasures.

When Raynor rose and Elizabeth's sapphire eyes met his, they were as warm as a lit window on a dark night.

Her warmth made him think of his talk with Jean. The head woman was convinced Elizabeth was what she appeared to be.

Mayhap he should at least give his wife an opportunity to prove herself. To do just that much would not be an irrevocable commitment on his part.

But what he might first do, Raynor realized, was beg forgiveness for the way he had spoken to Elizabeth the night Harrington's messenger came. In all fairness, he should not have reprimanded his wife before the whole assemblage.

"Elizabeth," he began, "there is something I have been wanting to say to you." He cleared his throat as she looked at him with curiosity and speculation.

He went on, more forcefully. "That night in the hall. I must beg you pardon for the way I spoke to you before the castlefolk. You are my wife and their lady. I owe you more honor than that."

Her eyes had grown rounder and rounder as he spoke, and her expression was one of amazement. Seeing this made Raynor slightly uncomfortable. Was she really so very surprised that he would admit to making a mistake? He bit back the comment that sprang to mind, then went on to finish what he had to say. "You know nothing of Harrington, and therefore can be excused that one mistake. I only ask that you be careful to refrain from mentioning the man or anything connected to him in the future."

She smiled, looking down at the ground as she replied. "How could I do other than accept such a magnanimous apology?"

Raynor watched her closely, for he sensed a hint of amusement in her tone. But when she raised her head and looked at him, her sapphire eyes were bright with happiness.

Suddenly Raynor's awkwardness left him, and he felt himself basking in the glow of her regard. Though he had been nervous as to how she would react to his apology, Elizabeth had not thrown it back in his face, as he had feared. Instead, she was behaving very well indeed. On impulse, he asked, "Would you care to help us make a swing?"

She smiled, and Raynor felt that the smile was for him and him alone. "I would be most glad to help."

Elizabeth watched the man before her as he carefully knotted the end of the rope, making sure that it was secure.

This was a day she had never thought to see. First Raynor had brought himself to beg her forgiveness, although that had come hand in hand with demands for her compliance in the matter of Willow's uncle. Then he had gone on to involve himself in an activity that had naught to do with either work or security.

Obviously, all things were possible.

This was her first indication that he might actually be willing to open up his heart. The knowledge was strangely exhilarating, though she knew his affection for his daughter had nothing to do with his feelings for her.

With the knot tied, Raynor took off his outer tunic, and Elizabeth felt a twinge in her lower belly. His tan pourpoint was open at the neck, revealing the strong column of his throat. As Raynor began to climb the tree, his wide shoulders flexed, and the rope tied about his flat belly grew taut. Elizabeth could not have moved from her stance beneath him had she tried while she marveled at the play of strong thighs in tight-fitting dark hose.

When he threw the rope down, it took her a moment to right herself and remember what she was about. Biting her lower lip, Elizabeth tried to calm her wayward thoughts as she held the bottom of the rope steady while he tied it to the branch.

What was wrong with her, that one noble action on Raynor's part could have her panting after him this way?

But that was how it had been since the beginning. Raynor had only had to be himself, and nothing more, for her to want him physically. That she could not deny. Her body's reaction to him had always been its own.

Once the rope was in place, Raynor flipped over the branch and slid down the rope. When he reached the ground, he grinned with evident pride in his accomplishment and said, "If it can hold my weight, there should be no problem with Willow. She's such a mite of a thing."

Elizabeth couldn't answer. The easy amicability of his manner completely disarmed her.

Was this Raynor as he might have been, had his life been different? For a moment, Elizabeth's heart tightened with sadness.

But she did not linger over the emotion. She knew that all the things that had shaped Raynor had made him the man who so irritated her, but so compelled her at the same time.

She also knew these feelings must stay hidden. Any hint of her attraction to him must be kept at bay, for it only seemed to drive him away. Elizabeth must control her reactions, not only for the sake of her pride, but for their relationship to retain this seemingly friendly footing.

Thus thinking, she answered offhandedly, "Mayhap I should try it out first." She watched Willow's small face.

The little girl had placed her mirror and comb carefully aside and was bouncing with excitement. "Me, me! Can I go first?"

"What think you, Raynor?" Elizabeth teased gently. "Should we trust our little treasure to your swing?"

His answer was unexpectedly low, and charged with an intense emotion that she could not identify. "Is she our little treasure, Elizabeth?"

When she glanced up at him, the look in Raynor's eyes made Elizabeth pause. Her breath caught in her throat, and her pulse quickened. His expression was eager, and at the same time uncertain. She held still as he took a step closer to her, bringing them within mere inches of each other. She held her breath, feeling that any wrong movement on her part could break the spell of intimacy that hovered like mist in the air around the three of them. Raynor, Elizabeth and their child.

She nodded, then spoke softly. "Aye, Raynor. If that is your wish, she could be our treasure. Yours and mine." The words hung between them, as real as an invitation. But Elizabeth knew not what to do from there.

She was dragged back to reality by a tug on her hand. "May I swing? May I swing now?"

Raynor recovered first, picking Willow up and setting her short legs over the huge knot of hemp. "Now hold tight," he instructed as he pushed her off, very gently.

The three of them played there for a time, more like a real family than Elizabeth had ever thought they could be.

Not that she allowed herself to believe Raynor was coming to accept their marriage. It was more as if he had realized that it was important to be a father to Willow, and was making an effort to accept Elizabeth as part of that equation, because of his daughter's love for her.

It was later, after Elizabeth called a halt to the game in order to make ready for the noon meal, that Raynor confirmed her belief.

As they walked back to the keep, Willow running on ahead, her black bag clutched in her hand, they were silent, but for once there was no tension in the silence.

It was Raynor who broke the quiet by saying, "Elizabeth, I have something to say to you."

She stopped as he did, turning to face him. "Yes?"

He did not meet her eyes. Instead, his fond gaze followed his daughter across the bailey. "I wish to thank you for your care of Willow. She is come to life since you arrived at Warwicke."

A warm glow washed over Elizabeth at his praise, but she could not take undue credit. "My lord, I have done nothing special. The child only had need of some attention. She was left too much to her own devices."

"Still," he said, as if the words cost him much, but had to be said, "I am grateful for your efforts. Many women would not have been so quick to take their husband's natural child to their bosom." He ended stiffly.

Elizabeth could not contain a self-conscious laugh. "But, my lord, can you not see that the circumstances of Willow's birth are not of her making? 'Twas not her fault her parents were not wed." She said this without thinking, simply wanting him to know that Willow's parentage was not of the least worry to her.

But she could tell when Raynor answered that he had taken offense. "I beg you, madame, to remember that you do not know all of what occurred in that situation." His tone grew thick with regret. "I would have wed Louisa in an instant, would she have agreed. But she, like many women, was set in her own mind and refused me."

Elizabeth blanched, not only at the implied reprimand, which she had not deserved, but also at the love in Raynor's voice when he spoke of Willow's mother.

Obviously Raynor had desired a marriage to Louisa. His love had been so great that he had been able to overcome his natural aversion to the state. Elizabeth had assumed that her husband's disregard for wedded bliss had always been a part of his makeup. Now she found that it was not, at least in connection to Willow's mother. The thought was like a naked blade in her belly.

But she did not wish for Raynor to see how jealous she was at hearing this. Her own tone was cool as winter wind. "I had no wish to pry into your relationship with the child's mother. I thought only to assure you that I did not hold her parentage against her, and add that she needed only the supervision and attention of a devoted parent. You, my lord, could have filled that void as well as I. I simply made the effort."

He had the grace to flush, and then he nodded jerkily. "I fear I had no idea of raising a child. I thought to leave her to the women of the keep. Many have children of their own and look after them well enough."

Elizabeth raised her hand. "I did not mean to offer criticism, my lord. I thought only to explain what I have done. You have no gentlewomen here, and the others have no real idea of raising a baron's daughter as she should be raised. Someday little Willow will have the task of running her own castle and folk. I but wish to see her properly trained for her station and responsibilities." Even as the bastard child of a baron, Willow could expect to make a good match.

"As you have been trained?" he asked.

She tried to read his voice for a hint as to why he had asked the question, but there was none. She could only answer him as if the query were a casual one. "Yes, as I have been. My mother took her duty to heart. I know how to make servants obey with enthusiasm. I can oversee the making of candles, food and clothing, and the preserving of stores for the winter. I can organize cleaning, dry herbs, entertain guests of high rank and keep ledgers with a legible hand." She shrugged, as if these accomplishments were nothing more than her duty. "I am as I was taught to be."

She looked into Raynor's eyes, willing him to see that she was not trying to take over his life, but only to live hers. To fulfill the work she had been trained to do.

Raynor stared at her for a long moment, then answered, "I begin to see why we are at odds." He looked away. "Mayhap I should simply leave you to it. I shall have to give the matter some thought."

With that, he turned and strode off.

Elizabeth was left staring after him, wondering what that last cryptic remark had meant.

That night, Raynor watched while Elizabeth went about her duties in the hall. The evening meal had been delicious, and served at the height of its readiness, as all the meals had been since the second day of Elizabeth's residence at Warwicke.

As he sat sharing a drink of ale with Bronic, Raynor realized he felt good, pleasantly full, relaxed and peaceful. His gaze went again to his wife, who was directing one of the churls in removing some soiled rushes.

As a heavy and unquestionably wistful sigh escaped him, he looked up to see Bronic studying him. Feeling that he had given away more of his thoughts than he would have liked, Raynor took a sip from his pewter cup.

But just then Bronic's voice interrupted his thoughts. "She is a good woman, the lady Elizabeth."

Unbidden Raynor recalled that one moment of suspicion of his brother, the day Elizabeth had taken out the castle windows. But as he had then, Raynor dismissed it immediately. He strove to keep any hint of reaction from his voice. "What makes you say so, brother?"

Bronic shook his head condescendingly, his square jaw jutting out. "It appears you are the only one who does not see the truth of this, Raynor. Your lady wife works from morning to night to see to the good and comfort of all in this keep. Not in my memory have we been so well cared for, and with so little complaint."

"She makes us soft," Raynor replied, fighting the stirrings of contentment inside himself. He was afraid to give in to those feelings, afraid of losing himself in Elizabeth. And not because she made his life comfortable.

His gaze went to her, held captive like an animal in a trap as she tossed her black hair, laughing softly as she said something that made the churl flush with pleasure. Elizabeth turned to beckon another boy, raising her arm, and he could not look away from the gentle curve of her breast in rich blue velvet.

Night and day he thought of little save Elizabeth and where she was, who she spoke to, what she said.

He had not so much as lain with her, and already he was slave to her wiles. Raynor ran an agitated hand through his thick, dark hair.

Almost against his will, he found himself telling his brother of the confusion in his heart.

As if sensing that Raynor was truly seeking some kind of answer, Bronic replied without his usual sarcasm. "What say you, Raynor?" He leaned forward. "In so many ways, Lady Elizabeth seems nigh on to being the perfect woman. She cares for Willow as if she was her own. She works alongside the castlefolk, making them love her without question. Your lady's gentleness and care of all of us is unstinting."

Raynor interrupted then, unable to let that last remark pass. "Not all."

"Aye, all," Bronic replied impatiently. "For you more than anyone else, Raynor. Have you not seen that, in spite of your ill humor and bad temper, she treats you with unfailing courtesy?" As Raynor's eyes widened in disbelief, Bronic added. "That is, until you drive her beyond it."

For a long moment, Raynor sat thinking. Though some of what his brother said could certainly be debated, most could not be denied. She was a good woman in all these areas. But there were other things about Elizabeth that were equally true, things that could not be passed over.

"On the other side of the coin," Raynor said, "she is headstrong, willful and demanding. She deliberately defies my every wish, and cares only for her own desires."

Bronic began to laugh, and Raynor scowled as the blond man spoke freely. "Brother mine, Lady Elizabeth cannot disobey wishes she knows nothing about. It does not occur to her to ask you so that you may be defied. She simply goes on as she thinks is best." He paused, pointing a blunt finger toward his brother. "The problem, Raynor, is that you and she are too much alike. Think on this. Do you feel you are disobeying your wife when you fail to consult her on a matter you are perfectly capable of deciding on your own?"

Raynor's scowl deepened. "'Tis not the same. I am lord of this keep." He raised his hand in a sweeping gesture. "The responsibility of all rests with me."

Bronic stood with a shrug. "As she feels it is with her." He turned and left a very confused Raynor staring after him.

Raynor remembered what Elizabeth had said to him earlier in the day, how she had been trained to do the tasks she performed. His impulse then had been that she should do so. But the thought of allowing her to have her will without his restraining hand...well, it was daunting, to say the least. How far would Elizabeth go, should he give her free reign?

His gaze went back to his wife, across the hall. Could he trust her to push no farther? Would she try to pry her way into the rest of his life, as his mother had done?

Elizabeth was now directing a woman in the cleaning of a tabletop. When she shook her head and took the cloth, bending to finish the task herself, the fabric of her blue cote stretched taut over the gentle swell of her bottom. Raynor felt a tightening in his groin, and shifted on his seat. But he was unable to look away as she straightened and smoothed the raven curls that had escaped her braid.

God, but she was beautiful, he told himself. There was no use in trying to deny it, even to himself—any man would find her so. But she was not some other man's, she was his, though in truth he knew nothing of her. Then, unbidden, a strange thought occurred to him.

Was it not odd that Bronic seemed to know so much of what Elizabeth was about? As soon as the thought was formed, Raynor pushed it aside in shame. He would not believe ill of his brother.

Elizabeth could feel Raynor's eyes upon her like a touch. Since the afternoon they'd spent with Willow, there was a new intensity in the way he looked at her.

She was near to screaming with frustration and confusion. What did he want from her? The heat of his gaze told its own story. But surely, if he desired her, Raynor would say so? She was his wife, and he had the right to take her when and where he would.

It was especially hurtful for Elizabeth to know that though he did not even act upon his desire for her, he still seemed to love Louisa. What traits had that gentle damsel possessed that Elizabeth did not? Had she been more beautiful, more kind, more caring? Who could say what strange fusion of qualities brought about the love of a man like Raynor?

Elizabeth knew she was jealous—oh, yes, without doubt, and of a woman who was near three years gone from this life. Though she did keep trying to remind herself that she should be gladdened to know that Raynor had loved Louisa. If he had been capable of loving once, then could he not come to care for her at least a little?

Though the possibility was remote, it seemed not so much so as before.

She knew that for Raynor to love her was beyond expectation. The circumstances of their marriage had seen to that. He would never be able to completely forgive her for what had happened. His pride and his need for the freedom to choose his own way were too strong for that.

The question was, could he learn to respect and honor her? Even that much would be as near to heaven as Elizabeth could imagine.

Long after she had left the hall and gone to her chamber for the night, these troubles would not cease plaguing Elizabeth. Her big bed sat ready, the heavy draperies pulled back invitingly on the warmth of the fire. Olwyn helped her to change into a sleeping gown of fine gauze, then left to seek her own rest.

But even after Olwyn had left, Elizabeth could not stop thinking about Raynor. Her desire to make him see that they must learn to live together with some small trace of harmony would not be dimmed this night.

Finally Elizabeth knew she could wait no more. There was never an opportunity in the day for her to speak with Raynor on any personal subject. Today, when they made the swing for Willow, had been the first time. And even then they had been within full sight of all who worked about the castle grounds.

How could she ever hope to make him understand, if she had no opportunity to tell him how she felt, to make him understand that it was important to make peace? His actions today with Willow made her think he might be ready to try.

Determined to act before she could change her mind, Elizabeth took her ruby velvet robe from the end of the bed and drew it on. She had no trouble locating Raynor's chamber, for it was the only room in the keep that she had not yet entered.

The chamber was bathed in the light from the fire, and she was surprised to see how neatly her husband lived. Two chests stood against the inner wall, their tops closed. Only a comb and a carefully folded cloak on one. The floor was bare, and there was no decoration save a coat of arms above the heavy curtained bed. The draperies looked clean, but the once-gold color had faded to dull yellow.

Elizabeth was appalled at the spareness of the chamber, and knew an intense desire to set it aright.

As baron of Warwicke, Raynor was deserving of some comforts. His people did not go without, as he cared well for them and made certain their homes and farms were in good repair.

But knowing how Raynor felt about her interfering, she would not change things without consulting him. Elizabeth made a mental note to speak to him about getting new carpets and draperies, if naught else.

But not this night. Tonight they had more important matters to discuss.

As she came farther into the room, Elizabeth heard the sound of someone moving in the bed.

She hesitated a moment, then squared her slender shoulders. "Raynor, it is I, Elizabeth."

A moment later, a head came out from between the bedclothes. It was not Raynor.

A mass of pale blond hair framed the pretty female face that looked at her with shock. It was the very same serving woman who had looked at her so resentfully on her first day at Warwicke. That resentment was now explained.

A blaze of red rose up to obscure Elizabeth's vision, and a throbbing rage filled her veins, making her limbs shake. How dare he! When he would not so much as touch her, his own lawfully wedded wife!

Without a moment's hesitation, Elizabeth moved to the bed and jerked the curtains open. She was not surprised to find the slut unclothed.

What did surprise her was that Raynor was not in the bed.

Disappointment at not being able to vent her spleen upon him made her seethe. Killing him would simply have

to wait until he returned. First she would deal with his leman. "Get up," Elizabeth growled.

The girl cowered there for a moment. Then, as if she suddenly realized she was fighting for her very position as Raynor's harlot, she raised her head, tossing her hair back from her shoulders to expose swelling breasts and a narrow waist. "I am waiting for my lord."

Elizabeth was not impressed by this view of the wench's charms. Ripping one of the bed curtains down, she tossed it to the little trollop. "I said get up!"

The girl cringed, but did not move. "You have no right to send me away. My lord Warwicke wants me in his bed."

Elizabeth felt a stab of pain in her belly at the knowledge that the words were true, but they did not sway her. She leaned closer. "On my authority as mistress in this keep, I order you to get out of that bed. Does my husband wish to rut with you, he will take you in the stable, or somewhere equally fitting. You will not now, nor ever again, venture into a place that is mine and mine alone."

The girl quaked, grabbing up the curtain and holding it over her nakedness, but she had not lost all her fight. She jumped down, standing with her head high, though tears streaked her pale cheeks. "Don't mistake, Lady Elizabeth. Everyone knows you don't share my lord's bed. 'Tis a disgrace that you won't have him, nor will you let him have another."

Elizabeth would have laughed, had the situation been less volatile. Did they really believe it was she who rejected Raynor?

If only the truth were known.

At that moment, she heard her husband's voice from the doorway. She spun around, ready to tear him to shreds with her tongue.

But the furious expression on his face, and what he said, made her tirade die aborning. "Hyla!" He strode toward the serf. "Get you from my chambers, and do not come back!"

The serving woman started toward him, dropping the cover so that he could see the voluptuous fruits she offered. "My lord..."

He simply picked the curtain up and threw it at her, the ice in his eyes freezing her where she stood. Raynor indicated Elizabeth with a sweep of his hand. "This lady is my wife, and the baroness of Warwicke. Do you ever again speak to her as you just did, I will have you whipped."

She shrank away from him with a gasp of denial. "Nay." Sniveling as if she had been struck, Hyla ran from the room.

Elizabeth was beyond speech. One moment she had been ready to berate her husband for not showing her the respect of keeping his leman from her own home, the next she was overcome to hear him speak of her with such deference.

Raynor rounded on Elizabeth, his anger a dull flame in his eyes. And in spite of the way he had just defended his wife, he seemed little pleased to see her. "To what do I owe this honor, wife?"

She pulled herself together, standing tall as she remembered that Raynor had actually been upholding her position as his baroness. Not Elizabeth herself. It was his fault that there was any need to do so. If he hadn't made his unhappiness with the marriage known, there would be no need. "I but came to speak with you, and inadvertently found your doxy in your bed," she answered resentfully. "Is there some reason I should not come to your rooms if I desire? I have more right to be here than that woman. You set me up to ridicule by sending her here."

He spoke slowly and carefully. "I did not send for her, nor any other. I have not in the time you have been at Warwicke." He finished quietly, "Though I know not why."

The last part was lost to insignificance as Elizabeth heard the truth in his statement. Raynor would not lie to her about this. He would not demean himself to do so.

Unaccountably she felt a strange flush of happiness. He had bedded no other. That was something, was it not? Though honesty told her the situation would not go on indefinitely.

At least he would not be rutting with Hyla. After what Raynor had said to her, she would not have the courage to place herself in his bed again. But Elizabeth knew the woman who replaced her would be no more acceptable in her eyes.

Thinking to have it out in the open at last, Elizabeth moved closer to him, her gaze catching his in the light of the fire. "Raynor, did you know that they all think I will not have you in my bed?" Her voice was low and uncertain. "What would the castlefolk say if they knew that it is you who will not have me?"

"Elizabeth..." he began, as if to stop her from going on.

But she was not to be halted. "Why do you keep yourself from me? I am your wife, Raynor. We are wed in the eyes of God and man. If you desire a woman, why can it not be me?"

She was so close she could feel the heat of him, and it was hotter and more radiant than the fire at her back. How she wanted this man, wanted his lips on hers, his arms around her.

He stood looking down at her, his expression strained as if he fought some inner battle, his hands clenched at his sides.

Their long-suppressed desire was a real entity between them, called to pulsing life just by Elizabeth's speaking the words. Her bated breath came from between parted lips. Her lids felt heavy as she looked into the darkening pools of his eyes.

Then it seemed he no longer had the will to resist her, or himself. Raynor reached out. Slowly, but without hesitation, he pulled her close. It was as if the inevitable had been accepted, then welcomed as his lips found hers.

She opened to him immediately, more ready for this moment than she had been for any in her life. Their previous encounters had done nothing but fuel this flickering desire that made her pulse race and her senses whirl. As he drew her tongue into his mouth, she groaned, a sweet ache pooling in her lower stomach.

With eager fingers, she pulled at the bottom of Raynor's tunic, wanting to feel his naked skin.

Hooking his hand over hers, Raynor stepped back and drew the garment over his head. He was bare beneath it, and Elizabeth's eager fingers moved to touch the smooth flesh of his chest. He sucked in a quick breath of pleasure, his lids coming down to mask the passion in his eyes. But Elizabeth had seen how he reacted to her touch, and she gloried in it.

Then he pulled her into his arms again, molding her to the hard contours of his masculine body. In complete abandon, Elizabeth threw her head back, allowing him full access as he pressed hot kisses to the column of her throat.

Trusting Raynor with some instinctive part of her mind, Elizabeth leaned into him. She trailed her hands over the hard lines of his back and shoulders. God, but he was a wonder, so much a man and so very beautiful to her.

How she had longed for this time, for the simple right to touch her husband, whom she desired beyond reason.

Through the haze of her passion, Elizabeth became aware of a sound behind her. Distantly she realized someone had come into the room.

Surely Raynor would send them away, make them realize they must not come into his chamber when he was here with his wife. But he simply stiffened under her hands, his supple muscles ridging with tension.

Elizabeth took a deep, ragged breath and pulled away from him. When she looked at his face, there was no emotion there. Turning to find out who had come in, Elizabeth saw Raynor's squire, Arthur.

Arthur stood there, seemingly struck dumb by what he was seeing. Raynor's sword hung forgotten in his arms. The boy seemed to come to his senses. "My pardon, Lord Warwicke. I did not know. I simply brought your sword...." Awkwardly he held the weapon up as proof. "I will go—"

"Nay, Arthur, stay," Raynor said at last, his voice devoid of emotion. "Lady Elizabeth was just leaving."

The words hit her with the force of blows. Even after what had just happened between them, she was being summarily dismissed. Once again he had shown how easily he could set her aside. As if she were nothing. Turning to look at her husband, her eyes on fire with anger and disillusion, Elizabeth raised her head high. Not for anything would she have let him see how much this rejection had hurt her.

"Aye," she said, "I was just leaving. My thanks to you, lord husband, for a lesson well learned."

As she left, Elizabeth remembered why she had gone to his room in the beginning.

They had not talked, as she had hoped.

Her hopes for a pax between them seemed foolish now, in the face of Raynor's latest rejection of her.

Chapter Nine

Once again, Raynor found his gaze wandering about the hall, his attention drifting from the case before him.

His fingers clenched around the arms of his high-backed chair. Where Elizabeth was concerned, it was as if he had no power over his own thoughts and emotions.

The previous day's events, the happy time they'd spent together with Willow, then the fierce eruption of passion between them in his room, had left them even more confused than before. He shook his head. Only Arthur's interruption had kept him from taking her then and there.

These events, and his growing attraction for his wife, his increasing desire to see her gentleness, honesty and forthright nature as genuine, made Raynor hope. And those feelings of hope were more terrifying to him than facing the fiercest foe in battle. For if he came to care for her, if he allowed himself to love her, it would be irrevocably.

The pull of her was that powerful and all-encompassing, and Raynor dreaded losing himself in anyone else to that extent. So much so that he felt compelled to do everything in his will to prevent it.

But was he not wrong for doing so? Was he a fool, as Bronic and Jean had told him? Was he tossing away a chance at happiness by continuing to reject Elizabeth?

Raynor knew he'd hurt her last eve, but he hadn't been able to stop himself. No matter how wrongly, he had simply reacted out of a need to keep her from seeing how much she affected him. In all honesty, he was sorry, but he did not know how to make amends. For he was not ready to commit himself to trusting Elizabeth. It was easy enough for Bronic to say she was simply independent. He did not have to live with knowing that his wife could turn that streak of willfulness against him at any moment.

He came back to reality when he realized he could no longer hear the villager talking.

God's blood, he thought. Today was his day for hearing his villeins' troubles, and he was attending nothing.

"Well, my lord?" the stocky farmer asked, his blue eyes puzzled. "Am I to be allowed to graze my sheep on the common with the others?" He nervously wiped a shock of sun-streaked hair from his forehead.

Raynor held up his hand. He knew this was no petty problem for the man. Even among the lower classes, there was a hierarchy, and those from the more influential families managed to dole out the best grazing lands among themselves. "Aye," Raynor nodded. "I will speak to John Marshal. If the warden has no objection of merit, you may."

With a smile of elation, the man bowed. "You have my thanks, my lord Warwicke." He turned then and left the hall.

Raynor looked to his bailif, a slightly rounded, neatly dressed man of no more than forty. The man spoke with a respectful nod to his master. "That is all for today."

The baron of Warwicke barely restrained a sigh as he rose and made his way from the room. He had no doubt that half the folk who had attended today's judgments would be returning in the next month. He had heard little of what had been said, and thus could not have made the kind of definitive decisions he usually did.

As the manorial court was sought only when the village courts had not proved successful, Raynor understood that his judgments were of great import to his people. He took their trust seriously, and usually gave them his full attention, no matter how insignificant some of the disputes seemed.

He had not done so this day.

The kitchen was hot, and Elizabeth wiped her brow with the back of her hand as she looked about her.

Several other women were working—peeling, mixing and kneading—about the rough-hewn tables. The fire in the hearth gave off a great deal of heat, but the large stone oven had to be hot for baking. A cauldron of stew hung over the flames, suspended on a chain that could be raised and lowered to regulate the heat. Along the walls hung various pots and cooking utensils. And despite the closeness of the chamber, there was an ordered air to the bustling activity.

Elizabeth had been here for the past hour, after being asked to portion out the spices for the day's baking. The scents of cinnamon, cloves and ginger wafted around her, and she breathed deeply. Ever since she was a child, she had loved to help with the baking of sweets.

Her slight frame gave lie to the sweet tooth that had made her the brunt of good-hearted teasing from her family.

With childlike enthusiasm, the lady of Warwicke sucked a bit of mince from her finger.

Eva, the cook, a slightly pudgy woman of eternal optimism, laughed, pointing a flour-covered finger. "Lady Elizabeth, never have I seen the like." She waved a hand to indicate her ample girth. "You'd best watch, or you'll be looking like me ere long."

Elizabeth smiled. "I have no fear, for I was thin as a child, and have worked mightily to fill myself out."

Another woman spoke up, rolling her eyes to emphasize her point. "I've not heard any complaints from her husband. In fact, Arthur had a pretty tale to tell this very morning."

A deep flush stained Elizabeth's cheeks. Obviously the squire had not kept last eve's events to himself. The castlefolk knew of the strain between her and her husband, and took Arthur's tale as a sign that all would be well between master and mistress.

She wished they would not discuss her relationship with Raynor so openly. But she knew the castlefolk had a slightly bawdy view of life, and meant no ill. That they teased her was only a sign of their affection.

Elizabeth also knew that the women would never treat her so familiarly in the hall. But here in the kitchen, she had entered Eva's domain. She accepted this with good grace.

Only one in the room seemed less than affectionate in her attitude toward the lady of Warwicke. Elizabeth was aware of Hyla, sitting beside the fire, peeling pears. She had not seen the woman since last night, when she had thrown her from her husband's bed. There was no amusement on Hyla's face as she listened to the women talking. She wore a stiff mask of anger, and jabbed her knife into a pear with barely suppressed resentment.

If the truth weren't so painful, Elizabeth might have laughed. Hyla need have no fear that Raynor had rejected her out of any feelings for his wife. Obviously the squire had not thought to mention that Raynor had sent Elizabeth from him at the first opportunity.

When she felt a hand brush against her skirts, Elizabeth looked down to see Willow.

"Good morrow, dearest." Elizabeth smiled, glad to see the little girl, but equally glad to change the subject.

"Will you play with me?" Willow asked, her wide brown eyes pleading.

Already Elizabeth loved the little one with all her heart, but she could not give in to that pleading. Willow must come to understand that there was a time for work and a time for play. It was an important part of her training. "Not now, Willow," Elizabeth told her gently. "Mayhap later. I must finish here first."

Willow's bottom lip protruded, but she said nothing, and Elizabeth was pleased. The child was coming along.

At that moment, a hush fell over the room, and Elizabeth looked up from her work.

Raynor stood in the wide doorway, looking tall and handsome with the sun gilding his brown hair and outlining his broad shoulders. He came into the kitchen hesitantly, as if unsure of his welcome.

Elizabeth grew still, uncertain of her reaction to seeing him here, especially after what had just been said. Not to mention the scene of the previous night.

After the way her husband had treated her last eve, it would be difficult to try to hold on to her resolve to get on with him. Even if he did appear the epitome of manhood, standing there so tall and strong in the entryway.

The cook turned and hurried to Raynor's side, bowing with deference. "What may I do for you, my lord Warwicke?" She was clearly pleased and honored that he should come into her kitchen.

Not once since she had been in Warwicke had Elizabeth seen him enter this chamber. Nervously she smoothed her hair back from her forehead, wondering what had brought Raynor here.

He answered very casually. "I wish for you to gather enough supplies to last three men for two days."

Elizabeth frowned. This was somewhat odd. Why had Raynor come with such a request himself? It was the kind of thing he usually left to his steward to oversee. Even as he talked with Eva, his gaze wandered about the room.

When Raynor's eyes met hers, he stopped, then glanced quickly away.

Stranger and stranger, she thought.

A moment later, he started toward her.

Elizabeth smoothed her hands over her skirt, knowing that the aged yellow tunic did not become her. She shrugged. There was naught to be done for it.

He stopped beside her and spoke pleasantly. "Good day, Lady Elizabeth." It was as if last night had never been.

She nodded, not meeting his gaze. "My lord."

He watched her add nutmeg to the vat of mince and stir. "You have no need to do this work," he said. "Eva has enough women to do the baking."

She stiffened, feeling she was being criticized. Facing him with a raised chin, she said, "I know that, my lord. I do this as my choice."

He nodded, and her shoulders relaxed. For some reason, he was even more ill at ease than she. This helped her find her equilibrium.

Raynor replied slowly, as if searching for the right words. "You may do as you like here. You are the lady of Warwicke. I am most sure your assistance is greatly valued."

Unaccountably, Elizabeth knew a surge of pleasure. She knew this was not an affirmation of affection, but she understood that Raynor was deliberately making an effort to be cordial. Was this his way of saying he was sorry for the way he had behaved last night? Judging from his nervous expression, it would seem to be. It was so unexpected that she could not remain unmoved in the face of such an overture. She met his gaze openly, smiling sweetly.

He returned the smile, then hesitantly reached toward her, wiping his finger across the skin beside her mouth. As her husband touched her, Elizabeth shivered, despite the heat of the room and the weight of the eyes that stared at them.

"You had mince on your face," he told her, holding up the finger.

Elizabeth raised her own hand to the spot he had touched, giggling. "I—"

But she stopped when he raised his finger to his mouth and licked the mince from it.

A strange flush of heat swelled in her thighs and trailed upward through her body.

Unexpectedly, into the quiet that had settled on the room, came the sound of a slap. It was followed by a startled wail.

Elizabeth looked about in confusion. Even when she located the direction of the sound and saw Willow holding a reddening cheek and Hyla standing over her with an angry stance, it took her a moment to realize what had happened.

Hyla's belligerent comment clarified the situation. "Brat! That will teach you to take food without asking!"

It was then that Elizabeth noticed the crushed mince pasty in Willow's little fist.

Rage filled Elizabeth, undulating through her with the sounds of Willow's crying. But before she could act, Raynor sprang from her side. He grabbed Hyla and dragged her to the door of the kitchen, casting her out into the courtyard.

Elizabeth and the other women moved to follow him out.

As Hyla screamed, trying to gain her feet, he shouted, pointing a finger that shook with rage, "Get you from Warwicke, and never return!"

A gasp arose from the gathering crowd. A woman alone in the world, without protection, had little hope of survival.

"Nay, my lord!" she cried in horror. "Do not cast me out! Beat me, but do not throw me out, I beg of you!"

Raynor looked around at the crowd. "No one, and I mean no one, is to give her shelter or assistance. This woman has dared to strike my daughter. I would have it known now that the same punishment will come to any who are so foolish as to think themselves above my wrath. Willow is my child, and as such has my protection." He pounded a fist against his wide chest. "I trust that will be remembered."

With that, he strode back into the kitchen and tenderly scooped his still-wailing daughter into his arms. Raynor then carried her from the courtyard, leaving none to doubt her worth to him.

Elizabeth stood as stunned as the rest.

Hyla had not stopped sobbing, and she turned glazed eyes to the people around her. "Please, will no one help me?" But none would meet her gaze. She was not well liked as it was, and no one would risk Raynor's wrath to offer her succor.

Though she had little sympathy for the woman, Elizabeth went into the kitchen and gathered some of the fresh-baked pastries and bread, wrapping them in a clean cloth. She then went to the shelf and cut a large slice of cheese. This she also wrapped in a cloth.

She took them out into the courtyard and handed them to Hyla. "Take this, and never come back," she told her. "Lord Raynor has done right in sending you away. Mayhap if you try, you will attain God's forgiveness for taking your own frustrations out on a helpless child."

With a snarl that was nothing akin to gratitude, Hyla grabbed the food from Elizabeth and scurried off.

Turning away, Elizabeth put the other woman from her mind. There was no sense in worrying about the banished serving woman. Her kind was like a cat, always managing to land on its feet. Elizabeth only hoped that it would be far from here.

Her thoughts turned to Raynor. It was only meet that the castlefolk should see how dear Willow was to him. At last Raynor was beginning to be able to openly show more of the loving man within him.

She remembered the way her husband had come into the kitchen. It was almost as if he had been looking for her. And he had been so very different, almost as if he were reaching out to her. A delicate flutter of hope rose in her breast. Could Raynor be coming to like her, at least a little?

That was not what she desired from her husband, but it would be a beginning of sorts.

She tried not to dwell on all the things she did want from Raynor, the desire he awakened in her with just a touch, the need to share his life.

Unbidden, her mind went back to the moment in the kitchen, when he had tasted the mince that he had taken from her mouth. With a groan, Elizabeth rested her hand over her lower belly.

It served no purpose to think about these things. She would do well to center her thoughts on less inflammatory matters. She must hope for nothing above friendship and peace with her husband. To even consider more was to open herself to disappointment and heartache. Last night was proof of that.

The next evening, Raynor returned to the keep exhausted from a day spent riding about his lands. He was weary beyond measure, but for all his efforts, he had not washed the thoughts of Elizabeth from his mind.

He knew Elizabeth had given food to Hyla even after he forbade anyone to help her. But he would not reprimand her. It would be useless to do so, though the deed reminded him of how headstrong Elizabeth was and made him wonder anew at the wisdom of trusting in her.

Yet he could not completely fault Elizabeth's kind act of helping a woman she had reason to despise.

Raynor realized banishing Hyla was a severe punishment. He had acted out of a pure, unsullied instinct to protect and defend his child. Nothing more.

Yet once he calmed, he'd felt a growing sense of responsibility for what had happened. If he had made it known all along that abuse of his daughter would not be tolerated, it might never have happened.

It had taken Elizabeth's arrival and subsequent attention to Willow to make him see that a parent must be involved in a child's daily life.

Elizabeth. She had changed so much in his life in the short weeks she had been at Warwicke. And it seemed that she was able to do so without even trying. Just by being herself, she made him see the world more clearly.

And therein lay Raynor's problem. Was he seeing things more clearly than before? Or was he becoming infatuated with a beautiful and cleverly manipulative woman? On the one hand, he wanted to believe in her, but on the other, he could not allow himself to.

Had his father felt this way about his mother in the beginning? Had he become so enraptured by her that he lost all ability to see her as she truly was?

Raynor opened the door to his chamber with a tired sigh. If only he could have the answers to his questions. If only he could see Elizabeth without her beauty and sensuality to color his thinking. Unfortunately, it was impossible. He was attracted to Elizabeth, more than he'd ever thought to be to any woman.

Images of her filled his nights with fantasies of heated flesh and passionate responses.

Raynor stopped on the threshold of his chamber. The big wooden tub had been set before the fire. Steam rose invitingly from its depths.

Too tired to question such bounty, Raynor sat down on the bench by the fire and began to remove his clothing. First came his shoes, hose and cross garters, then his tunic and pourpoint.

Soon he was chin-deep in the pleasantly hot water, its heat and buoyancy relieving his tired muscles. Before long he could feel his lids growing heavy and allowed them to close. This night he would miss going to the hall to eat.

He was exhausted from fighting his feelings for Elizabeth, and not sure anymore of why he did so.

Raynor awakened when the door opened behind him. He knew not how long he had been asleep. Judging by the much cooler temperature of the water, it had been for some time.

"Arthur," he said, thinking that it must be his squire, "did you finish cleaning my saddle?"

"It is I," came Elizabeth's voice, directly behind him.

With a start, he turned to face her.

She quieted him with gentle hands on his shoulders. "Nay, my lord. Do not get up, but let me attend to your bath."

"I have no need of assistance," he told her stiffly. For some reason, he felt painfully vulnerable with Elizabeth here like this. But Raynor would not let her see how shaken he was at the notion of her assisting him to bathe. He would prove, if only to himself, that he was capable of resisting his wife, that she held no sway over him. It was important for him to do so if he was ever going to be able to live with her in any semblance of harmony. He would be his own man!

He gave a brief nod, still struggling with the nearly overpowering urge to send her away. "My thanks for your help."

Unaware of his motives, Elizabeth smiled as she dipped the cloth she held ·in the water and smoothed it over his wide shoulders. Dear heaven, but Raynor was beautiful, his skin golden and smooth in the firelight.

Since the day Raynor had sent Hyla way, he'd seemed different. There was a barely concealed hunger in his eyes when he looked at her, and more than that, a deep yearning that went beyond the physical. It was the awareness of that yearning that had given Elizabeth the confidence to have this bath prepared for her husband. For some reason, it had become very important for her to be with him, to perform this wifely task as any other woman would for her husband. It was as if it might establish a new foundation for them, if he could accept her in this way.

Careful to keep her tone matter-of-fact, she said, "Lean forward and I will wash your hair." He did what she asked, allowing her to minister to his needs without demur. She felt hope rise like a new seedling in her breast.

Taking a pitcher from the floor beside the tub, Elizabeth poured water over his head, then lathered it with soap scented with sandalwood. The thick mass felt heavy in her fingers, and she knew a growing sense of wonder.

Never in the weeks they had been wed had she touched him so intimately, not even when they'd nearly been overcome by the force of their passion. Those times had been fraught with a tension and an overwhelming desire that blocked out all else.

This strong, virile man was her husband. By God's laws, she had the right to touch him this way, to feel the weight of his wet hair in her hands, to know the contours and touch of his body.

But Raynor did not want their relationship to be an intimate one, and if ever they were to attain some peace, she had to respect his wishes. Elizabeth must content herself with this moment, and what little closeness he could give.

Then, as Raynor leaned back, giving her silent permission to do as she would, Elizabeth realized there was no fooling herself. The reality of him naked and acquiescent beneath her hands was as heady as strong red wine. How she wanted him—not just his friendship, but his passion.

Without conscious thought, she dropped the cloth, soaped her hand, then ran her fingers over his skin. He grew perfectly still. It was as if he were waiting for some desired event, but could not move toward it. Slowly, and with infinite sensuality, Elizabeth traced his shoulders, then moved both hands around to glide down his chest.

She heard him sigh, but there was nothing of contentment in it. The sound was ragged, and as full of tension as a strung bow.

Her own heart galloped in her chest at an alarming pace. Not stopping to ponder the wisdom of her actions, or what Raynor's reaction might be, Elizabeth pressed her lips to the tender flesh at the back of his neck. She closed her eyes on the heat that filled her.

Raynor shivered beneath her lips, and her name escaped him in a desperate whisper. "Elizabeth."

"Raynor." She kissed him again, not knowing what she was doing, acting solely on her own impulses.

As her lips brushed his neck, Raynor knew he was lost. His body quivered with long-suppressed desire.

He turned to face her, wanting her to understand fully what was happening between them. Slowly he stood, his gaze never leaving her face as his body was exposed to her view.

Elizabeth drank in the sight of him, tall and golden, and beautiful beyond words. His manhood thrust proudly from a thatch of dark curls, and she marveled at the way it pulsed and reared toward her as she looked upon it.

Again he whispered her name, his voice husky with longing. "Elizabeth?"

She rose to face him, taking his hand. Her eyes were hot with her own passion. "Yes."

He stepped from the tub and took her in his arms, unable to hold himself back anymore. This moment had been coming since the first time he saw her. It was as inevitable as the phases of the moon, and just as powerful.

With a groan, Raynor caught her in his arms and carried her to his bed. He laid her down upon it and reached to take her gown from her, but his hands trembled with desire, and he was uncharacteristically clumsy.

With a muffled curse, he ripped the gown down the front. When the cloth caught halfway down, Elizabeth raised desperate fingers to help him. Soon her clothing was a ruined pile on the floor. But she was naked beneath her husband, and where his body touched hers there was fire.

As he lowered his dark head to suckle at her breasts, she gasped at the subsequent melting heat in her lower belly. Raynor's large hands traced her flesh with wonder and barely restrained passion. Where they lingered, the tender undersides of her breasts, her flat stomach and tapered hips, her skin flamed with awareness.

Unable to wait for another moment, Raynor rose above her. Telling himself this was her first time, and he must go slowly, so as not to hurt her, he moved carefully. Holding back with every ounce of his will, he took uneven, deep breaths, trying to think past the fierce erotic pounding of his blood. Sweat beaded on his brow, and he shuddered with the effort it cost him to control himself.

Elizabeth was on fire, her body aching and hungry for Raynor, needing to feel him inside her as she had never needed anything before. She knew in the deepest part of herself that only by being fully joined to him would this agonizing craving be eased.

With a gasp of desperation, she rose up, engulfing him in the hot moistness of her body. There was only a momentary hint of pain, as distant as the stars, before the pleasure engulfed her. She rocked toward him, feeling a spreading warmth of piercingly sweet tension rising up to block all thoughts of anything beyond the joy of it. And then she was lost as the rapture surged up to drown her.

Raynor cried out as he felt Elizabeth shudder beneath him. He could no longer keep back the tide of his own fulfillment, thrusting deep inside her as his seed burst forth in a raging torrent.

She held him to her, sobbing out her happiness. "Now you are mine."

For a moment, Raynor lay still, barely hearing her past the throbbing pleasure still pulsing inside him. Then her words sunk deep, wiping the fog of passion from his mind.

Now you are mine.

He rolled away from her and rose to kneel beside her on the bed. Not seeing the confusion and hurt in her eyes, he stared down at her as if she were a stranger.

He shook his head wildly and growled in frustration. Even now, as he looked at Elizabeth, overwhelmed by his dread of being owned and controlled by her, Raynor could not stop the tightening of desire in his body. He could not still the rush of wanting that the sight of her, flushed from his passion, brought to the fore.

He turned away, in an agony of confusion and hurt.

"Raynor." She sat up, holding out her hand. "What is it? What is wrong?"

He stood, picking up his discarded clothing from the floor, then began to pull them on.

"Raynor," she called out desperately, "answer me. You owe me that much."

His walnut eyes were dark and deep as a forest at midnight. "I owe you nothing." He went to the door. "And make no mistake, my lady, I belong to no one save myself."

The door shut behind him with a sickening finality.

Wrapping her arms around her knees, Elizabeth began to cry. They had gone from the heights of pleasure to the depths of despair too quickly. Reaction made her shake as if with palsy.

What had she said? It had been nothing more than a simple declaration of her own happiness at finally being with him. That and that alone had called up Raynor's fear of being subjugated by her.

Tears fell in hot trails down her pale cheeks. Dear God, what was to become of her?

She had become his wife at last, only to be rejected in the next moment. And so long as Raynor refused to overcome his misgivings about being ruled by a woman, naught would change. He had to see that giving of his heart did not mean thralldom.

Chapter Ten

Over the next days, Elizabeth did all she could to stay out of Raynor's path. It was not really a problem, because he seemed as bent on keeping clear of her.

One morning she awakened early to realize that she was allowing Raynor too much power over her. Since she had not done anything wrong, she could not change him. Her husband had to come to see her as she truly was and not as he imagined, and only he could make that happen.

She decided to go riding. Minerva had been sadly neglected over the past few days, and was surely eager to resume their morning rides. Even more, Elizabeth felt she could take some comfort in being with her old friend.

The mare did not look on Elizabeth with helpless sadness, as Olwyn did. The companion was aware of the trouble between Elizabeth and her husband. She had taken note of the torn gown Elizabeth had tried to hide in the bottom of her chest. But when the golden-haired woman questioned her, Elizabeth had refused to be drawn.

Though she took comfort from her woman, Elizabeth refused to discuss her marriage. It was for herself and Raynor to right the wrongs between them, thus telling Olwyn would serve no real purpose other than venting her spleen.

And, truth to tell, it would have hurt Elizabeth to admit how bad things were. She did not want to explain that Raynor was angry over having made love to her, that he felt doing so was somehow a detriment to his self-government.

For Elizabeth, the experience had been a glorious awakening. Raynor had seen it as an attempt to bind him.

Going to the stables, she asked for Minerva to be saddled. It was as she was waiting that Elizabeth realized she had forgotten her gloves. Hurriedly she made her way to her chambers to retrieve them.

The sight that met Elizabeth's eyes when she opened the door to her solar made her stop short in surprise. Olwyn and Bronic stood in the middle of the the room, locked in a passionate embrace.

Hearing her gasp, they started apart. As soon as Olwyn saw that it was Elizabeth, she stared at the stone floor, a deep crimson flush traveling up her neck and over her face.

Bronic had the grace to look slightly uncomfortable, but he was slow to take his arm from around her companion's slim waist.

This evidence of his care for Olwyn heartened Elizabeth. She met his proud gaze and smiled. Here was a man who knew how to share his feelings with a woman. Would that her own husband had learned the same trait.

Bronic grinned in return, obviously relieved that she did not disapprove. Though something did tell her that he would not have curtailed his pursuit of Olwyn even if Elizabeth had been against the relationship. As he drew his arm from around the golden-haired beauty, his hand lingered in a tender caress. He spoke to Olwyn gently, intimately. "I will see you when I return to the keep this eve."

Only then did Olwyn glance toward Elizabeth, and what she saw made her smile shyly. She nodded to the man. "Aye."

As he left them, Bronic paused at the door. "Good day, Lady Elizabeth, and thank you."

She inclined her head. "Good day."

When he was gone, Olwyn turned to Elizabeth, her face flushed, her light blue eyes clouded with renewed uncertainty. "It has never happened before. He simply came to ask me something.... I cannot even recall what now." The blush darkened again. "And I'm not sure what—"

With a raised hand, Elizabeth halted her. "There is no need to go on, Olwyn. He is a most agreeable knight, and I can well understand why you might succumb to his attentions. I well like him myself." She laughed, with teasingly arched brows. "Though clearly not as much as yourself."

As she finished, Elizabeth knew that what she said was true. Since learning that he was Raynor's brother, she'd watched the other man closely. In his pursuit of her companion, Bronic had made his presence known, turning up all the time. And he'd shown himself to be of good and honorable character.

Olwyn beamed, her whole being lighting up as she looked at the door through which he had recently left. "Aye, he is most agreeable."

Seeing the happiness on her face, Elizabeth knew a momentary twinge of loneliness. If only she were as free to express her affection for Raynor.

Olwyn spoke earnestly. "I would not leave you now, when you have no one else, my lady. I will continue to serve as your companion."

With a shake of her head, Elizabeth hurried to reassure her, though she felt a stab of pain at the truth of Olwyn's statement. She pushed down the emotion, for nothing could be gained by feeling sorry for herself. "Nay, you must go forward with your life. Have no fear for me, I will see to my own problems. You will allow your feelings for Bronic to take their own course."

Olwyn seemed unconvinced. "Elizabeth, you need not remain here. Either Henry or Stephen would have you, and gladly. There you might be happy again."

For a moment, Elizabeth was shocked beyond reason at such an idea. Then she wondered whence such a violent reaction had come. Surely it was not such an unreasonable notion that she might go to one of her brothers. They would indeed have her gladly.

But Elizabeth could not go. Her determination to make a marriage with Raynor had gone beyond the original stubborn determination to set her mistake right. Now the idea of living without Raynor, no matter how exasperating and unpleasant he might be, was abhorrent. The few glimpses she'd had of the lonely and hurting man inside him made her long to fill the void. "Nay." She held up a commanding hand. "Warwicke is my home now. I must make what I can of that."

With a smile of what she hoped was complete assurance, Elizabeth fetched her gloves and went to collect her mount.

It was only a few short minutes later that she was outside the keep and turning her horse away from Warwicke and her problems.

But they did not remain behind her, despite her intentions. Raynor's unhappiness and distrust of her hung over her like heavy, stifling smoke.

What Elizabeth had told Olwyn was true. No matter how painful things were for her here at Warwicke, the thought of leaving was excruciating. To never see Raynor smile at her in that sweetly yearning way, to never feel the touch of his hands... She shook her head. No. Difficult as it was, as long as she remained at Warwicke there was hope of making a life with him. Even if that hope was as distant as it now seemed.

She kneed her mount to a gallop, trying to clear her mind of the pain of remembering the coldness in his eyes after they'd made love. Her face burned at the memory of how she had given herself to him, losing all thought of anything save the way he made her feel. When he touched her, Elizabeth became nothing more than a creature of need and desire. No matter how she tried to block them out, the tormenting memories refused to leave her.

For those short moments while he'd held her, losing himself in her body, she had felt how much he needed her. But she was sure his very need was what kept him away. Raynor could not trust any woman after the way his mother had treated his father. And only he could overcome that mistrust.

As it was, the more he cared for Elizabeth, the more desperately he seemed to hold her away from him.

She let Minerva have her head as they raced across an open pasture. The warm June breeze tugged at her wimple and the skirt of her crimson velvet gown. But even the freedom of riding with the wind did not dispel her melancholy.

It was as Elizabeth reached the top of a particularly sharp rise that a horse and a male rider came into view at the edge of the forest before her. She slowed, unsure of whether to go on. After refusing the company of the stable boy, the lady was more conscious of her aloneness than she might have been. She was not a timid woman, having lived so many years at court with Stephen. But she knew no one in the region, and did not wish to put herself in undue jeopardy.

She had just turned to ride in the opposite direction when she heard her name shouted out. "Lady Warwicke!"

She looked back over her shoulder and saw the man moving toward her over the greensward. She hesitated.

He called out again. "Please wait, Lady Warwicke. I will not harm you."

Against reason, this convinced her. She knew that if he wished her harm, the man would certainly claim otherwise. But she felt no inner sense of disquiet, and that stayed her.

Then, for the first time in days, Elizabeth smiled. If naught else, living with Raynor had convinced her she could deal with most men.

The man who stopped before her on a dark brown stallion had a strongly made face, light brown hair and blue eyes, and seemed somehow familiar. She tried, but could not place him. "Have we met?" she asked with a puzzled frown.

He bowed. "Dear lady, we have. Though at that time you were Elizabeth Clayburn. It was some four years ago, at Windsor, when I came there. You were all of sixteen and newly arrived at court."

"You were with a lady," she replied, at last recalling the meeting. "Was she not your sister?"

"My stepsister, Louisa. I am Sir Nigel Harrington."

At that moment, Elizabeth understood that this was Willow's uncle, the very man whose name Raynor refused to even hear. And that would make his sister..."Louisa. Willow's mother." By concentrating, Elizabeth could call up a vague image of the other woman. If her memory served her, Louisa had been a small woman, with brown hair and eyes, like her daughter. This surprised Elizabeth, for she had always thought that Willow's coloring must be a lighter version of her father's.

He nodded as an expression of anger and pain passed over his features. "The very same."

Elizabeth stated the obvious. "That means you are Willow's uncle." She studied him for a long moment. She remembered how furious Raynor had become when this man simply sent a messenger to the keep. "Why is my husband so set against you?" she asked bluntly.

He shook his head, looking away from her as if he could not bear for her to see the pain in his eyes. "I know not. I loved Louisa." His voice took on a note of anger. "I have a right to see Willow. She is my flesh and blood, all that is left of our family. Warwicke thinks to keep her from me, but he has no right."

"Why would he do so?" she asked.

He looked to her then, his expression filled with longing. "I know not. I only know that he will not allow me to take the child and care for her as she should be."

Elizabeth knew she could ease his sadness on that score at least. "Have no more concern for that. I have taken over the child's care, and I must add that Raynor has begun to understand what he needs do to be a good father, as well."

Nigel's lips tightened for a moment, but he took a deep breath, then smiled sadly. "For that much, I must thank you, Lady Elizabeth. It will indeed ease my mind to know little Willow has you with her."

Then he went on, his gaze directed at the ground, and again she had the feeling that what he was saying was terribly painful for him to admit. "But I am a lonely man, with Louisa gone from this life. Willow is all I have in the world, and I've never so much as seen the little one. Just once, I wish to hold her in my arms. It would be like having a small piece of my sister returned to me. That is why I took my case before the king. Your husband refused me any access to her whatsoever. I had hoped Edward would understand my need to be with my niece. But the king did not listen to me." Harrington's voice rose in what appeared to be anger, but he quickly squelched it, shaking his head slowly. "His Majesty only heard Warwicke. He refused to see how much having the child would mean to me."

Elizabeth fidgeted in confusion. She had no idea why Raynor would deny Nigel Harrington even some small access to his dead sister's child. He seemed nothing but a lonely and hurting shell of a man.

Remembering the way Raynor had confessed his feelings for Louisa, Elizabeth could only think that Raynor was determined to keep his beloved's child to himself.

An idea crept into Elizabeth's mind. Mayhap she could do something to make Raynor change his mind about allowing Nigel to see Willow. That might teach him a lesson about sharing love, rather than clutching it so close.

She said, "I could speak to my husband on your behalf."

Nigel leaned toward her, his eyes alight with some inner fire. "Oh, if only you could, dear lady. Would that you could help us make some truce."

She raised a cautioning hand. "I must tell you true, before you take too much hope. I have little influence with my husband, and fear he will not heed what I ask of him."

With raised brows, Nigel looked at her with flattering disbelief. "It is difficult for me to believe that such a lovely woman could have so little influence upon her husband. Be assured that were you mine, I would move heaven and earth to gain you your way."

Elizabeth shrugged. This kind of ingratiating flattery was not unknown to her, thus she did not take it to heart. Her real concern was with making him see that he should not set his sights upon her ability to make Raynor change his mind. She said, "I do not speak out of false modesty, my lord Harrington. I tell you fact."

"Nonetheless," he told her, "I shall remain optimistic. This is the first sign of hope I have had. You must allow me that."

Elizabeth pulled up her reins. "As you will." Then she paused, as something else occurred to her. "How came you to be here this day? It is an odd thing that we should meet."

He looked down at his hand, where it rested on the pommel of his saddle. "I have a confession to make. I often ride close to Warwicke, hoping against hope that I will get even a small glimpse of the child." He looked at her, his eyes ingenuous. "It was only fortune that made your path cross mine."

Elizabeth studied him, wanting to warn Nigel again not to be too hopeful, then thought better of it. Who was she to rob another of hope? "I shall send word when I have news."

"I will take nary a breath in anticipation," he said.

She realized there was nothing she could say that would dull his enthusiasm, so there was no point in continuing to try. She only hoped Harrington was not setting himself up for a grave disappointment. He did not understand as clearly as she how little her husband valued her opinions.

Glancing upward, she saw the sun had climbed high overhead. "I have tarried long enough," she said. "I must return to Warwicke. I will be late for the meal as it is."

He did not try to detain her. "Again you have my thanks," he told her. "Go with God."

"Goodbye," she told him, and turned to ride for home.

For a moment after she left him, Elizabeth felt a glimmer of hope that she might actually succeed, despite her pessimism with Harrington. She clung to a vision of Raynor embracing her as he spoke of his gratitude for her bringing the two families together and ending their feud. But deep inside, Elizabeth knew it was not likely to happen. Now that she was alone, without the sadness in Nigel's eyes to prod her, Elizabeth knew her husband was not apt to even listen to her. She was a fool to have thought otherwise, even for a heartbeat. Raynor was angry enough with her. Any hint of perceived disloyalty was sure to feed his distrust and set him even more firmly against her.

But she raised her head high, feeling the wind on her flushed face. She would not cower from doing what was right simply because Raynor would be angry. It was not in her to do so.

Besides, it wasn't as if she risked their relationship by doing this. They had none to risk.

She relegated to the back of her consciousness the hope that this might bring her and Raynor closer together.

Elizabeth had resolved to broach the subject with her husband as soon as she had an opportunity. Unfortunately, one was not presented for several days.

When Raynor did not wish to see her, he was a master at making himself unavailable.

Finally Elizabeth knew she had to have it done or scream. With Olwyn acting as her scout, she waited up late one night. When the companion came to her with news that Raynor had returned to the keep, then gone to his chambers, Elizabeth gathered her courage about her and made her way there.

She did not bother to knock, knowing her husband would only refuse her admittance.

When she opened the door and stepped into his rooms, Raynor was seated before the fire, his long legs stretched out before him, a cup of wine in his hand. He started up from his slouched position as soon as he saw her.

"What do you here?" he growled.

She stood tall and straight, refusing to be intimidated. "I would have a word with you, my lord."

He set his cup on the floor and turned to face her. "Surely whatever you have to say can wait until the morrow. You are not welcome here."

A sharp stab of pain made her clench one fist to her chest. Then she told herself not to be foolish. She had expected no more from Raynor. Defiantly she faced him. "This will not wait, my lord. I have been trying to gain an audience with you for these four days now. It seems you are ever too busy." She raised haughty black brows. "Or might it be that you are avoiding me, as usual?"

Raynor had the grace to look abashed. There was no way for him to deny the truth of her charge. Avoiding her was exactly what he had been been doing since the night they had made love. He was completely confused about his own feelings. On the one hand, he knew Elizabeth was right. He did judge all women by his mother, but he could not bring himself to put those fears aside. It was a matter of self-preservation. No matter how much he might be tempted to see the good in Elizabeth, her care for Willow, her unselfish ability to work toward the good of Warwicke, the gentleness of her. All were overshadowed with doubt when he thought of her other traits. The stubbornness, willfulness and headstrong attitude that were also a part of her. How could he be certain those characteristic could be overcome?

Wishing to see her gone as quickly as possible, Raynor nodded jerkily. "Have your say, then, and leave me in peace."

She came a few steps farther into the room, but was careful to keep a distance between them. For some inexplicable reason, this annoyed him. But he forced the feelings aside, telling himself not to be a fool.

Elizabeth went on. "I want to ask you of a matter that I know will not please you...." She hesitated.

He stiffened, then shrugged with irritation. "Then why are you here, madame?" He looked away from her, telling himself not to allow her to provoke him.

She looked at him, her eyes meeting his challengingly. "Because it must needs be done. You do not frighten me, husband. I will not cower from a subject simply because you may not care to discuss it. What I do, I do because I feel it is right." Then she added hopefully, under her breath, "Mayhap when all is done you might have occasion to thank me."

He stared at her for a long moment that stretched her nerves to taut strings. Finally he nodded, and had she not known better, she would have sworn she saw admiration in his gaze.

He motioned toward the chair he had vacated. "Then, by all means, do what you will."

She came toward him and sat in the proffered seat, then wondered at the wisdom of this when she looked up at him, so tall and powerful above her.

He folded his arms over his broad chest. "Well?"

"I want you to hear me out before you say anything," she warned with a scathing glance. "I know you prefer not to listen to any other opinion besides your own, but this one time, you could try."

He scowled blackly, his dark brows meeting over his straight nose. "Get on with it."

She sat straighter in the chair and cleared her throat. "A few days ago, I was out riding, and I chanced upon a man."

His lips tightened. "A man?"

"Yes, someone you know. He...he told me of a...problem he is having with you, and I offered to intercede with you on his behalf."

His eyes had become dark pools of suspicion. "I hope, Elizabeth, that you are not talking of the one I suspect. It would be most foolish of you to even mention that name in my presence, or even in this keep, as I have forewarned you."

She stood, facing him with equal heat. "Why, Raynor? Why do you hate Lord Harrington so?"

His fist struck the wall near him with incredible force, and she saw blood appear on his knuckles. "I did warn you, woman. Why must you trespass where you are not wanted? Why must you meddle in affairs you do not understand?"

"Then pray help me to understand, my lord, why you would so despise one who is lonely and alone, as Lord Harrington is. He wants nothing so much as to see Willow, yet you deny him that, for some selfish reason of your own."

Before she knew what was happening, she was caught in a viselike grip as Raynor's hands closed on her shoulders. He drew her forward and up close to his face. As he leaned over her, his voice was filled with barely suppressed rage. "Harrington is not what he seems. If you have one jot of loyalty in you, you will hear me on this. I will not allow that man to see Willow. If you defy me this time, wife, you will pay. And I do not make that threat lightly."

She glared up at him, though her heart was pounding. "I told you, my lord husband, I do not fear you." Why did he always react like this, before she had an opportunity to even try to fathom his reasons?

He stared at her, fierce emotions flitting across his features with incredible speed. Then, as if he had fought some inner battle and won, he slowly took his hands from her shoulders, setting her away with finality. "I see that you do not."

He turned from her and walked several steps away. He did not look at her as he went on, and she could hear the exhaustion in his voice. "Elizabeth, I beg you. For your good and mine, and Willow's—especially for Willow's. As you love her, do not take this further. I will not ask you for promises. Obviously you feel no loyalty to me, and thus would not give them. But I plead with you, leave this lie. Louisa would turn over in her grave if she knew what you are trying to do."

Elizabeth didn't know what to say. She desperately wanted to comprehend, but he gave her no clue. "I want to do what is right, Raynor. If only you would tell me why it must be this way."

He shook his head. Without emotion, he replied, "I will not. I cannot."

She studied his broad back, shaking her head in defeat. "You will not let me into your life. You share nothing with me that helps me to understand you or makes me feel like a real wife. If you treated me at all as if I were a part of your world, it would help me to see things from your view, but you will give nothing."

Fighting feelings of betrayal, Raynor could not look at her, at the beauty and temptation of her. Her words barely registered in his mind, and not enough for comprehension. He'd known all along that Elizabeth would be trouble for him. That she would show her true colors eventually. Now that it was proving to be true, he felt no satisfaction in being right. Aligning herself with his worst enemy was surely the epitome of treachery.

Disappointment rocked him. He spoke cruelly, out of his pain. "Did you really think that bedding you once would so bind me that I would be moved to do what you wanted? And why Harrington, of all people? Surely you could have found some more obviously selfish favor to beg of me. That I could understand. How could helping Harrington be of any benefit to you? Why would you deceive me in this way, Elizabeth, unless you were deliberately trying to hurt me?"

"Deceive you?" she gasped. "I have not told you a falsehood since that day I said Stephen wanted you to dine alone with me. There was no deception here. I have come forward to tell you all. I offered to come to you because he was so sad, so alone. And I felt sympathy for him, not to hurt you. That is the simple truth."

A heaviness settled on his heart as Raynor heard her in silence. What about him? Why did she feel no sense of fealty toward her own husband? And as long as she had none, he could not trust her. What he would have given to trust someone, to love someone. Then Raynor stopped himself. He did not want her pity. But her loyalty he did have a right to expect.

He knew Elizabeth did not know why he hated Harrington. But that did not absolve her. She was his wife. Her first loyalty should be to him and to Willow, whom she had accepted as if she were her own daughter. And Raynor did not doubt, no matter how much he distrusted Elizabeth, that her love for the child was real.

Which only served to confuse him further.

She must actually believe that Nigel's seeing Willow was reasonable. His lips tightened. Did Elizabeth think Raynor such a petty man that he would hold such hatred against Nigel for no reason?

He could not tell Elizabeth the truth. He had promised Louisa never to reveal Willow's secret. And he meant to keep that vow, regardless of the cost to himself.

As his wife, Elizabeth should be willing to let this go, as he asked.

It was her duty.

How could she ever expect him to trust her if she felt no such responsibility to do the same?

Since the night they'd made love, Raynor had been lost in a sea of conflicting emotions. On the one hand, he feared what it would be like to give in to his growing feelings for Elizabeth. On the other, he felt compelled to be with her, to hold her in his arms, to share his life with her.

He'd realized shortly after leaving her that night that Elizabeth had not meant any wrong when she said he was hers. Considering the circumstances, it had simply been natural for her to feel some sense of his belonging to her.

And therein lay the problem. For Elizabeth, the giving of oneself was a normal part of their being together. For Raynor, it was torment. Fearing to lose himself in her as he did, panic rose up to block his throat at the very thought.

He'd not been able to go back and face her. The thought of belonging wholly to another had him as frightened as a boy in his first battle.

That, coupled with this incident, made him even more certain it would be nothing short of emotional suicide to give in to these feelings he had for his wife.

He kept his back to her, only allowing himself to turn when he heard the door open, then close. When he looked around, he was alone.

And that was just what he wanted. Wasn't it?

Elizabeth got little sleep that night.

Tears burned behind her eyes, but she refused to shed them. Weeping would solve nothing.

What she needed to do was think.

This was her life, like it or nay. And Raynor was her husband. She had to find some way to make things better.

No matter how hard she tried, she could not understand why Raynor was so dead set against Willow's uncle. If only he would tell her something, give her some reason to believe he was behaving rationally.

She knew in her own case that Raynor was completely blind when it came to the truth of who she was. He refused to see that she was nothing like his mother. Nothing she did or said could convince him otherwise.

Was he being just as obstinate when it came to Nigel Harrington?

But what gave her the most pause, and made her hesitate to take the matter any further, was what Raynor had said about Louisa.

Why would Louisa wish to keep her own stepbrother from her child? Obviously they had been close at some time. This was evidenced by Lord Harrington's obvious love for a little girl he'd never even seen.

Elizabeth knew she had to find out.

If she tried, it was possible that she could start to unravel some of the problems in her life. If Raynor was truly acting for some good reason, then perhaps she could find some equal ground with him.

Mayhap then they could try to come to terms with what was really keeping them apart—Raynor's inability to believe in himself and his own feelings.

Chapter Eleven

When dawn broke outside his window, Raynor gave up trying to sleep, and dressed. He made his way past the barely stirring occupants of the hall and out to the stables.

After a bracing ride, he went to the practice field. The intense physical activity did nothing to clear the night's events from his mind. Though the sweat soaked his hair and dripped from his back, Raynor could find no peace.

Calling for Arthur, he had a horse brought forth. This day was as good as any to begin the boy's training with the lance. He could not allow his personal problems to keep him from fulfilling his responsibilities.

Though Raynor saw the barely restrained excitement on his squire's face, he did not share it, as he might have.

The man could think of little save the heated words he had exchanged with his wife.

Had he been fair to Elizabeth? If he considered the situation, he had to ask himself what she really had done, aside from bringing up a subject she'd agreed had been ordered not to.

Elizabeth had spoken with Harrington. Raynor could not stop the spasm of anger that tightened his stomach at the very idea of his wife conversing with the knave. But in all fairness, she had not gone looking for Harrington. The bastard had approached her.

Yet what was important was that she must understand that she could not continue with this plan of uniting them. It could not happen, now or ever. Surely Raynor had convinced her to go no further with the matter.

If he could not trust Elizabeth to help him keep Harrington away from Willow, there was no hope for them. She must see that he had the right of this, without knowing any more than she did right now.

But was it his own fault that she had not listened to him? Her accusations echoed in his mind. Was it true that he had not tried to let her into his life?

He knew it was difficult for him to speak of things like his mother or his relationship with Louisa. But the fact was that he had told Elizabeth more than he had anyone in his life. Even with Louisa, who had been his friend since childhood, he had not spoken of his mother. And she had never pried. It was one of the things that had drawn them together. She had had her secrets, and he his. It had been understood between them.

He had already told Elizabeth something of his relationship with Louisa. More than that he could not do, not without risking Willow's secret.

Had Elizabeth spoken true when she said she hadn't lied to him since that fateful night in Windsor, when she'd told him Stephen wanted him to stay and dine despite his absence? Raynor could not help feeling he knew the truth of this. Ofttimes they had fought and disagreed, but she'd never cowered from telling him exactly what was in her mind. No matter how it angered him.

Even now, when she knew how enraged he would become if she brought up the subject of Harrington, Elizabeth had sought him out and had her say.

Raynor raked his hand through his dirt-encrusted hair. If only there were some way out of this dilemma.

As Arthur rode to the end of the list, he called out to his overlord. Raynor shook his head to clear it, knowing he should be more attentive to the moment. He could recall how excited he had been on first taking up the lance.

If Arthur was anything like himself, he would not admit to the ache in his leaden arms at the end of the day.

And so it was. Raynor kept him charging at the target until the boy was making a visible effort to hold the long weapon steady. Arthur would be so sore on the morrow he would do well to lift his own hands. But that was as it must be. In battle a knight must needs hold his lance for hours without tiring. This was only the beginning for Arthur.

And as he worked with the boy, Raynor wondered if such a beginning could be made with his wife.

Was it thus with a marriage? Did one have need to work to the point of pain in order to gain? He had seen all the pain on one side in the case of his father and mother.

What Raynor did know was that he had been very hard on Elizabeth.

Perhaps if he went to her, tried, not to explain more fully, but to speak with less anger. Might she then be more acquiescent to his wishes?

The concept was a new one for Raynor. And he felt no small amount of anxiety at the thought of facing Elizabeth, after the way he had treated her last night. Would she reject his attempt at a reconciliation?

In the past, Elizabeth had accepted any small overtures of friendship graciously. He remembered the day he had apologized for reprimanding her before the people in the hall. She had made no cutting remarks, nor any attempt to condemn him. It had been completely unlike the way his mother had treated his father. That woman had used every situation to further her dominance over her husband.

Nay, Elizabeth had not given him reason to think she would use any sign of kindness on his part against him.

Now that he looked at it, Raynor could see that she had in fact acted openly to try to attain some peace with him.

Even knowing these things, Raynor did not think he would have an easy time of coming to trust in her. Nor could he force Elizabeth to feel any fealty toward him. What he could do was earn it, by showing some for her.

Raynor knew it would not be easy to overcome his old self-protective habits. But he had to try, if not for his sake, then for his daughter's. In the matter of Willow's safety, his pride was secondary.

He must somehow convince Elizabeth that he had only Willow's happiness at heart, even though he could not explain why.

Some hours later, after giving Arthur leave to go ease his muscles in the river, Raynor turned toward the keep.

There was no sense in putting off what must be done.

When he questioned the head serving woman as to his wife's whereabouts, Jean told him Elizabeth was in her solar.

Going to the stairs that led to the third story of the keep, Raynor wiped his suddenly sweaty palms on his filthy tunic. Looking down at himself, he realized he had best go to his chamber and cleanse himself.

As he hurriedly washed and changed into fresh garments, Raynor knew it was foolish to feel such sickening nervousness in the pit of his stomach. Elizabeth was his wife. But he could not slow the erratic beating of his heart. This was the first time in his memory he had ever deliberately acted to appease any woman, and the idea was not a restful one.

On reaching the door to her solar, Raynor stood perfectly still for a long moment. Then, taking a deep breath, he opened it.

What Raynor saw when he opened the portal caused his heart beat to escalate to a deafening thrum in his ears. For the space of a drumbeat, he could only stand there, struck dumb with shock and betrayal.

Elizabeth and his brother, Bronic, stood locked in an intimate embrace beside the window. The whole scene was illuminated in startling detail by the afternoon sunlight. Bronic was close against her back, his hands on the white flesh exposed by her torn gown. Elizabeth was making no attempt to break away, but squirmed toward him wildly.

A hot slice of memory pierced his pain—Elizabeth's hands over Raynor's own as she had helped him rip her gown from her body in her haste to be naked beneath him.

In the blink of an eye, the vision was gone, but the gut-wrenching agony of what he was seeing remained. Of all people, he had trusted Bronic most. And Elizabeth. God, but her licentiousness struck as deep as a lance.

All this Raynor observed in no more time than it would have taken to cough. Immediately Bronic swung around to face him. "Raynor, come. You must help me."

Staggered as he was by the lack of remorse on his brother's face, it was a moment before Raynor understood what Bronic was saying. But even then he stood rooted to the stone floor, unable to grasp what the words meant.

Elizabeth looked around as Bronic spoke, her beautiful sapphire eyes glazed with passion. Raynor felt his stomach roll with nausea. The perfidy of the woman.

Still he could not move.

Through the fog of despair covering his mind, Raynor heard a voice behind him. "Excuse me, my lord Warwicke."

He frowned in confusion. What was this now? Someone else wanted to come into the solar, to view this unholy melee? Surely the whole world had gone mad.

He swung around and looked into Olwyn's face.

"Your pardon, my lord," she said again. She held up a tray laden with wine, bread and meat.

The sight of the mundane items freed Raynor from the spell that held him immobile.

With lightning-quick speed, he leapt across the room and tore Bronic away from his wife.

Raynor heard Olwyn gasp as she saw what was happening. But, to Raynor's surprise, her voice was full of concern as she hastily set the tray on the table and rushed to her lady's side. "Lady Elizabeth, what has happened?"

Raynor looked to her with fury as he jerked Elizabeth back against him. "Is that not obvious?" His tortured gaze went to Bronic. "And with my own brother!" Elizabeth struggled against his grasp, but he held her fast.

Bronic gave a grunt of surprise and irritation. "Have you lost what sense you were born with, Raynor? If I was less fearful for your wife, I would throttle you. As it is, the accusation is so ridiculous I would not dignify it with a reply."

Curling his lips, Raynor indicated his wife's torn cote. "Then pray tell what is this?" So furious was Raynor that he didn't even notice Elizabeth's indrawn breath of outrage.

Elizabeth jerked herself free, then swung around to land a stinging blow on Raynor's cheek. "How dare you, you insufferable knave?" She moved some distance away and stood staring up at him, her hands on her hips. A white ring appeared around Elizabeth's red lips, so tightly did she press them, and her chest heaved with the agitation of her breathing.

Raynor knew a twinge of unease at this show of self-righteous rage, but he quickly dismissed it. How dare *he?* It was she who had dared too much. There was no way for her to disprove the evidence of his own eyes. Hands clenching and unclenching at his sides, Raynor took a step toward her.

Bronic stopped him by sliding between them. "Do not, brother, else you will make a bigger fool of yourself than you already have."

Then, as if Raynor were not even important enough to warrant his continued attention, Bronic turned worried blue eyes to Olwyn. "Your lady has been bitten on the back by a spider." At Olwyn's cry of fear, he raised his hand. "There is no real danger, as it was not poisonous. I am certain, because I found and killed it. But you should have a look at the welt. It may need dressing."

As realization of what he had done sank deep, Raynor stood there, his breath escaping in a hiss of shock.

A spider.

He looked to Elizabeth, but she would not meet his gaze. But as she raised an unsteady hand to pull her torn gown higher on her shoulder, the truth was evident in her hurt expression.

Heaven above, what had he done? Raynor ran shaking hands over his face.

Torment clouded his features as he looked to his brother. "Bronic, I . . ."

Bronic would not face Raynor, and his lean jaw flexed with the effort it took to speak evenly. "Only out of the love I bear you do I forgive what you have thought this day, Raynor. I would not now or ever take to your wife's bed. I thought we two knew each other better than for you to think so. In all these years, you have never before, by deed or word, caused me to think you did not hold me in deepest regard. Because of that, I will do my utmost to forget what has been wrought here this day."

The blond man turned to Elizabeth, who stood silent and pale, as Olwyn looked on helplessly. "It is your lady wife who must have the most trouble in absolving you, Raynor. For she has had none of the good of you."

With that, he strode from the room.

Olwyn went to Elizabeth, going behind her to gently pull aside the torn remnants of her amber velvet cote.

Spurred to action, Raynor moved to set the companion aside. Guilt and anguish at what he had just done drove him to whisper huskily, "Nay, I will see to her." But as he touched her, Elizabeth flinched. And Raynor did, too.

Olwyn waited for Elizabeth to tell her what to do, her uncertain gaze on Raynor.

"Tell her to go," he pleaded, his voice raspy with pain. Elizabeth looked at the floor. "Do as he says."

As soon as Olwyn was gone, Elizabeth moved to stand some feet from her husband, facing him with a defiantly raised chin, despite the sorrow in her blue eyes.

He reached toward her. "I... Forgive me, Elizabeth. I saw Bronic, and I thought... I lost control."

She snarled, "'Tis obvious what you thought, husband." Her throat tightened around threatening tears that she had no wish to shed before this madman. "How could you, Raynor? Have I ever given you cause to believe I would—?"

His fingers curled around handfuls of his own hair. "Nay, you have not. It was me, only me. But what was he doing here? Why was Bronic with you?" His voice was wild with desperation.

It galled her to explain anything to him after what had happened just now and the previous night. He gave nothing of himself, simply expecting her to trust in him and his judgment. It was intolerable, especially when Raynor had not even a modicum of faith in her.

She said as much. "My dear lord, I feel no responsibility to appease you, when you tell me nothing of what you do and why. But for your brother's sake I will say this. He comes to see Olwyn. You are so blind to everything but your own problems that you see nothing of what others feel. Bronic loves Olwyn, and she him."

As soon as the words were out, he knew she spoke fact. It had been there for him to see. When he looked back on it, every time he had seen Bronic with Elizabeth, every single time, Olwyn had also been present. He recalled the many excuses Bronic made to visit the keep in the middle of the day, times when Elizabeth would not be there.

He beat his fist against his palm. "God, but I have been a fool. I have no defense, Elizabeth. I know this will make no difference now, after what I have done, but I want you to know that I came here not to make more war with you, but seeking peace." He shook his head in self-derision. "I know not what has come over me in these last months since we met. As you have accused, I seem to have lost my mind."

"Indeed you have," she told him coldly. "Now I would thank you to leave me."

He knew she had a right to ask him to go, but he couldn't, not like this. He had to try and set things right, not because of Willow, but because he had wronged Elizabeth, and terribly.

For weeks now he'd been able to concentrate on little save Elizabeth. Never had he had such overpowering feelings for a woman.

Why, he'd been willing to fight his own brother for touching her. Two short months ago he'd not have believed such a thing possible. He would have said no woman was worth a conflict with his brother, and that Bronic would be welcome to have any woman who might come between them.

For Raynor, women were nothing more than a means to satisfy a natural bodily urge, no one more special than any other. But what he felt for Elizabeth went beyond that. There was no sense in these emotions he was experiencing. When he saw Bronic with her, he'd known a feeling of possession he'd never imagined possible.

Until Elizabeth came into his life, he'd known neither peace nor laughter. And what little he had now was only in her presence.

He moved close to where she stood, stiff and unyielding, staring out the window. In the past, Elizabeth had been quick to forgive him his boorish ways, but somehow he knew this time was not the same. And Raynor could not fault her for that. He'd done the unpardonable in accusing her of dallying with Bronic. He only wished there were some way to make amends.

Elizabeth's tattered cote had slipped down to bare one silken shoulder. At the edge of the cloth, he could see what looked like the spider bite, an angry welt that must hurt her. Would that he could take that pain to himself.

Remorse made him reach out to her. Tenderly he pushed the garment aside and bent to place his mouth to the spot in a show of contrition. "Elizabeth, please forgive me."

She gave a start as his mouth touched her, then grew still.

Slowly, then, so slowly he almost felt he was imagining the motion, Elizabeth turned to face him. Only when she spoke did he know it was real. "Raynor." Her tone was filled with confusion and bitterness. "Why do you behave thus? What have I done to make you hate me so? I am sorry you were forced into a marriage you did not desire, but must I pay for that mistake for the rest of my life?"

An ache settled in his chest at hearing how much he had hurt her. A contrite Raynor raised his hand and placed a finger over her lips. "Nay, Elizabeth. You have done nothing. The marriage was no more your fault than mine. I have come to see that. I made my own choice in staying with you that night, when I knew Stephen would not be present. That decision was mine, and mine alone. And hate you I do not—never that. My feelings toward you are vast and uncountable, but hatred does not number among them."

Taking his hand from her mouth, Elizabeth gazed up at him, her eyes no longer bitter, but filled with sadness. "Oh, Raynor," she said with a sigh. "That admission is something, at least. Yet I fear there is little future for us."

He moved closer, his eyes boring into hers. The words cut deep, but he could not allow himself to believe them. Surely he had not wounded her so badly that he could never set it right. She must give him time to prove that he was worthy of another chance.

"Must we speak of the future now?" he asked. The events of the past hour had left him aching and lonely at the thought of losing her. Mayhap by tomorrow they would be better able to sort things out.

For such a commanding, powerful man, Raynor appeared so unexpectedly sad and tired, staring down at her like that, Elizabeth could not find it in her to further berate him.

As she looked up at her husband, Elizabeth realized that at this moment, with his eyes dark with remorse and loneliness, he was more appealing than he had ever been. It was as if in opening himself up, even this little bit, he had exposed an empty space inside him. And it was a place she longed to fill with all her being.

A voice inside her begged caution. Could she trust her feelings to this man, this wounded, abrasive, beautiful man?

Even as her mind cried nay, her heart thudded with hope. Raynor had made no protestation of love, and for that she was glad. It was best to be honest. What feelings he had, Raynor had not put name to, any more than she could have her own for him. Perhaps in time the love would come for them.

And if it did not... She gave a mental shrug. Then respect, honor, companionship and, yes, desire might have to suffice.

For the desire was there inside Elizabeth, as always, just below the surface. And as she acknowledged it, it cried out for attention. Not since the night they'd made love had Raynor touched her. Though she'd tried with all her might to forget that night, and the things she'd experienced, the memories would not leave her. She longed to be held in his arms and reach that pinnacle again.

Her gaze went to his hands, which he held stiffly at his sides, those hands that had touched her so intimately, brought her such pleasure. Elizabeth's breasts grew taut and heavy, while a spreading warmth grew inside her.

Something of what she was feeling must have communicated itself to Raynor, for he was watching her with uncertainty and a growing sensual awareness. But he did not make a move to touch her. He seemed unsure of how he would be welcomed after what had gone between them.

Knowing it was up to her to let her husband know that she did indeed want him, Elizabeth reached up and put a slender hand to his face. "Raynor."

Understanding the act as an invitation, Raynor nevertheless felt the need to be quite certain Elizabeth wanted him, as it appeared. After the terrible mistake he had made about her and Bronic, he wished to be quite sure that his perceptions of the moment were true ones.

But the heat of her gaze warmed his blood like a fire warmed wine. He felt himself spiraling down into that ready well of longing inside him. Carefully, he must go carefully, so as not to push her away.

Raynor leaned close to her, his eyes dark with longing. "I know I have wronged you this day, and many times in the past. But now...what I see in your eyes makes me think..." He held her gaze with his as he sought the answers to his questions. "Your eyes tell me that you want us to be together. Do you want that, Elizabeth? Do you want me?"

Standing perfectly still, he waited for her reply, knowing he would accept her answer without question. Not even needing her as much as he did at this moment would Raynor hurt her again this day.

Without question, Elizabeth knew that reply could only be yes, and she was near overcome with joy that he would be so reverent in his query. "Yes, my husband. I do want you."

Raynor wanted to be tender, to hold her sweetly and gently. But Elizabeth would have none of that. When he took her in his arms, her lips found his with unerring eagerness. Her lips opened, and she drew his tongue into the sweet, wet interior of her mouth.

Raynor gasped and lifted her against the hard wall of his chest. His fingers tangled in the glorious mass of her hair, and he pressed her head to his as he kissed her fully, allowing her to feel the force of his pent-up desires. And she welcomed him with greedy abandon, her hands clasping his shoulders. She threw her head back and cried aloud as his head dipped to the bodice of her gown, where it sagged over her bosom.

With his teeth Raynor tore the cloth aside, and his mouth closed over one rigid peak. As he drew on the bud, she cried out his name, clutching his head to her with all her strength, and he chuckled deep in his throat.

Pleasure surged in aching waves from her breasts to the juncture of her thighs. Elizabeth clung to him desperately, trying to open her legs, to bring that aching part of her into contact with him. But her skirts hampered her, and she rolled her head from side to side in frustration. "Take me, Raynor. Do not wait. I have longed for you."

Her pleas did not go unheeded. Raynor wanted to love her for hours, trace every perfect contour of her body, but the fierce throbbing of his blood must be answered. It was as if the jealousy and anger he'd experienced had opened a path to his innermost emotions. His manhood rose, turgid and nearly painful beneath his clothing.

He slid her slowly down his body until she moaned, bucking against him, and he throbbed anew.

As Elizabeth reached to run her hand down his back to his buttocks, Raynor arched against her, having no will to control his reaction to her touch. And wanting none.

This was his woman, his wife, and she desired him.

And there in the solar, where anyone could enter, they tumbled to the floor, each pulling at the other's clothing.

He tried to rise, unable to take off his tunic with her so close. But Elizabeth held him with surprising strength as she breathed in his ear, "No, Raynor. Please, let it be now. I burn for you."

He acquiesced, reaching down to pull up her gown. His senses reeled when he drew up the cloth and found her bare to his questing fingers.

As with the first time they had made love, she was already slick with desire, and he marveled that her response could so easily match his own and more.

She was all woman, his Elizabeth. All woman, and unafraid to experience the passion that was her right.

Trembling in his need to become one with her flesh, Raynor tugged at the front of his own clothing, finally succeeding in undoing the belt that held his drawers in place. Elizabeth reached to help him, her breath coming in hoarse gasps.

Raynor could not withhold a moan when she pulled him down to her ready flesh, her long legs going about him as he slipped inside her.

She cried out her joy, moving with a powerful longing that drove Raynor to lose all track of himself. They were one entity, fused by heat and desire.

He kissed her, and gasped as she instinctively took his tongue in the same primitive rhythm that held their straining bodies. She arched backward, and he kissed the sensuous line of her throat. As they moved, thrusting and straining toward completion, her gown pulled down, and one bare breast became exposed to his heated gaze.

The nipple tautened and swelled like a ripe raspberry as her pleasure sharpened and she cried out his name. "Raynor, Raynor, Raynor..."

Then she stiffened beneath him. Her inner muscles spasmed around him as a sharp cry of fulfillment escaped her lips. He leaned forward and kissed her, sucking greedily on her bottom lip.

No more than a heartbeat later, Raynor felt his own seed spill forth in an explosion of joy, and he thrust deep inside her, feeling her clutch him to her with arms and legs as the spasms eased and he lay still.

He began to roll away, but she held him to her. "Nay, do not go from me."

He took a deep breath to calm his rapid breathing. "I do not wish to crush you."

She laughed sleepily. "If you did not in the past moments, I do not see how you can."

Chuckling softly, he made no reply, but rolled over so that she was lying upon his chest with their bodies still joined. She sighed, relaxing against him. "That is not so very bad."

"Nay," he replied quietly, kissing the top of her tousled black curls. "It is not."

When Elizabeth woke, she was in her own dark room, in her bed, tucked between cool sheets, and the shadows had grown quite long in the room.

Without even looking for him, Elizabeth knew that Raynor was gone. The chamber did not feel of his presence.

She could only assume that he had brought her here, for Elizabeth remembered nothing after he had rolled beneath her. She flushed hotly as she recalled how wildly she had responded to him. It seemed that where Raynor was concerned her passion was boundless.

But what embarrassed her even more was having fallen asleep. Evidently the events of the afternoon had so exhausted her that she could fall asleep on her lover's chest, then be moved to her own bed without even awakening.

Lord, now that she thought on it, what they had done was near mad. Anyone could have come upon them in the solar.

Mayhap Olwyn had kept everyone away, knowing Raynor and Elizabeth were there together. She offered up a silent prayer of thanks for her companion.

Just then the door from the solar opened to admit that same woman.

Olwyn stood in the opening, coloring as she saw that Elizabeth was awake. "I did not mean to awaken you," she said. "I did have some concern for you when Lord Raynor told me you had fallen asleep. I thought perhaps the spider bite... Or mayhap your husband had upset..."

Elizabeth did not meet her eyes. "Oh, nay, there is no cause for concern. I was simply tired."

She glanced at Olwyn, then away, feeling guilty for the concerned expression on the other's face. "Really, Olwyn," she said earnestly, "there is no need to worry. I am fine, and Lord Raynor did nothing to upset me. He apologized most graciously for what he had said. I think we ended with an understanding of sorts." She flushed to the tips of her toes as she recalled how the conversation had ended.

Olwyn nodded, taking in the deep red tone of her mistress's bared throat and swollen lips. It took no skill to read what had happened here.

Olwyn looked at the floor. "All is well with you and Lord Warwicke now?"

Elizabeth thought for a long moment. What could she reply? Though things were better between herself and her husband than ever before, Elizabeth did not make the mistake of believing that all was well. Raynor had made no protestations of commitment or devotion. She was under no illusion that one pretty apology and an unrestrained burst of passion would cure all that ailed them.

Raynor was still the same man, with all his distrust of women and love. Slowly Elizabeth shook her head, not wanting to lie to her woman, nor wanting to dwell on what life might be like if he never overcame his fears. "In truth, I can not answer that question, Olwyn. Raynor is... well...Raynor. What will come is only for God to know."

Rising from the bed, Elizabeth went to the window, as if the golden glow of the setting sun might hold the answer to her future. If only it did, if only what was to come could be so bright.

Then something came to Elizabeth as she stood there. Raynor had once loved Louisa, that much was clear. He had trusted in her word and judgments so deeply that a word from her had made him a bitter enemy to her stepbrother, Nigel Harrington. Louisa's word had carried and still did carry great weight with Raynor.

If Elizabeth could come to understand what Raynor's relationship with her had been like, to see the other woman as Raynor might have seen her, then possibly she would have the answer to her problem.

Not that Elizabeth thought she could be like Louisa, or even had any desire to be so. But she did believe that this might help her to unlock the secret of solving this in her own way.

And that she was determined to do, now more than ever. There had to be a way for her and Raynor to come together, without the past acting as a wedge to keep them apart.

Chapter Twelve

The knowledge Elizabeth sought came the very next morning, in an unexpected way and from an equally unexpected source.

As she was working in the storerooms with the head woman, Jean, Elizabeth was startled to see the woman sit down on a bag of beetroot and burst into tears.

Not wishing to pry, but feeling as if she must offer some kind of comfort, Elizabeth said, "Jean, what is the matter? Is there aught I can do to help you?"

Jean turned to her mistress, her gray eyes damp. "It's my girl, Hyla, my lady. I am sorry she's caused so much trouble for you and Lord Raynor. She was ever a spoiled child. Her father could never say a word of no to her, and it's been my cross to bear since he died, when she was twelve."

Elizabeth's eyes widened in surprise. "Hyla is your daughter? I had no idea."

"Aye, she's my very own. Though after what she did to little Willow, I rue the day I bore her. Lord Raynor did right to send her away. She's had her nose bent since you came, thinking you took Lord Raynor from her. When I saw how it was going to be, I sent her right off to the kitchens with Eva. I thought there she'd stay out of your path."

Elizabeth blanched, remembering what had happened to Hyla in the kitchen. "I did her no harm."

"And well I know that," Jean answered, nodding her head as she looked at the floor. "I... know as how you found her in Lord Raynor's room, my lady."

A flush of color darkened Elizabeth's cream cheeks. "Really, I would rather not discuss that matter. It is most personal, and I would thank you not to speak of it, Jean." Everyone in the keep must know of that ill-fated eve, Elizabeth thought.

Jean rushed to explain. "I meant no familiarity, lady. I but try to explain something. Hyla admitted to me that Lord Raynor had not sent for her. She only knew he did not share your bed, and hoped to win him back." She hurried on earnestly as Elizabeth's blush deepened. "But, Lady Elizabeth, she could not win him *back* to her. For Lord Raynor was never hers. Oh, he may have bedded her at one time. But that is all there was. Hyla was not his woman, any more than any other. 'Tis doubtful Lord Raynor would recall her very name, were she not before him. He is not a man to take a woman to his heart. Has not been for a very long time."

Then Jean turned to Elizabeth with a hesitant expression. "Lady Elizabeth, may I speak freely? 'Tis of Lord Raynor."

Brows arching in surprise, Elizabeth considered this carefully. How much more freely could Jean speak? Besides, whenever someone began a speech with those words, it was relatively certain that the listener would not like what was to come.

But something kept Elizabeth from halting the servant. Jean said it was of Raynor that she wished to speak, and wasn't overcoming her own reticence worth the possibility of learning something of her husband? After giving Jean a further searching look, Elizabeth nodded. "You may say what is in your heart."

"I am glad you have come here, my lady. Lord Raynor needed someone to take him out of the past. He also has need of someone to love him—and to love."

For a moment, Elizabeth could think of no reply. She was gladdened that the servant felt she had been good for her husband, but at the same time felt awkward about talking this way with anyone. It was simply not in her nature to do so. Even with Olwyn she was reticent about discussing such things.

She was sure the people of the keep knew most every detail of their lord and lady's private life. It would be near impossible for them not to. They all lived and worked in this small world called Warwicke together.

Just when Elizabeth was thinking that it was surely time to tell Jean that she could go no farther, the serving woman went on. "I've not seen lord Raynor so alive since before Lady Louisa died."

Now Elizabeth's attention was pricked, and she knew that no matter how far this conversation strayed, she would not halt it. Everything in her longed to know of Raynor's relationship with Louisa. Surely understanding that would help her to know the man she had married. Thus thinking, she found herself encouraging the other woman. "What do you mean?"

"Why, just that, my lady. Lord Warwicke had just begun to come into himself after his mother died. She was a one, I can tell you." Jean shook her head sadly. "Never gave the boy a moment's rest from her nagging and demanding. He was nineteen when she passed on, and it was the first real peace he'd ever known. While she was alive, she prodded and pushed and tried to control her son as she had the old lord." The servant sat up straighter, smiling with pride. "But Lord Raynor, he'd have none of her controlling his every act. Though I know it took much out of him, her never letting up. As I said, in the years after her death, he became more cheerful, like. You see, he didn't have to fight her anymore, and guard his back against her manipulations. I'm sure it was like the weight of the castle being taken off of his shoulders.''

Elizabeth tried to imagine her husband's mother and what she must have been like. It was difficult. Her own mother had been a partner and friend to her father. And as far as her children—including her daughter—were concerned, she'd taught them to think and act for themselves. Elizabeth frowned. ''Was she really so very terrible? 'Tis hard to believe anyone could be.''

Jean's lips thinned in condemnation. ''Aye, that one was. Her, she couldn't love anyone but herself. In my whole fifty years, I've not seen another who had so little care for anything or anyone around her. 'Tis hard to believe she birthed two such men as Lord Raynor and Sir Bronic. Never would so much as even tell Bronic who his father might be, though I heard them arguing about it often enough when he grew old enough to understand.'' The woman hesitated. ''I know 'tis not really my place to criticize my betters this way, but that one was no lady. Mayhap by birth, but not in her heart.'' Her face was slightly defiant when she turned to Elizabeth.

For the first time, Elizabeth wondered what it would have been like for Bronic, not even knowing his father's name. No wonder he and Raynor were close—they'd had no others. But curiosity about Louisa pushed even this thought aside. ''Tell me of Louisa. What happened when she came? What did she do to change Raynor back to the way he had been?''

The serving woman shook her gray head. '' 'Twas not that way. Lady Louisa, she was sweet as spring, and as kind.''

''Mayhap it was her death that turned him sour toward life,'' Elizabeth offered, thinking aloud.

''Nay. It happened when she arrived.''

"When she arrived?" Elizabeth asked, incredulous. It made no sense. If Raynor loved her, and she was all Jean said, he should have been overjoyed to have her with him.

Jean looked as puzzled as Elizabeth felt. "Aye, my lord Raynor seemed to grow angry again at just that time, though he treated his lady as if she was made from glass. That, you see, was only six months before Willow was born. I was here that day, helping to deliver the child. Louisa was a wee thing, with narrow hips, and the babe was large. A plump, healthy babe she was, our Willow." Jean's eyes clouded over with sorrow. "Lady Louisa took two days to birth her, and after that we couldn't stop the bleeding."

Though she felt sadness at hearing of Louisa's death, Elizabeth also knew a growing confusion as the story sunk deep. It took more than six months to conceive, then birth, a plump healthy child. Elizabeth had seen a six-month babe her mother had helped deliver once. It had been a small, weak infant, and had died within a matter of hours. "So Louisa must have already been with child when she came here to live with Raynor," Elizabeth mused aloud. "How and where did they meet? Surely not at Harrington."

Jean shrugged. "Lady Louisa was never a guest in this keep before that time. I would have known of it. But she and my lord could have met anywhere, for aught I know, though I did not hear of him riding to Harrington. It had been a long while since my lord Warwicke was like to visit with Louisa and Nigel. Though they had been great companions in earlier years, we'd seen naught of them in quite a time."

Elizabeth's black brows drew down as a new thought came to her. "Could Raynor have been angry because he suspected the child might be another's?"

"Oh, no, my lady. As I told you, Lord Raynor treated Lady Louisa as if she was made of glass. He was ever helping her about and asking after the babe, making sure Lady Louisa had everything she could want. Besides, Lord Raynor has never denied being little Willow's father. In fact, he has proclaimed that he was from the very beginning.''

That Elizabeth knew was true. Raynor was ever clear on the fact that he was Willow's father.

Jean went on, oblivious of Elizabeth's thoughts. ''But something was wrong. Lord Warwicke had a mad in him that all could see. And when Lord Harrington came to the keep, demanding to take his sister home, Lady Louisa set up such a fuss, screaming and carrying on. Lord Raynor became so crazed, we all thought he might go out and kill him with his bare hands.''

''Well.'' Elizabeth arched her brows. ''What did Raynor expect Lord Harrington to do? Louisa was his sister, pregnant and living with a man who was not her husband. How would Raynor feel in the same situation? Lord Harrington must have been beside himself with worry. I can only wonder why Raynor would choose to turn his unexplained anger on him. Even though Louisa did not wish to return home, Raynor might have tried to understand the other man's position.'' Elizabeth knew her own brothers would raze the very keep of any man who tried to hold her under similar circumstances.

''I know nothing of that, my lady. But I do know that when Lord Harrington brought his men and stood outside the keep, calling for his sister, it was Lady Louisa who cried and threatened to throw herself from the battlements did Lord Raynor give her over.''

Elizabeth sat down on a barrel of last year's apples. Threatening to throw herself from the battlements seemed more than a hysterical remark made simply to get one's way. Raynor had said Louisa would turn over in her grave at the idea of Elizabeth trying to help her brother see Willow. At the time she had wondered if mayhap Raynor was only projecting his own dislike to Louisa. Obviously that was not the case. For some reason, Louisa had hated her stepbrother, hated him to the point of threatening to kill herself to keep from going home. Whether this was because she couldn't bear to lose Raynor, or due to some fault of her stepbrother's, Elizabeth had no idea.

But one thing was clear. For some reason known only to herself—and, most certainly, Raynor—Louisa had not wanted Nigel to have contact with herself or her child.

This would bear some considering. But, though the reasons for Louisa's attitude were still unclear, Elizabeth knew she had no right to overlook the wishes of Willow's own mother. If Louisa had wanted them to have no contact, she would certainly not try to interfere by helping the knight in his quest to see Willow. Nigel was on his own.

No matter how hurt he was over being without the child, Louisa had wished it this way. And Elizabeth would see to it that her wishes were carried out.

But even as she made this decision Elizabeth knew it was more for Raynor than any other reason. Even though he refused to tell her anything about what had happened between Louisa and Nigel—and she was now certain that therein lay the crux of the feud—Elizabeth was coming to see that Raynor did not act without reason.

Despite his ill nature and quick temper, he was a man who made the utmost effort to judge and behave fairly.

Raynor always acted from his own logic. It was one of the things that drew her to him, even as it irritated her. Even when Raynor was angry with her, he'd felt he had reason. Whether it was that he thought she had trapped him into a marriage he didn't want, or even that he was vehemently set against being manipulated as his father had been.

Raynor seemed to have a deep-seated reason for disliking Nigel Harrington, and that had become good enough reason for her.

If they were ever to have a real marriage, she must learn
to put her faith in her husband. One of them must try to
have a little faith in the other, and it might as well be her.
Perhaps if he saw her making an effort to believe in him,
he could begin to believe in her—in them.

Once outside the cold cellar, Elizabeth felt the heat of
the day like a blanket over the keep and grounds.

There was an unrelieved stillness to the air, and the castlefolk moved about their daily work listlessly. The under-
arms and backs of their rough-woven wool garments were
dark with perspiration. There was no hum of conversation to distract from the hot, radiant sun that rode high in
the afternoon sky. Flies buzzed noisily about the goats that
roamed the bailey, eating grass. Even the goats showed
little energy as they flicked the pests away with their tails.

Taking a deep breath, but finding no relief in it, Elizabeth pushed her hair back from her forehead. Olwyn had
braided the thick mass to keep it back, but it still felt heavy
and hot. Never could Elizabeth remember such a warm
day, even in July.

Willow came across the yard toward to her, her wild
curls tousled and damp with perspiration. She looked up
at Elizabeth with apathetic brown eyes. "It is hot."

The statement could not have been more true. Elizabeth ran a gentle hand over the tousled curls. "Yes, dearling, it is. Why don't you go to my solar? I'm sure Olwyn
has opened the windows."

Willow sighed heavily. "'Tis hot there too."

Elizabeth realized that the child needed to cool off
badly.

And, aside from that, Elizabeth could do with a little
cooling off herself. She'd been through much in the past
days, and could use a little time to think, away from the
busy life of the castle.

First she fetched a blanket. Then, going to the kitchen, she asked Eva to prepare a basket of food for them. Taking the food with a smile of gratitude, for she knew Eva was already busy with the preparations for the evening meal, Elizabeth grasped Willow's hand and led her from the keep.

She waved to the watchman as she went through the gate. He returned her salute, but seemed no more enthusiastic about moving than anyone else.

They followed the path that led toward the village, before turning off to go toward the river. It was then that Elizabeth saw a rider approaching them from the direction of the village. Even at a distance, Elizabeth could see it was her husband. There was no mistaking that thick, dark hair, or the mount he rode.

"Papa!" Willow called. She ran down the path toward him.

Elizabeth hung back, not certain as to how Raynor would behave toward her today. After the way she had given herself with such abandon, she felt uncharacteristically shy.

And she also felt slightly uncomfortable about the things she had discussed with Jean. She was now closer to really understanding her husband than ever before. But Elizabeth had a feeling Raynor would not approve of her conversation with the head woman.

She watched as Raynor stopped his horse and dismounted, walking the last few feet to meet his daughter. He scooped her up in his arms and moved toward Elizabeth as he gave Willow a kiss on her pink cheek.

Now Elizabeth could see the warmth and pleasure in his eyes. But she was not reassured about how he would react to her. His happiness was surely from being with his daughter.

But as he came closer, Elizabeth saw that his smile did not fade. He seemed not wary at meeting her, as in the past, but a little unsure himself.

Even as Elizabeth wondered at this, her heart gave a tiny flutter of hope.

Raynor stopped a few feet from her. "Elizabeth."

She nodded. "My lord."

Willow looked to Elizabeth, her arm looped trustingly around her father's neck. "Can Papa come with us?"

Raynor indicated the basket and blanket in Elizabeth's arms. "You are going on a picnic."

"Yes," she said, feeling silly now for taking the time out of her busy day for a picnic. Surely Raynor would not wish to occupy himself with such pursuits. She turned to Willow. "Sweeting, your father is a busy man. I am sure he has no time for picnicking today."

Raynor stopped her with a surprised look. "Nay, Elizabeth. I would like to accompany you, if I am welcome to do so. But perhaps you do not have enough for three."

A flush of pleasure colored Elizabeth's pale cheeks, though she told herself he was coming with them for Willow's sake. "You would be most welcome my lord." She raised the basket. "Eva has sent more than we two could eat."

"Oh, yes, we have much," Willow agreed her brown eyes earnest on his. "If there is not enough, you can have mine, Papa. I'm not so very hungry."

Raynor's face softened in an expression of abject love as he reached out to pull his daughter close against his neck. "I thank you for that, little one," he said huskily.

Elizabeth had to turn away to hide the tears that started to fill her eyes at the expression of overwhelming love, tenderness and gratitude on his face. How cruel fate was, that this gentle man should feel such gratitude for a child's kindness.

She turned toward the river to hide her reaction. She knew Raynor would not be glad of her sympathy. He was too proud a man. "We should get started," she said, wiping a hand over her damp brow. "It is hot."

They started down the path, woman, child and man. Raynor continued to lead the horse that followed docilely behind them, the reins tucked under his arm. Crickets chirped in the dry grass as they passed, and the sound was strangely soothing. A peaceful quiet settled between them.

Almost like a family, Elizabeth thought.

She stopped herself. She was allowing her fantasy to go too far. She only set herself up for heartache by expecting too much. Better to take whatever Raynor might be able to give.

Suddenly she was too aware of the perspiration trickling between her shoulder blades and the tiredness in her limbs. If only her relationship with this man were not such a constant battle.

Gratefully Elizabeth moved into the shade of the trees that grew along the slow moving river. Once inside the stand of oak, beech and walnut, she felt as if she had entered another world.

The presence of the trees and water cooled the air by at least ten degrees. And there was a peaceful stillness in the glade. The only sounds were those of an occasional bird's song, or a butterfly fluttering softly over the tops of purple irises and yellow tulips. The water was clear, but not too deep, and the ground was covered in a soft bed of grass and moss.

Elizabeth could see why this spot was a favorite one among the occupants of Warwicke. They often came here for swimming and fishing.

If she hadn't been so occupied with worrying over her relationship with Raynor, she might have come sooner herself. Elizabeth sent a surreptitious glance toward her husband.

Raynor was setting Willow down upon the soft carpet of green. He seemed unaware of his wife as he spoke softly to his chattering daughter, and Elizabeth felt a twinge of loneliness. His deep brown eyes were soft with care and amusement when he looked down into her little face, which was lit with pleasure at being with her father.

His love for Louisa was evident in the love he showed their child.

What would it be like for Raynor to love her as he had Louisa? Elizabeth's mind could not call up such an image.

Knowing she was not helping herself by thinking of anything so ridiculous, she set the picnic basket on the ground. Then she busied herself spreading the blanket, listening to their quiet conversation while they moved off toward the river together, obviously forgetting her presence.

Unaccountably, she found herself blinking back tears.

She told herself not to be foolish. She should be glad Raynor and Willow were growing so close. That was as it should be.

But she couldn't help wishing that she was a part of their closeness.

Resolutely she turned to unload the basket.

Surely they would come back hungry.

But before she had even finished opening the lid, she felt a hand on her arm. She looked up into Willow's merry brown eyes. "Elizabeth, may I wade in the water? Papa said I must ask."

Elizabeth looked over the child's head, with its halo of golden-brown curls, then up into the eyes of the man who stood behind her. He was smiling, his face more relaxed than she had ever seen it. Her heart gave a lurch of longing at that smile.

Taking a breath to calm her racing pulse, Elizabeth turned back to Willow, nodding. "Of course, sweeting, but be careful not to go out too far. I've heard the water is deep in the middle."

Willow danced away excitedly.

Raynor moved to take her place, and as Elizabeth looked up, her gaze locked with his. Into the resulting stillness, he spoke softly. "Why don't you join us? Then you can be certain there is no danger."

Elizabeth waved at the basket, flushing. "I... You don't really need me. You are Willow's father. I'm sure you can keep her from harm."

For a moment Raynor made no reply, but then he held out his hand. "Come. We do need you. Not for Willow's sake, but for mine. I wish to spend some time with you."

Swallowing hard, Elizabeth stared up at him. What did he mean?

She told herself not to read more into what he was saying than a simple invitation. But the warm welcome and, yes, desire in his gaze made that difficult. His eyes were like a dark but strangely inviting night.

Almost without volition, Elizabeth placed her hand in his. She rose to follow him, and to her surprise he did not release her hand, but tucked it close to his side.

The contact with the warmth of his body caused a delicious shiver to run up her arm, then down her spine. She glanced up at Raynor and found him watching her with a knowing grin.

She blushed, turning to Willow, where she waited at the edge of the river, her shoes and hose a disordered pile on the mossy bank.

To Elizabeth's further surprise, Raynor sat down and began to remove his own footwear. She watched him as he pulled his hose down, for a moment exposing the long, muscular length of his thigh, before his tunic covered him again. Her breath caught, and her heart began to hammer in an erratic rhythm.

He glanced up at her, this time seemingly oblivious of her reaction. "Are you not going to join us?"

Willow grabbed her hand, her feet patting the ground in an uneven rhythm. "Yes, yes, Elizabeth, you too."

"But it's been years," she countered helplessly.

"All the more reason to do so," Raynor told her, his eyes sparkling with mischief.

"I'll get my gown soaked."

He moved toward her, grabbing up the ends of her trailing cote. Artfully he began to tie the garment about her waist. "If we fix it like so, it will be fine," he said, then backed away to examine his handiwork. "And even if you do get wet," he added with a matter-of-fact shrug, "'twill dry soon enough in this heat."

Elizabeth recognized the reckless side of his nature taking over. Even though there was no danger in wading in the river, the idea appealed to the unconventional in him.

Without even knowing why she was doing so, Elizabeth nodded. "Yes, I will come wading."

With the decision made, she wasted no time in ridding herself of her own hose and shoes.

As she stood, Willow took Elizabeth's hand, clutching it tightly. Obviously the little girl was a bit nervous, as well as excited about what she was about to do. Elizabeth gave her tiny fingers a gentle squeeze of reassurance.

Thinking to help allay the child's fears, Elizabeth stepped in first. She gasped in surprise as the chilly water swirled about her ankles. "'Tis . . . very cool." She looked up to see Raynor's amused expression.

Raynor waded in next, with a husky chuckle. "Aye, but not too cool. We shall be accustomed in only a moment."

Elizabeth was already discovering the truth of his words. She turned to Willow, urging her to step in. "Just come slowly."

Her eyes dancing with a mixture of joy and fear, Willow dipped her toes in the water, then jumped in. Water sprayed up to dot the other two, and they all laughed aloud.

The memory of the next hour was to become one of the most precious of Elizabeth's life.

Raynor was warm and playful, as she'd never seen him, splashing both her and Willow with gleeful abandon.

Elizabeth had to repay him in kind, and they ended with all of them getting quite soaked.

When Elizabeth deemed they had had enough of the water, she had to lure them out with reminders that lunch awaited them on shore.

Because they were now wet from the splashing, Raynor suggested they move the blanket out into the sun. Readily Elizabeth agreed.

The three of them feasted on bread, cheese, meat and watered wine. They ate with a hearty relish born of their play in the river.

Willow finished her portion quickly. Then, giving a beatific smile, she settled back on the blanket to sleep.

By now their clothing had dried in the heat of the July sun, and Raynor carefully pulled the blanket into the shade. He smiled down at his daughter as he did so, saying, "Her skin is so fair. I would not have her burned."

This time, Elizabeth felt no twinge of loneliness, for she felt as if she were part of them.

It was this sense of belonging that gave her the courage to ask Raynor a question as he settled back on the blanket beside her. "Was Louisa fair, as Willow is?"

He stretched out on his back, pillowing his head on his bent arm. He stared into the treetops for so long that Elizabeth thought he was not going to answer. Then, softly, he said, "Aye, she was. Willow's coloring is just as her mother's."

Elizabeth knew an incredible surge of happiness. Raynor had answered her. This was the first time he had spoken of anything personal without anger prodding him on.

Mayhap this day did mark a change in their relationship, though she did not know what might have brought the change about. Could the mistake he had made about her and Bronic the previous day have taught him a lesson? Was Raynor ready to try to make a marriage with her? To trust?

Good sense told Elizabeth not to question too much, but to enjoy this moment while she could. It might not last.

Knowing this could be her one chance to tell Raynor some of the things she most dearly wanted to say, Elizabeth spoke. "Louisa was a fool, you know. Not to have married you was a frightful mistake on her part."

He grew incredibly still, not looking at her. "What do you mean?"

She bit her lip, hoping she had not hurt him, but needing to say the things in her heart. "I mean she could have saved you so much grief in making you her husband and Willow's legitimate father."

He spoke softly, and Elizabeth thought she heard a note of disappointment in his voice. "I see you think of the child. No doubt you are right, but I have claimed her as I aught, so there is no use wishing Louisa had wed me to make the babe legitimate." He turned to Willow, and Elizabeth could hear the love in his tone, even though she couldn't read his face. "I could care for the child no more if I had been wed to her mother."

Taking a deep breath, Elizabeth urged herself on, to say what she really wanted to. "I mean not only for Willow, but for you. It was wrong of her to hurt you so. You are a good and loving father, and would have made her a husband such as women dream of. She was a fool to reject your love."

There, she had said it. Would he guess how much of her own feelings were behind the words? Would he see how much she had come to care for him?

Slowly Raynor rose up to face her, his expression carefully blank. Why was Elizabeth speaking to him this way? She seemed almost angry with Louisa for not having loved him. Though he searched hard, there was nothing in her face to mark the emotions behind her words.

But he knew he had to explain something to Elizabeth, to make her understand how it had been between himself and Louisa. He began hesitantly. "Elizabeth, you have some misconception of Louisa's and my relationship. There was no love between us, as you imagine. It was more as a brother and sister that we cared for each other. We had known one another since early childhood. My parents cared little what Bronic and I did, so long as we caused them no trouble. We wandered the wood between here and Harrington at will. It was there, in the forest, that we met Louisa and Nigel. She was Bronic's age, just two years younger than my eleven, and Nigel was thirteen." For once there was no hatred in his voice when he spoke the other man's name. "We became fast friends, the four of us." He frowned. "Though even then, Nigel seemed somewhat jealous of her. He was ever challenging Louisa to do some dangerous feat. I suppose it was her inheritance, even then. You see, Louisa was to have nearly all. Her mother had come to his father a wealthy widow. Everything that had been her husband's was to pass to Louisa. Harrington only had use of the money and lands until Louisa married or reached her majority." Raynor heard Elizabeth's gasp of surprise, but said nothing more. He knew that he was coming as close to explaining what had happened to Louisa as he ever could. For some reason, it had become important to him for Elizabeth to know how it had been between him and Willow's mother. That he had felt protective and loving toward her, but not as a lover.

Elizabeth said, "Is that the cause of the bad blood between you and Lord Harrington? That he was jealous over Louisa's inheritance?" Then Elizabeth stopped, with a hand over her lips. "Nay, I'm sorry I asked, Raynor. I made a promise not to question you further on that. It is just that I want so desperately to understand. Pray forget I spoke."

Raynor forced himself to relax the muscles that had grown taut at her queries. A growing hope rose inside him. Elizabeth had done what she said she would, withdrawing her own questions, without a word from him. Mayhap they could come to have something together.

He sent a fond glance to his sleeping daughter. It seemed even more important than before for his wife to know him. "Louisa was so like Willow. Bright and alive and loving, but too trusting of the world around her. Even when we were children I felt it was my duty to protect her. Nigel's father cared little for her, and she was lonely."

He looked at Elizabeth, willing her to comprehend how it had been. "She was the sister of my heart, if not my sister by birth."

Elizabeth gazed back at him, then spoke, as if she could not prevent herself from saying what was in her mind. "But you had a child together?"

Raynor frowned. She had him there. From Elizabeth's position, what he was saying could not make any sense. He wanted to, but could not, tell her the truth. He could not betray Louisa's trust in him, even for Elizabeth.

He leaned closer to her, his eyes pleading for understanding. "Elizabeth, I have asked you for little in the time we have been married. This once I ask that you believe me when I tell that Louisa refused to marry me because she did not love me in that way and she knew I felt the same of her. She insisted that I be free to love where I would." He shook his head sadly. "I did everything I could to convince her, and still Louisa would not be swayed. But it was not to hurt me. What she did was out of love for me."

For a long moment, Elizabeth watched him. Then, as she looked into his dark eyes, she came to a decision. How could she doubt the truth of what he said? It was there for her to see in the unshuttered pain in his gaze. For reasons known only to them, Raynor and Louisa had taken comfort from each other in the form of physical love. But that love had not been enough to sustain a marriage, and they had known it.

Elizabeth's heart swelled with emotion. There had been no constraint on Raynor to tell her of this. He had done so out of unselfishness. He had not been able to allow her to think ill of Louisa.

No matter what else Raynor might be, he was loyal and caring to a fault to those whom he had given his heart.

She did not know if Raynor would ever come to completely accept and trust in her that way, but he was no longer resentful of her presence here. That must suffice.

Unable to voice her thoughts aloud, Elizabeth looked to Willow. The child who had been produced by Louisa's and Raynor's devotion to each other.

Would that she could have Raynor's child. That much, at least, would be something. If she could not openly show her care for him, she could love his child.

Driving her fear of speaking her thoughts into the deepest part of her, Elizabeth turned to her husband. "I wish I could someday bear a child. Your child and mine." She held his gaze, her own blue eyes dark with longing.

For a moment, he did nothing. Then, slowly and inevitably he leaned toward her, pausing when his lips were a mere whisper away.

She could feel his breath, sweet from the wine they had drunk, and a heavy, honeyed languor oozed through her body to pool in her belly. She closed her eyes, feeling the perspiration that beaded on her upper lip. His tongue flicked out to lick it away, and she sighed.

His lips found hers, and she found herself pulled close to the hard wall of his chest. Squirming in Raynor's arms, she tried to get closer to him, but her cote was tangled under her and she fumbled awkwardly, trying not to break the contact of their mouths.

With a deep chuckle, Raynor lifted her and settled her on his lap.

Elizabeth melted against him, glorying in the strength of his arms around her, his heart beating beneath her hand, as his tongue danced with hers.

Through the haze of longing invoked by his embrace, Elizabeth heard a muffled giggle. She started, drawing back from her husband.

Willow was sitting up, looking at them with amusement and a little surprise. "Papa, you're kissing Elizabeth."

Slowly, and with obvious regret, he eased Elizabeth off his lap. "Aye, I was, moppet. Does that bother you?"

Jumping up with a cheery laugh, she threw her arms around Elizabeth's neck to give her a hearty kiss on the cheek. "Oh, nay. I am most glad. Elizabeth is soft, and nice to kiss."

His eyes met her over Willow's head. "That she is, dearling. That she is."

Chapter Thirteen

Elizabeth did not know exactly what had happened between them the previous day by the river, but something had changed. Raynor's gaze had a new warmth that dredged up hopes she was afraid to put a name to.

As Elizabeth paused in the doorway of the great hall, she saw that her husband was already seated at table. It almost seemed he might have been watching for her, because his gaze was trained on the spot where she stood, and a wide smile curved his lips.

Her own mouth quirked upward in response.

Seeing the pleasure in his dark gaze, Elizabeth felt a sense of happiness and genuine hope for their future together growing inside her.

Surely now things could only improve for them. This very morning she had sent a messenger to inform Nigel Harrington that she would not be meeting him again. Elizabeth did feel some guilt about not telling him in person, but nothing must be allowed to jeopardize the very new emotions between her and her husband. What they were experiencing was as fresh and fragile as a drop of dew on a rose petal and Elizabeth felt she must go very carefully, so as not to disturb it.

But Elizabeth was not the only one to take note of Raynor's eagerness. The trestle tables were filled, the occupants of the keep breaking their fast in preparation for the day's labors. Many elbows were pressed to fellow diners' sides while she made her way toward her grinning husband.

A newfound shyness made her avoid Raynor's gaze as she settled herself next to him at table. But she felt his attention on her like a cloak, and she could not keep herself from glancing up at him.

He smiled softly. "Good morn, wife." There was a note of possession in the word *wife*.

Elizabeth looked down at her clasped hands. Though she tried not to, Elizabeth still felt the weight of all those pairs of watching eyes.

She answered her husband quietly. "Good morrow, Raynor." His name felt strangely intimate on her tongue. Rarely had she called him by it, except in the heat of passion. A faint blush stole over her ivory cheeks.

Raynor's smile widened, as if he knew her thoughts.

Looking to where Bronic sat, in his accustomed place beside Raynor, Elizabeth saw that his face showed both amusement and speculation. Clearly he was interested at seeing the couple getting along so well, especially after what Raynor had accused them of only days ago.

If Raynor was aware of his brother's scrutiny, he gave no indication that it bothered him. He continued to gaze on Elizabeth with unconcealed pleasure.

When the tray of cooked venison was brought in, Raynor carefully chose the tenderest portions and placed them before Elizabeth. This he had done before, but now, unlike the other times, he allowed his hand to brush hers, where it lay on the table. Elizabeth felt an unexpected flush of heat through her body, and nearly gasped aloud. It never ceased to amaze her that Raynor could awaken her so with just a touch. From beneath the veil of her black lashes, she glanced toward him, and found her husband watching her with tender fascination, as if he were hungry for the sight of her.

"Is there aught else you desire, Elizabeth?" he asked, his tone low, as he poured out her drink himself. This new solicitude from Raynor was welcome, but disconcerting at the same time.

Hesitantly Elizabeth shook her head. "Nay, my lord, you have been most considerate." She felt more unsure of herself and her position than at any time in her life.

"I trust you slept well?" he asked, as if sensing her confusion.

Elizabeth smiled hesitantly. It almost seemed he was trying to put her at her ease, and for that Elizabeth was grateful. But she also knew a sense of impatience. Why must they try to come to know each other before so many curious stares? She knew the castlefolk wished them well, but that did nothing to ease the strain of being the object of so much attention, however well-meaning.

And despite Raynor's obvious approval of her at this moment, she felt unsure. There lurked in Elizabeth memories of other times when she had allowed her husband to see how much she wanted him. Those times he had reacted by pushing her away.

Would he do so again?

Elizabeth could not bear the notion of that happening with the whole keep looking on. As she looked up into her husband's handsome face, which grew dearer to her daily, Elizabeth's mind began to form an idea.

She only hoped that Raynor would understand it as a chance for a new beginning for them.

That eve, when Raynor returned to the keep, there was a message awaiting him in his chamber.

Elizabeth requested him to sup in her solar.

Raynor turned away from Arthur, who had come to help him change for the evening meal. But he could feel the boy's eyes on his back.

Holding the note in his hand, Raynor hesitated. He did not know what reply he would give. It was true that he was coming to care for Elizabeth. But that care was new to him, and as yet untried.

What was she about, to ask him to sup with her?

He recalled the last time he had done so. That night at Windsor, when they had been found together.

And this very morning, when they had breakfasted together. Though he could not quite put his finger on the reason, she seemed different. Elizabeth had spoken very little, and looked at him even less. Mayhap it was because the change in their relationship was as new to her as it was to him. Now he was not so sure.

Uneasiness washed through him, and he shifted uncomfortably. Now that his wife had seen that he was coming to care for her, was she setting him up for some purpose of her own, to get him in a position of intimacy so that she could use his attraction to her against him? Would he now discover that she was indeed trying to manipulate and control him?

The silence stretched on.

"My lord?" Arthur questioned, standing ready with his clean tunic.

Raynor glanced at him and away. "My wife has invited me to sup in her solar."

Arthur simply blinked at him, then at the brown tunic he held. "You would like something finer, my lord?" he asked.

Raynor knew a moment of discomfort at the notion that Arthur would think him eager to please his wife by dressing more grandly.

Then, irritated with himself, Raynor sat on the chair by the empty hearth. What did he care if Arthur assumed he might want something finer to wear for an intimate dinner with his wife? There was no reason to be embarrassed about being asked to come to her solar. It was not unheard-of for a wife to invite her husband for an evening alone.

But even as he told himself these things, Raynor knew this was not so of himself and Elizabeth.

It was no secret that they did not behave as a loving couple. They had been anything but close since Elizabeth's coming to Warwicke, and despite his original efforts to make thing appear normal, everyone in the keep knew it.

It was not surprising, really, that Arthur would assume this was a special occasion.

Then something else occurred to the lord of Warwicke. Arthur had also assumed that Raynor would be accepting Elizabeth's invitation.

This was what finally swayed him. Since they had picnicked with Willow two days before, Raynor had felt closer to Elizabeth. He had told her things he'd never said to anyone else, never thought to say to anyone. And she'd listened without judging, and, even more importantly, without asking questions he did not wish to answer.

Raynor could think of no good reason why he should not go. It seemed only right, when he had decided to try to be a husband to her. But Raynor's trepidation did not completely leave him. The wounds of his past were difficult to leave behind him.

He could not help asking himself why Elizabeth would care about him. Louisa, Bronic, and now Willow, were the only people who had ever really loved him. But they had clearly needed him as much as he had them.

His wife was a different matter. She was strong, resourceful and intelligent. She had a family that would accept her return with joy. Of that he had no doubt. So why did she want him—need him? The lord of Warwicke had no answer. But mayhap he should try to find out.

He looked at Arthur, who still waited with the appearance of patience. Raynor nearly smiled, knowing how difficult a pose this was for the boy.

With a sigh of resignation, he said, "Get the green velvet tunic and the black pourpoint."

With a nod, Arthur moved to do as he was bidden.

As he readied himself for the meeting with his wife, Raynor's unease began to be overlaid by a growing sense of anticipation.

Clearly he recalled the first time he had dined with his wife alone. It had ended in his being married to the maddening, beautiful, endlessly intriguing woman.

Somewhere inside him lurked the question of whether the request had anything to do with her admitted wish to have a child. His child.

Elizabeth had prepared her chambers carefully.

The table was set up in the middle of the solar. Her own pewter plate and glasses were arranged on top. A cool jug of wine waited to be poured. A host of candles had been lit and placed about the chamber. Their soft golden light flickered over the highly polished surface of the table and chairs, and created mysterious shadows in the dim corners of the room.

Elizabeth moved restlessly to the window and peered out into the warm darkness.

Would he come?

She ran her hands over the scarlet velvet of her skirt, then checked the ribbon Olwyn had tied around her hair at the nape of her neck. She'd left the glossy mass loose except for that ribbon.

As she lowered her hand, she realized it was trembling. Elizabeth clasped her fingers together to still the quivering, but it did no good.

But the nervousness that had gripped her since she'd decided to invite her husband to dine would not leave her.

Had she made a mistake in inviting Raynor to her solar? Would he even accept? What if he was not yet prepared to go so far as to put himself within her domain?

Surely he would know that which was relegated to the back of her mind, but which was just as compelling as her need to have peace with him. Did he sense what she hoped for, desired with all her being?

Her cheeks burned. How could he not know, after what she had told him the day of the picnic? She'd come right out and admitted that she wished to bear his child, their child.

Her hand went to her flat stomach. What would it feel like to have Raynor's baby moving inside her?

Elizabeth only wished she knew what he would do. Raynor was a man who needed to make his own decision, act on his own desires and thoughts. Perhaps she should have waited for him to come to her. Would he feel she was pushing him, trying to control him?

With a sigh, she put her hand to her forehead.

There was no use in torturing herself this way. Either he would come or he would not.

Her gaze went to the door.

But surely, if he meant to come, he would be here by now. The portal remained firmly closed.

Her attention strayed outside the window. Her gaze sweeping the inky blackness of the night, Elizabeth tried to force her stiff muscles to relax.

Just when she thought she would scream with the tension, she heard the door slowly open.

Afraid to turn, in case it was someone else, and not Raynor, Elizabeth stood perfectly still until he spoke her name. "Elizabeth."

She remembered the first time she had heard that voice, in the antechamber at Windsor. Even though it had only been a matter of months, the changes in her life made that time seem infinitely long ago. Now, as then, she knew an image of rough fingers in brown velvet when she heard him speak. That husky edge always set her senses on edge in a very sensuously pleasing way.

Slowly she turned to face him, a soft smile curving her red lips. "My lord husband, you are come."

As she faced him, there was a heady sweetness in his gaze that made her head swim and her breath quicken. In that moment, she knew that she had done the right thing in asking him to come to her.

He bowed formally. "I am most pleased to be invited." Where he stood, his face was in shadow, but she knew he was watching her. She felt the touch of his gaze upon her face, her neck, then down over the deep neckline of her cote. A heady warmth suffused her, and she longed to throw herself into his arms.

Slowly, Elizabeth thought, go slowly.

She moved toward the table and picked up the jug of cooled wine. "Will you drink, my lord?"

"Yes."

She poured a cup and held it out to him.

Without warning, she had several vivid flashes of memory of that first time they'd dined together in Stephen's house...pouring him wine...talking...the kiss they'd shared.

So much had happened since then, so many changes in her life and his.

He took the offered libation, and she prepared one for herself. As Elizabeth turned back to him, he raised his glass. "To the future."

Surprised, she raised her own glass. "Aye, to the future."

Uncertainty kept her from tasting the wine as she took a drink, but she felt its heat course over her tongue and down her throat. Yet it was no more warming than his manner. Raynor seemed so accepting of her, and their being together here. This was more than she'd even dared dream of.

To cover her confusion, Elizabeth motioned toward the meal awaiting them. "Olwyn brought this some time ago. The cook said you liked eels, so I asked her to prepare your favorite recipe. She was most eager to do so." Elizabeth smiled at him, and heard him catch his breath.

When Elizabeth looked at him askance, he said, "My lady wife, do you have any inkling of how lovely you are when you smile? Your eyes sparkle like the finest of sapphires."

She blushed to the roots of her dark hair. In her lifetime, she'd been flattered by many men, and more eloquently. But none of those compliments had meant so much as this one from her husband. Raynor was not a man who bandied pretty words about until they were meaningless from overuse. What he said came from the depths of his heart, and thus meant more than any poem or song of technical merit.

Happiness dampened her eyes as she gazed up at him. "Raynor."

He looked away, suddenly seeming shy, and that surprised her. She'd not thought to see the powerful and commanding Raynor blushing like a young squire.

But she could hardly fault him. She, too, felt out of her depth, with this new softness between them.

Thinking to give them something to do, she asked. "Will you take your sup?"

He sat in the indicated chair. Rather than take the other seat, Elizabeth moved to stand behind Raynor. Acting as his squire, she served her husband eels, venison and fresh white bread. He appeared surprised that she would perform this humble service for him, but he said nothing.

It was as if neither of them wanted to break the sweet enchantment that held them in its gossamer spell.

Finally he asked, "Will you not take your leisure with me, my lady wife?"

"Nay, my lord. I have no hunger."

How could she tell him that at this moment she could not possibly eat? Her stomach was aflutter with hope and longing. Elizabeth could not say she wanted to run her fingers through the weight of his hair, where it grew along his nape. That she longed to push the dark mass aside and press her lips to the tender spot at the joining of neck and shoulder.

He did not answer, but she could feel his attention on her as she stood beside his chair. Elizabeth wanted him to feel that she cared about him. That she wanted to be a wife to him, to see to his needs—and his desires.

She closed her eyes on that last thought. Patience was what she needed. She and Raynor had experienced only the physical side of love. And while her body cried out for fulfillment, she wanted more. Elizabeth knew Raynor must come to see that she desired him for all he was, his smile, the sound of his voice, the touch of his hand, his kindness, his loyalty, his devotion.

In short, the essence of Raynor.

Elizabeth thought all of this as she continued to serve him from the dishes on the table. She was in such a state of agitation that she didn't really know if the food was still warm enough. But if her husband found anything amiss, he made no comment.

The room was quiet while she moved about, seeing to his comfort. But it was a sultry silence, evoked by their heightened senses and the warmth of the night. Only the occasional call of an owl came to them on the soft summer breeze that wafted through the window.

Raynor was dazed by the soft rose scent of his wife as she stood so close behind him, her attention trained on his every need. When she leaned close to serve him another one of the eels he hadn't even tasted, her hair fell over her shoulder, and a long strand clung to the velvet of his sleeve. Raynor wanted to reach out and grasp the stray curl, to wind it round his finger, thus bringing her close to him. He did not, swallowing back his growing need to touch her.

But only a moment later, as Elizabeth reached across him to refill his wine goblet and her breast brushed against his arm, Raynor could no longer hold himself back. His large, callused hand closed over hers and he turned it palm up to face him. He looked down at her fingers, marveling at how pale they were, resting in his own sun-browned ones.

She was so fair, his lady wife. Slowly he traced his own fingers over her palm.

She closed her eyes, trying with all her might to remember that she must make Raynor see that she wanted him for all he was. That before they made love again, there must be some understanding and harmony between them.

Then he raised her palm to his mouth, and she was lost, drowning in the heady sensation of his lips on the tender flesh. It was no use even attempting to resist, she thought, as her belly twisted in a spasm of longing.

Bending close to his ear, she whispered, her voice raspy with ill-concealed passion, "Oh, my lord, my husband. How I long to feel you inside me again."

With a rough gasp, Raynor pushed back his chair.

Neither of them paid any attention when it fell over onto the floor.

His arms closed around her, his lips finding hers. Raynor's kiss seared her to her very soul.

Elizabeth's breath came in ragged drafts as his open mouth left hers to press hot kisses down her throat. His tongue flicked over the rapidly beating pulse in her neck, and she moaned with sweet wanting as she tipped her head back to give him better access to the sensitive flesh.

When his head dipped to the deep neckline of her gown, she held his dark head against her with both hands. Her fingers curled in the thick mane of his hair.

He nudged aside the edge of her cote and tunic, exposing one deep pink nipple. As he raked it gently with his teeth, it hardened. Raynor sighed, taking the small raspberry firmness into his mouth to suckle.

Elizabeth arched against him and felt the hard length of his manhood against her stomach. She was on fire, her body straining against his.

As if aware of her struggle, Raynor put his large hand on her buttocks and lifted her high against him. Her legs felt boneless, and quivered as she tried to open them. Elizabeth whimpered softly when her clothing hindered her desire.

Barely able to think over the throbbing in her blood, Elizabeth cried out, "Raynor, Raynor, I want you!"

He raised his head, looking down at her with walnut eyes, dark with passion. Then he kissed her, hard and long, before scooping her up in his arms to carry her to her bedchamber.

The room was dark, save for the light of one candle that Olwyn had lit earlier in the evening. The bed—her bed— was a huge, hulking shape in the center of the room, its hangings pulled back in welcome.

Raynor held her face up for his kiss as he laid her in the deep shadows of the bed.

"Take me now, my husband!" she gasped, arching against him.

Her lips clung to his as he pulled away to look down at her. He cupped her fevered cheek in his large hand. Raynor longed to do just that. He was roused to the point of agony, his blood a rushing torrent of need in his veins. But he would not hurry this time. Pressing his fingers gently to her lips, he whispered huskily, "Softly, Elizabeth. I will not have you in such haste this night. I would love you properly, as you should be loved, here in your bed, where I have dreamed of having you since the first time I saw it in the back of the wagon. The fact that I could see nothing of its shape beneath the cloth that covered it only made my imagination work harder at visualizing you in it—naked and wanting.''

As he spoke, Elizabeth shivered at the image he brought to her mind. ''If only I had known,'' she whispered, kissing his hard fingers, then leaning up to kiss his lips. ''For every time I looked at it I thought of little else but us there together.''

He raised her up on her knees, his gaze holding her. ''I shall see you as I thought of you—now.''

Elizabeth kissed him again, her mouth open and inviting. ''Aye, now.''

He eased her clothing from under her, and before she knew it Elizabeth was indeed naked to his scorching gaze.

Almost reverently, Raynor leaned forward and kissed the swell of her firm, high breasts, his voice a hoarse whisper. ''You are lovely. So lovely my breath is taken from me.''

Elizabeth swallowed hard, feeling the honeyed dampness at her thighs. She leaned back into the softness of the bed, her hand held toward him in invitation. ''I need you, Raynor. Love me.''

''I will, until you cry out with joy,'' he told her. He stood then, removing his own clothing quickly, but with no awkward haste. It was as if this moment were perfectly choreographed by some benevolent goddess of love, for Elizabeth knew no embarrassment or false modesty as he looked down at her. She held herself proudly, feeling beautiful as never before beneath his hot stare.

Before, their couplings had been too hurried, too desperate. But now Elizabeth looked at Raynor, truly marveling at the perfection of his hard body in the soft light of the candle flame. His shoulders were wide, his waist was flat and ridged with muscle, his hips and thighs were well sculptured. "It is you who are beautiful, Raynor," she told him with unfeigned wonder.

He came to her then, stretching out to hold her against the whole length of him.

His lips traced fiery trails over her heated flesh, down her throat and over her breasts. When his mouth closed on one peak and then the other, Elizabeth reached out to hold him to her, her breath coming more quickly. When she thought she would surely scream with the passion burning inside her, Raynor's head dipped lower, and his hot tongue laved her quivering belly. And she knew she would surely ignite.

Aflame with desire, Elizabeth pulled him up to her in desperation, her whole being centered on the pleasure he evoked.

Her lips met his as she reached out to feel the shape of his strong back. Her fingers slipped down to the rounded hills of his buttocks, and he gasped aloud, arching toward her even as his manhood jerked against her stomach.

Elizabeth moaned, her body heavy with desire, opening her legs without conscious thought. How she wanted him, needed him inside her, filling the ache only he could assuage.

Raynor's fingers dipped to the thatch of black curls at the apex of her thighs, and he found her slick and wet with desire.

Slowly and lingeringly, he slid along the slim length of her. "Now, now!" she cried out. "I can bear no more!"

Shaking with his own pleasure, Raynor rose up over her, kissing her open mouth, his tongue flicking hers.

Elizabeth was past coherent thought, pushed to the bounds of reality by the passion that raged through her. She made a unintelligible sound deep in her throat.

When she reached out to him desperately, he positioned himself between her legs. As he entered her buttery darkness, she wrapped her legs around him with a cry of pleasure.

"Elizabeth, you unman me," he cried though clenched teeth, trying desperately to gain control of himself.

"Nay, Raynor, never that." She rocked toward him, and the motion brought deliciously radiant sensations from deep inside her. "I want all the manliness of you, Raynor." Elizabeth began to move her head from side to side as she sought release from this all-consuming fire. "Help me."

He rocked with her then, unable to prevent himself.

And as he thrust deep inside her, he heard her moan, calling his name with the force of her fulfillment. "Raynor!"

He gasped, and stiffened above her. He felt himself spill into her like a river entering the ocean, and a great sea of pleasure closed over his head.

Sometime later, Elizabeth wakened in the darkness of her bed. A body, large and warm, curled against her back. The pleasantly heavy weight of an arm held her close against him.

Raynor.

She placed her hand over his where it rested on her belly.

A great swell of happiness rose up to block her throat. Dear heaven, how she loved him, more than life or reason. This difficult man, with all his foibles, had come to mean more to her than anyone.

He was her life, her joy, her soul.

She lifted his hand to press a tender kiss upon its tanned back. That hand, so strong and yet so tender, was a source of protection, as well as pleasure. Never need she worry about the future with Raynor at her side. He would see she was safe and cared for.

And care for her he must, at least a little, even though he had not said the words. His gentle loving had given him away. And though it might not yet be love he felt for her, that could someday come.

She became aware that Raynor's other hand, the one beneath her, had tightened on her breast.

He was not sleeping.

Slowly his finger circled her nipple, which hardened under the gentle stimulation. "You are awake, wife," he said, his breath warm on her ear.

Elizabeth sighed with pleasure, rolling onto her back to smile up at him in the enveloping darkness. "Yes, husband, I am awake. As are you."

As his hand moved to her other breast, she felt him stir against her side. He chuckled softly. "Aye, that I am. A most happy coincidence."

Chapter Fourteen

When Elizabeth woke, Raynor was gone from her bed, but the sweet memory of his caresses remained.

She blushed, thinking of the things they had done, things she'd not imagined in her wildest fantasies. Never had she dreamed that a man and woman could experience such deep and satisfying passion as she and Raynor had.

For she knew that he had felt it, too.

His tender lovemaking, the hoarse abandon of his own cries, told her he had known her wonder.

Surely this was just the beginning. Raynor would come to her tonight, and each night thereafter. Even if it wasn't the love she craved, mayhap in time their union would turn to that.

Elizabeth forced down a sharp twinge of regret that Raynor did not love her as she now realized she loved him. There was no sense whatsoever in mourning what was not. She should focus on what was. And even this awakening tenderness he showed toward her was more than Elizabeth had ever hoped for.

With determination to face the future with optimism, Elizabeth threw back the covers and leapt from her bed.

The day, and Raynor, awaited her.

When she called for Olwyn to assist her in dressing for the day, Elizabeth's queries as to her husband's whereabouts were met with a disappointing reply. She was told that Raynor had gone to the practice field with his brother. Her teeth worrying her bottom lip, Elizabeth tried to suppress her disappointment. She had hoped they might spend this day together.

It seemed obvious that Raynor did not have the same desire. Determinedly she told herself to remember her resolve to allow him to come to her in his own time. That was the only way for him to truly learn to trust in her.

So thinking, Elizabeth decided not to sit and brood. It would be best to occupy herself and her mind until she saw her husband again. Though, with the memory of the previous night to heat her blood, patience would prove a hard-won virtue this day.

Resolutely she began to ready herself for her daily ride.

Raynor spent the early part of the morning in sword practice with his brother.

Both were proficient in this area, and Raynor enjoyed the contests. Today he had a hard time losing himself as he usually did in the sheer pleasure of matching skill and wits as Bronic's sword clashed against his own.

He'd left Elizabeth's bed as the first hint of dawn tinted the windows in her chamber a pale gold. In the dim light he'd found Elizabeth breathtakingly beautiful. Almost too beautiful to leave, with her black hair spread across the white of the pillows and the slender warmth of her curled against his side.

Not in all his twenty-seven years had Raynor thought that any woman could come to mean so much to him, much more than mere physical attraction could explain.

It was true that he desired Elizabeth—to distraction.

More than that, he wanted to lie down beside her and rest his mind. He longed to hold her every night as he had last night. He wanted to fill her with his sons and watch them grow up under her firm but tender care.

Was this love?

He wasn't sure that he would put that name to his feelings. But if 'twas not love, it certainly felt like it.

Too late, he parried Bronic's downward thrust and took an unexpectedly heavy blow across his hip.

Bronic stopped short. Having turned his weapon to land the blow with its flat side at the last moment, he knew he hadn't cut his brother. He was surprised the swing had made contact. Few about the keep could best Raynor with sword. He was lithe and fast, despite his large build.

Throwing his sword to the ground as Raynor grunted with pain, Bronic scowled, his blond brows meeting over his nose. In doing so, he unknowingly heightening his resemblance to Raynor. "What are you about, Raynor? Arthur could have blocked that thrust."

Shrugging, Raynor gave a rueful laugh, not meeting Bronic's eyes. "Aye, you are right in that. I know not what is the matter with me."

Bronic gave him a long, knowing glance. "You may not, brother, but 'tis no secret to anyone else."

Raynor's tanned complexion darkened as he blushed deeply. "I see."

"Why do you not just stop fighting it? You love her, Raynor. Elizabeth is a good woman, and if you would just allow yourself, you'd see she is as like our mother as the she-goat is to the mare. Elizabeth is a fine filly, full of spirit and intelligence. It is time you opened your eyes and saw that she is good for you and worthy of your faith and love."

Raynor watched him without speaking. How could he tell Bronic that he longed for nothing so much as to trust and believe in Elizabeth? Slowly he answered, "'Tis not so easily done as all that. I have seen the good she has done, felt the sweetness of being with her, and the more I want her the more I fear a betrayal, no matter how I tell myself I am a fool, that she is not like mother." He looked to his brother for understanding. "Bronic, I cannot just say I will trust her, and do it."

Bronic shook his head in consternation. "Aye, you can. If you but let yourself."

Was it that simple? Raynor asked himself. Could he just set aside his fears of being manipulated and controlled as his father had been? And control him Elizabeth could, without great effort, should she choose to do so. She had become the focus of his every thought and deed.

The question was, would she?

Bronic would have him believe not. What could Bronic gain by falsely urging him to trust in Elizabeth? Nothing that Raynor could see.

Could it be that Bronic was so besotted with the lovely Olwyn that he wished to see others in the same state of bliss?

As his brother's gaze remained unwavering on him, Raynor knew this was not so. Never in their years together had Bronic acted for anything other than his good. It was inconceivable that he would do otherwise now.

Slowly Raynor held out his sword.

Bronic took it with a grin. "Your lady is out riding. I saw her leave the castle just a little while ago. You were too busy fighting off my skillful attacks to take note."

For that, Raynor clouted his brother on the shoulder with a hard fist.

Bronic's reply was a rueful laugh.

Then, his expression changing to one of affection, Raynor reached out and clasped Bronic's shoulder. "You have my thanks, brother," he said.

Raynor knew Bronic would understand that he was thanking him not for the information, but for his support.

With that, Raynor turned toward the stables to get his own horse. Mayhap, if he hurried, he could catch up to Elizabeth.

* * *

Elizabeth allowed Minerva to have her head, and they raced freely over their usual route across the landscape.

But as she came to the top of a rise and saw a man and horse ahead of her on the path, Elizabeth slowed. Her heart sank, for even at this distance she could see that it was Nigel Harrington.

He was mad to have come here, after she had told him nay. And in his madness he could destroy all she held dear.

She knew she should ride for the keep and tell Raynor he was here, allow her husband to deal with his enemy as he would. But something stopped her. She did not want Nigel's death on her head, for surely that was what would happen if Raynor discovered him here. The man was a source of anger and frustration for them, but did he deserve to lose his life for that?

Elizabeth was tempted to turn and ride for the keep, to avoid Nigel and the sure disaster he represented, but she could not. Fear of meeting him again would make her a prisoner in the keep. And that she could not accept. Nigel must be made to understand that she would not assist him.

Even as these thoughts passed through her mind, Nigel rode toward her, calling out her name.

She brought Minerva to a halt, waiting for him, her lips thinned in anger.

As soon as he reached her, Nigel leapt from his mount and strode toward her, leading his horse. He was clearly excited at seeing her, greeting her effusively. "Lady Elizabeth, I am so happy to see you."

"I fear I cannot say the same in regard to you, my lord. Why are you come here? Did you not get my message?"

His lean jaw flexed with what appeared to be anger, but he quelled it immediately, raising sorrowful blue eyes to her. "I did, but I hoped there was some mistake."

"There was no mistake, Lord Harrington," Elizabeth answered stiffly. "'Tis a most difficult situation you place me in. I can do nothing for you. Nor do I have the desire to do so. My loyalty is to my husband." She pulled up the horse's reins, ready to put this situation and Nigel Harrington behind her. "I will say that I am sorry for offering false hope though, I did warn you. No, I must go, and you must not return here. If you do, I shall surely be bound to inform Raynor, and he will deal with you in his own way."

Nigel rushed toward her, his normally placid features twisted in anger. "Foolish bitch!"

Raynor lost no time in following after his wife. He didn't know exactly what he would say or do when he found her, he only knew he must see her. He felt alone and incomplete without Elizabeth at his side, and he was done with denying it.

He would let whatever came after today take care of itself.

Without care for what the guard at the gate might think, he galloped off in the direction the man told him Elizabeth had taken. It was really no effort to follow her, for the path was a well-traveled one.

If he hadn't been so bent on getting to his wife, Raynor might have paused to admire the deep blue of the sky, the peaceful beauty of green meadows, deep forest and colorful wildflowers. But he was oblivious of these things on all but a subconscious level.

All he could think about was Elizabeth, and their chances of having a real life together.

Raynor was coming out of a hollow in the land and just starting up another slope when he chanced to look up ahead of him.

What he saw made his heart stop in his chest. When it began beating again, it was a heavy, aching thing inside him.

At the top of the rise was Elizabeth, and she was not alone. A man, holding the reins of a gray stallion, stood beside her. And even from this distance the prickling along the back of his neck told Raynor it was Nigel Harrington.

His dread enemy.

Betrayed, by Elizabeth.

For a disorienting moment, a haze of rage and disappointment rose up to obscure his vision. Raynor ached at the loss of what might have been. Then he quickly counted himself a fool for ever having contemplated a future that included any kind of trust between them.

All the while he'd been rocked by the discovery of her perfidy, his horse had carried him forward. And now Raynor was close enough to identify Harrington more clearly.

Elizabeth's horse was drawn close to Harrington, who stood on the ground next to her. He had his hand on her arm. It was a very intimate scene, and Raynor's blood throbbed at seeing the other man touching his wife.

As Raynor approached, he realized the two were so deep in conversation that they didn't even notice his arrival. This only served to further fuel his fury.

His pain was too great for him even to contemplate what he would do about Elizabeth's betrayal. As to Nigel Harrington, there was no question.

He must die.

Drawing his sword without slowing his mount, Raynor let out a cry of challenge. "Stand ready, Harrington!"

The other man looked up to see his enemy descending. It seemed to take only a moment for the threat of Raynor's presence to register on him. With a harsh sound of anger, Harrington swept Elizabeth from her horse to hold her before him. "Come then, Warwicke!" he bellowed.

Raynor felt a stab of sheer panic pierce his chest as he realized Nigel meant to use Elizabeth as a shield.

And in that moment, Raynor lost himself, body, mind and soul. He loved her, for now, for all time. For one heart-wrenching second, he knew a sweet relief that was cleansing in its intensity. At long last, the feelings he'd tried so hard to suppress found release. But, just as quickly, that joy was gone, replaced by the reality that Elizabeth did not deserve his love. She had betrayed him.

Without even pausing to consider, Raynor pulled hard on the reins. No matter what his wife had done, he could not endanger her, even to get to Harrington. His stallion reared at the sudden halt, pawing the air wildly. For a moment, Raynor had some difficulty keeping his seat, but he managed to do so.

When he'd calmed his horse, his gaze went to Elizabeth, who stood before Nigel, her sapphire eyes round with horror and guilt.

His heart sank even further.

If he'd had any doubt as to her culpability, seeing her shamefaced reaction settled it once and for all.

"Come then, Warwicke," Nigel gibed again, his light blue eyes alight with cruelty. He tightened his hold on Elizabeth. "Do you not wish my death above all things? What makes you hesitate?" Then he laughed, as if this last question were indeed very funny.

Raynor clenched his teeth on the rage that made his blood thrum. He did wish for Nigel's death above all things. But he could not risk harming Elizabeth.

Nigel seemed to sense Raynor's defeat, for he laughed spitefully. "Lay away your sword, Warwicke."

Raynor hesitated.

"Did you hear me, Raynor?" the other man growled. He reached into his belt and withdrew a small but viciously sharp-looking knife. Without preamble, he pressed it to the pale column of Elizabeth's throat. "I will kill her, and gladly. If only for the sake of seeing you suffer as you have made me."

Raynor knew Harrington was telling the truth.

Elizabeth's eyes pleaded with her husband as the knife pricked her throat and a drop of blood stained her creamy flesh.

Raynor's heart throbbed anew at the sight of her blood, spilled by his enemy's weapon. Seeing her sustain even the slightest injury was like a hot knife in his gut.

God help him, but he loved her for good or ill. And no matter what she had done, he could not change that.

He was trapped by his own heart, just as he'd always feared. Raynor was completely incapable of acting in his own interests because of his feelings for a woman. The knowledge should have been staggering, but he only felt a strange sense of inevitability.

He'd been born to love Elizabeth. It was as inescapable as time, and just as unstoppable.

With a bellow of frustration and rage, Raynor cast his sword aside.

Nigel threw back his head and laughed with triumph.

Fixing the other man with a gaze that fairly bled hatred, Raynor growled harshly, "Harm her further and I shall kill you slowly. And only after torture so exquisitely painful you will beg for that end."

He turned his tormented gaze to his wife, his eyes dark as umber. Despite his anger, Elizabeth could see fear for her clearly etched on his harshly chiseled face.

In that moment, Elizabeth knew he loved her.

But what good would come of that love, she did not know. For it was equally clear that he thought she had betrayed him. Love, fear and hatred warred on his face as he met her gaze.

And was it not true? Had she not betrayed him by even speaking with Harrington? She should have ridden for the keep and fetched Raynor immediately.

Tears sprang to her eyes even though she fought against shedding them. It was too much. To at last discover he loved her, only to have him hate her, too. She could not bear it.

Somehow she must make Raynor see that she had not meant to do ill.

Elizabeth held out her hand. In spite of the knife pricking her throat she cried, "Raynor! It is not as you believe! I did not ask him to come here! My only sin is one of omission. I knew you would kill him if I told you he was come!"

"Quiet, slut," Nigel growled, and pulled her head farther back. The knife stung, and she felt a new trickle of wet on her throat.

"Harrington, I will kill you," Raynor threatened, starting forward. But he stopped short when Nigel held her even tighter. If Raynor had heard her words, he gave no sign, for his eyes remained hard on hers.

Nigel taunted, "You, my lord fool, are in no position to make such rash statements. Were I you, I would not waste breath on them." To Elizabeth's horror and surprise, he chuckled, seeming to enjoy this game immensely. "I could kill her this instant, and you could do nothing."

Elizabeth knew she had been wrong, wrong to protect this man's life. Obviously he was mad, whether over losing the members of his family or for some other reason. It mattered not why. What did matter was that he clearly was incapable of ever being an uncle to Willow.

Raynor had had the right of it all along. She longed to tell him she was sorry.

But what he said next made a chill of despair run down her spine.

Raynor fairly spat the words. "You and she are of like mind, Harrington. She is as faithless as you in her loyalties. But be that as it may, the woman is my wife, and what I have I keep to me."

Nigel laughed again, almost gleefully. "Oh, Raynor, my most clever opponent. You could not be more wrong in your assessment of your wife." He gave Elizabeth's black hair a vicious tug. "It is I who have been betrayed by her. She sent a message telling me she would not help me to see Willow. I came here to try to make her change her mind, to see reason, but she refused."

The expression on Raynor's face did not change. Would nothing sway him? Even as Elizabeth wondered why Nigel would defend her by explaining what had really happened, her answer came.

Nigel snickered. "I wish you to know, Raynor, that she has been loyal to you, that she loves you as you do her. It will give me great pleasure to think of your agony while I take her myself. For take her I will."

Raynor leapt to the ground and started toward them, but Nigel pushed the knife deeper to Elizabeth's throat, and she cried out in pain as the blood trickled afresh. "Stay back, or she will die here before your very eyes."

Elizabeth watched the frustration and helplessness play over her husband's face. She longed to help him. Raynor was a man who hated not being able to control his surroundings. This would be agonizing for him.

Nigel spoke again, his tone unexpectedly reasonable. "There is a way, Warwicke."

Warily Raynor watched him, saying nothing.

The other man went on when he saw that no reply was forthcoming. "Willow. You bring the child to me, and your wife is yours."

Raynor tipped back his head and howled his rage and frustration like a wolf caught in a trap.

Despite his previous bravado, she felt Nigel tremble behind her.

And even Elizabeth, who loved him, was not immune to the stark fury in her husband.

"Never! Not while there is a breath in my body!" Raynor screamed. "You will not lay a filthy hand upon her!"

Nigel answered Raynor with nearly equal fury, the obsession with having what he wanted obviously driving him beyond his fear. "You bastard!" he cried. "Who are you to deny me my right? She is my own flesh—my daughter. Not yours, as you so boldly lie. For lie you do. I know you do not believe the child is yours. You could not. I know Louisa told you I raped her. You can't deny me my right to my child. I will stand for it no longer."

Elizabeth felt the words like a cold shock of ice through her veins. What was he saying? Nigel was Willow's father? He was Louisa's brother, although only by marriage. And he'd just admitted he'd raped her.

"No!" Raynor shouted, trying to deny the facts even now.

But one look at her husband's face told Elizabeth the truth of it. It was there for her to see, in the taut line of his jaw, the hatred burning in his eyes as he focused all his attention on the man behind her.

Were Elizabeth not so filled with anger, revulsion and fear herself, she would have found it in her heart to almost feel sympathy for the man who held her. For when Raynor did get his chance for revenge—and there was no doubt he would, judging by the look in his dark eyes—she would not wish to be in Nigel's place.

Then, as the truth of what Nigel had just said sank into her, so many things became suddenly clear. Jean had said Louisa had birthed the babe only six months after arriving at Warwicke. Elizabeth had thought he might be jealous that the babe was not his, but Raynor's anger at that time had been caused by the knowledge that his friend had been raped by her own stepbrother. It explained why Raynor had appeared so angry to the serving woman, even while he was so unstintingly kind to Louisa. And this also explained why Louisa had hated her brother, had been the one to beg Raynor to keep her child from seeing him.

Raynor's determination to convince everyone that Willow was his child now made sense.

Raynor was past the point of speech. He stood there, his attention a fixed point of hatred. He'd neither blinked nor showed any sign of acknowledging anything Nigel said since that one-word denial after Harrington divulged the fact that he was Willow's father.

As if realizing he would get no further with Raynor at this moment, Nigel began to back toward his horse. Even as he climbed atop the gray, he never let up the pressure of the knife on Elizabeth's throat.

She was forced to follow him.

Raynor never moved, but watched them intently for some opportunity to act.

The blade was so tightly pressed to her throat that Elizabeth was incapable of even speaking. Fear made her follow Nigel Harrington's every movement. An even greater fear of what he would do to her once he got her to his own castle made Elizabeth watchful of any opportunity to break free from her captor. Soon she found herself seated before him on the gray, her hope dwindling like mist in sunshine.

Still holding tightly to her, Nigel rode up to Minerva and gave her a sadistic kick in the side. The horse reared and galloped away. Then he did the same to Raynor's mount. Now there would be no way for her husband to ride after them.

As they swung around to ride away, she tried to turn her head, to meet Raynor's gaze one last time, to plead with him to forgive her. Nigel prevented her with another tug on her hair. Tears came to her eyes, but they were not from physical pain.

It was only when they were nearly to the edge of the clearing that her chance came.

A rabbit bolted across their path, and Nigel's horse shied. He reached down to grab at the reins with the hand holding the knife.

Realizing that it was this moment or none, Elizabeth pulled free of his flailing arms and threw herself to the ground.

The stallion reared above her, and she covered her head with her arms as she screamed.

The slashing hooves came down but scant inches from her face, and she screamed again. It was then that Elizabeth felt herself being dragged free of the impending danger. Strong arms lifted her away and up into a protective circle.

For a moment she was disoriented by the speed with which the rescue had occurred.

"Are you hurt?" Raynor asked through her confusion.

Though she was shaking, Elizabeth raised her head from his chest to look at him. "Nay." Her breath came in uneven gasps.

"I will kill him!" Raynor shouted in a voice that left no doubt that he was making not a threat, but a promise.

It had all happened so quickly that Nigel was still working to get his mount under control. When he saw that Raynor's attention was on him now, instead of Elizabeth, he gave the animal a vicious kick, sending it surging forward, away from his enemy. Yet his cowardice did not stop him from calling out a warning over his shoulder. "You will pay for this, Warwicke, and dearly."

With a cry of rage, Raynor raced across the clearing after him, clearly ready to kill his enemy with his bare hands. "Come back, you bastard. Fight me. Fight me!"

Desperately Elizabeth called after her husband, "Raynor, this will serve no purpose! You have no weapon, and can never catch him without your horse. Let him go. He is too much a coward to come back and face you."

Raynor dropped to his knees on the grass, panting as if he had run for leagues.

Elizabeth knew he was fighting hard to control the rage that drove him, the hatred that made him lust for Nigel Harrington's blood. She knew she had to leave him to fight his demons alone. There was naught she could do until he had driven them from himself.

Besides, Elizabeth knew Raynor would not thank her for anything she might say on the subject. The look on his face when he found her with Nigel had told everything.

She wanted to lie down and cry, herself.

But she did not. It would gain them nothing.

More for something to do than from any notion that he would want her to, Elizabeth began to look for Raynor's sword in the thick grass. All the while, she tried not to look at Raynor, who had not moved from where he knelt.

Just as she finally located the weapon and bent to raise it from the ground, she felt a hand on her arm.

Elizabeth started, turning awkwardly to face him. She looked into Raynor's eyes. They were cold as stone. Her chest ached with the loss of what happiness they'd found in these past few days. She was filled with an aching emptiness.

All her life she'd known how to manage things and people, to smooth over difficult situations without effort. It was a gift she possessed.

But with Raynor it was not the same. Her own future happiness hinged on whether or not he accepted her.

This was one time she could not fix things.

Either forgiveness and understanding came from inside her husband, or it did not. She could only pray that it would in time.

Turning away from her, as if it hurt him to continue to look upon her, Raynor said, "We had best return to the keep."

It was in that moment that something inside Elizabeth broke, like a wineskin filled too full. During the months of their marriage, she had done her utmost to remain calm, to be fair to Raynor, to give him time to adjust to their marriage. To her.

But Elizabeth had reached her end. She, too, had married a stranger and started a new life without having time to become accustomed to the notion. And not once in their relationship had Raynor ever made concession for that.

From inside her, the tears gushed forth.

She raised her hands to her face to stop them. But they came all the harder. As a chocking gasp escaped her, Raynor swung around.

When he spoke, the amazement in his voice was all too apparent. "You . . . you are crying."

Elizabeth lowered her hands to look at him, though she continued to weep as if her heart were indeed broken. "Are you surprised, husband, that I might cry?"

He shook his head. "It's just that I have not seen—"

Elizabeth stamped her foot in utter frustration. "You have not seen. My lord Raynor. You see very little but what you wish to. I know that I am not without fault, my lord. I know that I made a dreadful mistake in not riding directly to the keep and telling you Nigel was here. But I knew you would kill him, and I could not live with being the cause of his death. It did occur to me that I could just ride back to the keep, and thus avoid speaking with him at all, but I did not wish to live under the threat of his possible return. I thought I could simply tell him to go, and he would." Then Elizabeth straightened her shoulders and tossed her head proudly as she waved a hand at him. "'Tis true you are my husband, and I owe my loyalties to you first. But you think only of yourself and your honor. What of mine? At the time, it seemed a small thing to save a fool's life by warning him away. I did not know of the things he had done...what he was. You had told me nothing."

She went on. "But you expect all of me and nothing of yourself. You want loyalty from me and give none in return. You immediately assumed I had come here with the intention of betraying you. And it will always be thus with us, Raynor." Elizabeth clasped her hand to her chest. "Because you do not see me. You see through the eyes of the past, and the wrongs others have done you. Did you truly care for me and believe in me, you would trust that I would not do you ill, and look for some other explanation."

A strange ache settled in Raynor's chest as he looked down at his wife. Her eyes were dark as a rain-drenched midnight. Gone was the sparkling sapphire he'd come to love. And by his own fault.

Elizabeth was right. He should have given her a chance to explain. Raynor stood looking at her with growing sadness. And she was right about other things. Not once had he been able to see her without the pain of his childhood clouding his vision. She'd just been held at knifepoint, and all he could think of was his own pride. It was wrong of him, and the time for seeing past his hurts had come.

Raynor could not speak, because of the lump of pain in his throat. Desperately he held out his arms in appeal and whispered, "Forgive me, love."

For long moments, she simply watched him as if she could not believe her eyes. Then, with a cry of joy, she came to him.

Raynor held her hard against him, barely crediting that she would be willing to forgive him yet again. Elizabeth was indeed completely unlike his mother. She knew how to love and to give of herself unstintingly. There was but one thing between them now. The lie he had told her and the world about being Willow's father. But though Nigel had told Elizabeth the truth of the situation, Raynor still could not speak of it. Even now he could not betray Louisa's trust in him by admitting the facts to Elizabeth, regardless of how much he wanted to prove his commitment to her. At long last, he drew back to speak, trying to explain without explaining. "Elizabeth . . . about Willow . . . I cannot . . ."

She hushed him with a finger on his lips. "Nay, Raynor, say no more. I understand, and there is no need for you to go on. You have done what you must to shelter her. You are like the wolf, and once another has been admitted to your small pack, you protect and keep them no matter what cost to yourself. How I have longed to be allowed into that select group you love so well. To openly show you my love."

For a long moment, he simply stood there trying to comprehend her words. Then he reached toward her with a groan, pulling her back into his arms. "You love me." His tone was hoarse with amazement. He rained kisses on her face and throat.

She wrapped her arms around him, holding to him with something bordering on desperation. "Of course I love you. How could I not?"

She drew back slightly, trying to read the expression in his eyes. "But what of your feelings? I swear on my life that I meant no harm in speaking to Harrington. I knew I loved you, and that I had to do as you asked, without explanation, as far as Willow was concerned. It was the only way for us to begin any kind of life together. I thought you might be coming to accept our marriage just a little, and I wanted nothing to jeopardize that. Besides, I'd seen for myself how much you love Willow, and I knew you would only act for her good."

He kissed Elizabeth again, then looked down at her, his eyes dark with pain. "I admit that when I saw you with Harrington my heart did a turn. It hurt to think you had come to meet him after I had asked you not to."

He hugged her tightly, as if he would never let her go. "But what hurt even more was seeing you in danger. I knew then that I loved you, no matter what you had done. For good or ill, my heart was given into your keeping. When I saw him with that knife...when I thought he might..."

Elizabeth pulled away from him and saw his pained expression. "I knew. I could see it in your eyes, Raynor." She reached up to touch his face. "But I could also see that it brought you no joy to love me. Is that how it must be, Raynor? The next time you are faced with the choice of trusting in me or doubting, which will you decide? Is there no happiness for you in loving me?"

He stared at her, his gaze holding hers. When he spoke, it was slowly, every word enunciated as if he were determined to make her see that he spoke from his soul. "Aye, Elizabeth, there is happiness in loving. Greater than I ever dreamed of. The months that we have been together have been the strangest, most maddening, happiest times of my life. Before I met you, I wasn't even alive. You helped me come out of myself and learn to see the good things around me, my daughter, you. When you showed me that you were willing to believe in me, I realized I must look inside myself and find the same faith in you. You've been nothing but honest with me. Even about our marriage. You took the blame for that on yourself, and though I let you, not all of it was yours. It was I who kissed you that night, not because you asked me, but because I could not stop myself. Even then there was something about you that drew me, despite my efforts to deny it. I have learned my lesson in this. There will be no more doubts."

At the expression of unwavering love in his eyes, Elizabeth cast her uncertainty aside with a cry of gladness. "Raynor, I love you, and I do believe in you, also."

"As I do you," he said, going down on one knee before her. "Elizabeth, my wife and my love. I pledge to love, honor and care for you all the days of my life. It is I who should be asking for forgiveness. Will you...forgive me...for taking so long to discover that I cannot live without you?"

She knelt down with him, tears pouring down her ivory cheeks, her blue eyes shining. "There is nothing to forgive. You acted out of your own pain. I can simply rejoice in the fact that you now love me. I add my pledge to yours, to love, honor and care for you all the days of my life."

Their lips met across the space that separated them, sealing their love for all time to come.

But even as he took her in his arms, Elizabeth knew that as long as the specter of Nigel Harrington lingered, they could not find real contentment. Now that she knew what he had done to his own stepsister, she understood why Raynor hated the man.

But mayhap she was wrong, and the confrontation with Raynor had put enough fear in Harrington to make him leave them be, despite his threats.

Elizabeth could only pray it was so.

Chapter Fifteen

Standing at the top of the steps to the keep, Elizabeth squeezed her husband's arm close against her side. He returned the pressure as she looked around the cluttered courtyard with a smile of happiness.

Raynor had arranged this celebration in honor of their newfound joy. On the night he told her of it, Raynor had held Elizabeth close in the darkness of their bed, telling her that he wanted everyone to share in their happiness.

He felt he'd been clear enough about his displeasure with their marriage. Now he wanted one and all to see how very much Elizabeth meant to him.

Hence here they were, some eight days later, surrounded by happy faces, vivid color and bustling activity.

It was like a fair.

Tents were set up all about the castle grounds, their colors bright in the afternoon sunshine. The narrow walkways between these were crowded with the occupants of both keep and village. When those folk closest to the steps of the keep saw Elizabeth and Raynor emerge from inside, they cheered a welcome.

All understood that this day was marked as a celebration of their lord's wedding, no matter that it came some months late. The people of the keep who knew Elizabeth had already come to love her for her generosity and fairness. The others had learned of her by reputation alone. But since word had been good of this new lady of Warwicke, they were willing to offer the couple their best wishes without restraint.

Both Elizabeth and Raynor waved to the crowd of well-wishers and started down the stairs, Elizabeth leading Willow by her free hand.

The little girl seemed spellbound by the sights before her, and she looked up at Elizabeth with shining eyes.

Elizabeth laughed as she turned to Raynor. "Nothing could have pleased her more, my love."

He looked into Elizabeth's sapphire gaze, and for a moment he couldn't think past the swell of happiness in his chest. That she loved him, this beautiful, giving woman, would be a source of joy for the rest of his life. Raynor could not resist pressing his lips to those sweet red ones, however briefly. "I wanted her to enjoy this day with us."

They moved through the crowd together, man, wife and child. But progress was slow, as the three paused to accept many wishes of congratulations as they went.

They also paused often to gaze upon the many sights that greeted them along the route.

Many of the booths contained merchants selling unusual and exotic goods. There were books in one, various knives in another, cloth of rich and brilliant color in yet another. Some even sold food, though there was to be a massive meal later, at which one and all would be welcome.

As they strolled past one particular booth, Raynor stopped when the merchant called out to him. The man reached across the barrier and handed the lord of Warwicke an odd-looking doll with strings that attached its arms and legs to sticks. By holding the doll by these sticks Raynor was able to make it move about as if by magic. When Raynor tried to pay, the man waved his arms and declared the toy a gift.

After offering his thanks, Raynor handed the object to his daughter with a flourish. "My lady."

Willow was completely entranced, and accepted the toy with enormous brown eyes. "Thank you, Papa," she breathed. She turned to the robust merchant, who smiled widely, showing large, widely spaced teeth. "My thanks to you."

When she tried to make it work as her father had done, the toy refused to obey her tiny hands, but she did not cry, merely looking to Elizabeth for help. Elizabeth laughed and told her that it would simply take some practice to work the thing properly. With a determined expression, Willow tucked it under her arm.

Elizabeth and Raynor exchanged a tolerant glance. They thanked the man again and moved on.

As she watched the little girl, Elizabeth could see that, despite the fact that she was not related to Raynor by blood, she was often like him in her manner. He often placed things beneath his arm just that way to carry them.

Elizabeth realized she was wearing a ridiculous grin, then also realized that she didn't care. Never had she been so happy as she was at this moment.

She had her husband and her child—for she did think of Willow as her own, as surely as if she had borne the little girl herself. No matter that she hoped to give birth to Raynor's babe, Willow would ever be her daughter in all but flesh.

Drawing a deep breath of sheer happiness as they moved along, Elizabeth caught a deliciously spicy scent and realized that she was hungry. Glancing about, Elizabeth saw that the clove-and-cinnamon-laden smell of roasted pears came from a booth to her right.

She looked up at Raynor from beneath her black lashes. "I find I am famished, my lord husband. I fear I was most wakeful during the night, and need more sustenance than usual." From the darkening of his walnut eyes, Elizabeth knew he understood what she was saying. They had made love until the wee hours of the morning, when they had fallen into each other's arms, sated, at least for that moment.

Raynor smiled down at her, his expression warm with suppressed desire. He leaned close to her ear. ''Ah, my lovely maid, I had best feed you then, for I would see you have enough strength to sustain the same level of activity this eve.''

A pretty blush colored her creamy skin, and her blue eyes brightened. ''You are most considerate of my health and happiness, my dearest lord.''

He laughed, kissing her with barely held longing, and her toes fair curled with response as she thought of the coming night with anticipation.

Then, with great reluctance, Raynor turned to purchase the three of them roasted pears.

The fruit was delicious, and just the right temperature to hold in the hand. When hers was gone, Elizabeth licked her fingers with delight, blushing anew when Raynor took her hand to flick away a morsel with his own tongue.

She gasped at the heat that coursed through her lower belly. ''Raynor, not before the child! What will she think?''

A bawdy chuckle escaped him, and then he sobered, meeting her uncertain gaze. ''She will think nothing but that I love her mother very much.'' He turned to Willow, who watched them with a grin as she finished her pear. ''Is that not true, little one? Do you not see how I love your mother?''

''Aye, you love her.'' She nodded sagely. ''And I love Mother, too.''

Elizabeth's heart soared at the words. It was the first time Willow had addressed her in this manner, and she determined anew to be worthy of the title. She, too, would protect Willow from all that might hurt her, regardless of the cost, and that included Nigel Harrington. She leaned down and gave the tiny girl a hug.

When Elizabeth looked up at Raynor, he seemed to sense how much the moment meant to her, to them as a family, for he reached down and picked Willow up. They continued on that way, their daughter nestled in the crook of his arm.

In the center of the rows of tents, a space had been left clear. As they entered it, Elizabeth saw that the area had not been left bare by accident. A loose crowd of observers were grouped around a troupe of acrobatic entertainers who performed at its center.

As they stopped to watch the exhibition, Elizabeth saw Olwyn in the crowd across from her. And the serving woman was not alone.

At her side stood Bronic.

Clearly he had decided to make his suit known to all. The very attentive air he directed toward the tall blond woman told the world of his feelings. Though he did not touch her in this public setting, Bronic's attention and care were totally centered on Olwyn.

And hers on him. She seemed oblivious of everything as she stared up into the golden-haired man's blue eyes.

Elizabeth could not prevent herself smiling as she nudged Raynor.

He looked where she directed, then smiled himself. His expression when he turned to his wife was one of gladness. "I am well pleased," he said. "Bronic loves her. I hope she will make him as happy as you have me."

Elizabeth nodded. "They are most suited to each other." Her shrug was teasingly smug. "Though I knew that from the very beginning."

Her husband raised dark brows. "Oh, did you now?"

"Aye," she told him. "As I knew we were."

As if he could not help himself, Raynor kissed her, to Willow's pleased laughter.

Elizabeth realized he had been right before. It was good for Willow to see them happy, to see them loving each other.

But feeling her pulse beat increase so drastically with just that simple kiss, Elizabeth knew it would be best for her to turn her attention to something else. At least for the moment.

When they were alone, now, that would be another matter entirely.

The acrobats were a true wonder. There were five of them, dressed in colorful costumes of brightly patterned reds and blues. And they appeared to have no small amount of skill in their work. Having seen such performances before, at the king's court, Elizabeth felt she had some basis for deciding this.

She watched as a man climbed atop the shoulders of his fellow, then stood on his hands while the one beneath hopped on one leg.

The crowd of onlookers cheered in encouragement while the men went on to demonstrate other such astounding feats. They made human towers, walked on their hands while singing, and tumbled over and about one another in wild abandon.

Willow clapped happily in her father's arms at each new trick, and they began to bow and smile in her direction, obviously marking her as the daughter of the house. Elizabeth felt Willow was truly an adorable child, but she also knew this deference was part of the performance.

She shrugged. It was no shame for these men to pay special attention to the family of the one who might give them a few coppers. They had to earn their livelihood.

Besides, Willow was enjoying the special attention greatly, if her squeals of delight were any indication.

While the five began to string a sturdy line from the stone wall to a heavy post in the ground, Raynor turned to set Willow on the ground beside Elizabeth. When he straightened, he smiled at her warmly. "I have just re-membered something I have to do, Elizabeth. Would you be so good as to excuse me for a few minutes?"

Pensively she frowned. The barely suppressed excite-ment in his dark eyes made her wonder what he was about. But she said nothing. Raynor was up to something, but she trusted him enough to know it was something good. The frown disappeared.

She smiled at her husband, lazily, seductively. "Aye, my lord. But do not be so very long that I forget who brought me to the fair."

He gave her a swift, hard hug, whispering intimate re-minders of exactly why she would not forget him. The words, however hurried and low, left her feeling weak at the knees, and even more eager for night to fall.

He held her away from him then, his eyes knowing as he saw the desire in hers. "I will return ere long. Stay right here."

"Yes," she answered breathlessly.

As Raynor left them, she watched his broad back with an incredible sense of yearning. And unaccountably she was reminded of the loneliness she'd known so many times in the past, watching his back as he walked away from her. Quickly Elizabeth set the thought aside. All that was gone. Raynor could accept his love for her now, and would not reject her again.

Elizabeth came out of her reverie when she felt a tug on her skirt. Looking down, she saw Willow studying her strangely.

"Well?" the child questioned.

"What is it, love?" Elizabeth asked. "I am sorry I was not attending that first time."

"Why are the men putting up that rope?" She pointed a chubby finger toward the scene before them.

"Well, I cannot imagine," Elizabeth told Willow, her blue eyes round with feigned wonder. "But if we watch, we are sure to find out. Don't you think?'' Elizabeth did have some idea of what was to happen, but she didn't want to give it away and spoil Willow's delight in the possible surprise of seeing the men walk on that piece of rope.

Soon the next phase of the act began, and Elizabeth saw that her suspicions had proved true. And the expression of complete amazement and awe on Willow's face told her she had been right to keep the knowledge to herself.

Soon Elizabeth's gaze was as rapt as the child's.

The men had certainly been agile on the ground. But what was amazing was that they were equally gifted in performing on the thin rope. They did more acrobatics, climbed into pyramids, jumped and pirouetted. Never had Elizabeth seen anything more amazing.

Elizabeth found herself cheering them on with the rest of the crowd. When she looked about, she saw that the throng of onlookers was now quite heavy. Some of the crowd began to throw coins, which were quickly scooped up by the ones who took their respective turns on the ground.

After the man on the rope had done a backward somersault, Elizabeth looked down to see how Willow was reacting to this new amazement, and realized the child was no longer beside her.

Immediately Elizabeth glanced across the circle of faces to where Olwyn had been standing before. Mayhap Willow had gone to her. Olwyn was no longer there. Searching the crowd, Elizabeth could find neither her companion nor the child.

An unbidden sense of dread rose up inside her like oil in water, covering the surface of her contentment. There were many strangers in the keep. It was not safe for the child to be wandering about alone. But Elizabeth fought to push the feeling down. Willow had simply wandered away. Perhaps she had even seen Olwyn leave the area, and was with her at this very moment.

Yes, she told herself with determination. She would surely find them together.

With this in mind, she set off in search of them.

And as she moved through the now thick crowds, watching for any sign of those she sought, she began to wonder where Raynor was. He had said he would not be long. Elizabeth had no idea of how long she had watched the acrobats, but it had surely been some time.

She became doubly determined to find Willow before Raynor realized she was missing. For Elizabeth did not want to worry him. He was fearful for the child at the best of times. This incident must not be allowed to mar the day he had worked so hard to provide them.

It was only a moment later that Elizabeth spied Olwyn standing beside Jean, who was attending one of the cooking fires, where a whole pig turned on the spit. Willow was not with them. Elizabeth's heart sank, and as she approached, the two women looked at her.

Obviously Olwyn saw by Elizabeth's expression that something was wrong. "What is it?" she asked.

Elizabeth made no effort to hide her burgeoning panic now. "Willow—have you seen her?"

Olwyn shook her head, grasping the situation immediately. Her expression grew fixed with worry. "Nay, not since I saw her with you at the performers. How long has she been missing?"

"Oh, dear me, Lord!" Jean cried in a harsh voice, causing Elizabeth to turn to her. The woman held her hand to her bosom, and her face was white with dread.

"What is it?" Elizabeth asked.

"My girl Hyla, she was here in the keep, not more than minutes ago!"

"Yes?" Elizabeth prodded. Hyla had been banned from the keep, and should certainly not be there, but what had that to do with Willow? Surely the woman could not wish to seriously harm the child.

"Oh, my lady! I should have called the guards and had her taken away, I should! As soon as she told me!"

"Told you what?" Elizabeth was near to screaming in frustration.

But Jean rattled on as if she hadn't heard. "Yes, that's what I should have done, as soon as she told me she was living at Harrington keep. But she said she'd only come back to see me. Not to make any mischief. Even asked me where little Willow might be. Said she wanted to be sure and stay clear of her and Lord Raynor and his lady."

Elizabeth felt her heart sink to her shoes, and she swayed as the blood rushed in her head. Dear God, no. Nigel. As panic rose up to grip her throat, Elizabeth grabbed Jean by the shoulders and shook her. "Think now, how long has it been since you spoke with her?"

Jean was crying now. "Oh, some time, my lady. She's gone and done it, hasn't she? Taken our babe?"

Think, Elizabeth told herself, you must think of what to do. Letting go of the other woman, Elizabeth turned to Olwyn. "Go and find Raynor. Tell him what has happened. I will go on ahead. Mayhap, if I am quick, I can catch up to them."

Olwyn did not hesitate as she rushed across the crowded courtyard.

Without another word, Elizabeth ran toward the stables. On horseback she would be much more likely to catch them. When her heavy gown hindered her progress, she lifted it high, completely oblivious of the stares cast her way.

She knew she had to act, and immediately, if she had any hope of rescuing the child before Hyla reached Harrington with her. After that, nothing short of war would see Willow returned to them. And that Elizabeth did not believe her husband would do. Not with the child inside the keep. If Elizabeth did not succeed now, Nigel would have won. Raynor would not risk harming her to get her back.

Even in the event that a long and tedious siege was undertaken, Willow would suffer with the rest of the castle's occupants, until they ultimately ran out of food and water.

'Twas untenable.

Guilt drove Elizabeth on, uncaring of the people she jostled in her haste. Willow had been left in her care, and she had failed to protect her. How could Raynor ever forgive her if Willow was lost to the very man who had raped her mother?

As she reached the stables, Elizabeth saw a sight that heartened her greatly and gave her hope that her quest would succeed. A black palfrey stood saddled and ready for mounting in the yard outside. It was a fine specimen of horseflesh with a proud head and glossy coat. Obviously this was the prized possession of some wealthy merchant's wife. Save the boy who held the reins, there was no one about, and this seemed odd, but Elizabeth chose not to question her good fortune.

Without a word to the startled boy, she hefted her skirts even higher and climbed atop the mare. She then reached around the horse's neck and pulled the reins from the boy's hands, even as she kicked the beast to a gallop.

She gained the outside easily and sped down the hard-packed dirt road in the direction of Harrington. Leaning low over the horse's back, Elizabeth prayed that she would overtake them before it was too late.

For several miles, Elizabeth rode on, hardly thinking past the pain in her heart. She knew nothing beyond the need to reach her child and see her safely returned to her husband.

Then, unexpectedly, she came around a bend and saw them on the road ahead of her. But when she did, her heart sank. For not only could she clearly see Willow, sitting before Hyla on a spotted mare, but there was Nigel Harrington himself, resting atop his own stallion, only a few feet from where Hyla had stopped.

Even as she watched, Hyla awkwardly nudged her horse closer to Nigel's when he reached out his arms.

Elizabeth's skin crawled at the idea of Harrington touching Willow, and before she had a chance to think on the wisdom of her actions, she gave a kick and her mount sprang forward.

But even as she reached them, she knew she would have to have her hands free to grab the child. Dropping the reins and trusting to her skill as a horsewoman to make the mare obey her by simple command of her gripping thighs, Elizabeth was between the other two before they even noticed her approach.

Taking a deep breath, she reached for Willow and brought her into her lap without so much as slowing. Elation filled her for that one split second, as Willow realized who she was and clung to her.

But the joy proved short-lived when her mare came to a halt with a jolt that nearly tore the child from her arms.

Elizabeth swung around and found herself looking into the mad gaze of Nigel Harrington. He smiled coldly, showing her reins in his hands. He must have grabbed them as she flew past. Elizabeth knew a sickening rush of disappointment and then fear. Although she held a sobbing Willow close against her, they were not free.

What would he do with them now?

Nigel Harrington gave a harsh laugh. "Now I have you both. Better and better. Warwicke will rue the day he crossed me."

Something inside Elizabeth exploded, and she screamed, "Filthy cur! How dare you even speak my husband's name! You are not fit to breathe the same air as one such as he!"

"Not fit?" he growled. "Why are you women ever blind to what Warwicke truly is? He wants Willow for her inheritance. You know, don't you, that everything of her mother's went to her? It was entailed through direct descendant, even if that was a female." His voice rose. "My father only married Louisa's mother to bring her money to Harrington. Louisa knew that everything but Harrington keep was hers. I asked her to marry me. We could have gotten a dispensation, ours not being a true blood tie. But she wouldn't have me. Though she made a pretense of saying it was because she didn't love me, I knew Louisa thought she was too good for me. Me, a Harrington. My ancestors came here with the Conqueror. But I showed her." He laughed bitterly. "I made certain she had a bit of Harrington blood in her."

Bile rose in Elizabeth's throat at his cruelty. "Vile despoiler," she spat.

Nigel leaned forward and slapped her face. "Do not press me, woman. You are in no position to make insults."

Elizabeth leaned back, stunned, as she moved one hand to her cheek. "You are mad." She shook her head. "Have you not caused enough harm? Why, why must you take Willow? How could you hope to gain? The king has declared Raynor the child's father. He will not allow you to keep her in the end, no matter that you take her now. You gain nothing but to cause us all pain."

Nigel laughed again. "My dear Lady Warwicke. You are quite wrong. By taking the child, I draw Warwicke from his den. Once he is disposed of, I become her only living relative. Not only do I repay him for keeping her from me, I also become the executor of all her wealth."

Elizabeth was not impressed with this bravado. "You may find Raynor is not so very easy to kill. Taking Willow does not make him more vulnerable to you. He has no need of a shield to protect him from you." She knew he was remembering the way he had used her as such by the angry flush that stained his cheeks. Just as she had meant him to.

Hyla spoke, surprising Elizabeth, who had forgotten her presence. "My lord. Should we not go?"

"Aye, we should," Nigel agreed. "We have lingered here overlong as it is. I would be at Harrington before Warwicke knows of this. For clearly he does not as yet, or you, lady Elizabeth, would not have come alone."

The observation was not one she could refute, so Elizabeth said nothing, only biting her lip in consternation. She could only pray that Olwyn had found Raynor quickly, and that he would come after them.

With an expression of triumph, Nigel began to lead them back down the road toward his keep. Hyla stayed close beside him, her own face filled with spiteful pleasure every time she turned to glare at Elizabeth.

They had gone only a short distance when a dearly familiar voice hailed them from behind. With a gasp of joy, Elizabeth swung around to see Raynor bearing down upon them.

Nigel's face was a tapestry of fear, rage and frustration when he saw his mortal enemy closing in on him. With a cry of fury, he threw Elizabeth's reins to Hyla. "Hold them while I dispose of Warwicke."

He drew his sword just in time, for Raynor was immediately upon him.

Elizabeth held Willow's face close against her shoulder, so she could not see the battle. But the child flinched at the first clash of steel against steel, and began to weep all the harder.

To Elizabeth's dismay, Nigel met her husband's attack with more skill and fervor than she would have guessed. He seemed to be a proficient swordsman, despite his past lack of bravery where Raynor was concerned.

Both men clung to their wildly dancing mounts as they fought on, each plainly wanting nothing so much as the other's blood.

Elizabeth held her breath in fear, for she knew that a tumble from his horse could easily render Raynor vulnerable to Nigel's flashing sword. But he kept his seat, and before long it was clear that the black-hearted knight was no match for Raynor. With each thrust and swing, he was further beaten back.

When finally the death blow came, Nigel looked at Raynor in shocked surprise, then crumpled off his horse to lie still upon the grass.

It was a moment before any of them could react. Then, as if realizing that her protector could no longer be of any benefit to her, Hyla cried out and attempted to escape.

But she was no experienced rider, and her mare did not instantly react to her signals.

By that time, Raynor had seen what she was about and easily caught her, only a few feet away.

Looking up at Raynor, atop his horse, his hand on her mount's neck to prevent her from escaping, Hyla's expression was filled with panic. When she spoke, her voice was rife with desperation, her eyes pleading with Raynor to heed her. "My lord Warwicke, let me go and I will tell you all."

Raynor's lips were thin with anger. "All what?"

Hyla pointed to Elizabeth. "Of her. It was your lady wife who helped us. She gave me the child when I went to the keep."

Elizabeth was aghast at the complete brashness of the lie. Surely Hyla must know that her story could be disproved! Elizabeth had no care for that. It was fear of Raynor's reaction to the tale that froze her blood in her veins and made her heart ache with sadness. Would he look at her as he had that time when he came upon her with Nigel Harrington? However briefly, would she see the shadow of doubt cloud his face, and know that deep within himself he held back?

As if he had read her very mind, Raynor looked fully on his wife as he replied to Hyla's accusations. "You lie. My lady wife would not betray me or our daughter in thought or deed."

A great cacophony of joy sounded in Elizabeth's heart at the trust and love in her husband's eyes.

At that moment, when they two were lost in each other's eyes, Hyla gave a desperate kick and was away, hanging precariously to the horse's back. Raynor began to go after her again, but Elizabeth stopped him. "We will find her, love. Right now, we had best take Willow home. She is most disturbed by what has happened here."

Raynor looked down at his daughter, who had stopped sobbing, but clung to her mother as if she would never let go. "Aye. I can see you are right. My men follow close behind, and I will set them to find her when we meet them on the road."

Elizabeth bent and raised Willow's tear-streaked face. "All will be well now. We are going home." When Willow buried her head against Elizabeth's shoulder again, she looked to Raynor with a frown of worry.

He leaned forward to take her hand for a brief moment, his eyes dark with emotion. "Have no fear, love. She will be all right, with your tender care to heal her heart."

That night, with Willow safely tucked in her own bed, Raynor held Elizabeth close in theirs. As she snuggled into his sheltering embrace, Elizabeth felt him shudder. "What is it, love?" she asked, reaching up to touch his face and finding it damp. "Raynor, do not cry, my dearest. We returned to you safe and well."

He took a deep breath, and when he spoke his voice was husky with emotion. "I weep with happiness, wife. So grateful am I to God for your life. The emptiness I felt at nearly losing both you and Willow is now filled with a love so deep it makes me ache just here." He put her slender hand to his hard, bare chest. "You are my life, my reason for living."

"God was surely with us," she replied, raising up to kiss him tenderly. "When I went to the stables, a horse stood there already saddled. I must remember to find the lady who owns the beast and thank her."

"Then you must thank yourself, love, for the mare was to be my marriage gift to you. It was what I had gone to get when I left you. A fight had broken out between two men who had taken too much wine, and I was delayed."

Elizabeth hugged him tightly. "She is mine? Oh Raynor, 'tis a most beautiful gift. Thank you. Nothing could have been more welcome than that surefooted sable mare. She carried me to Willow."

Raynor pulled her down to him, holding her so tightly she could scarce breathe, but Elizabeth reveled in the embrace. "Why did you go alone?" he whispered. "I was just inside the stables there, but by the time the lad had come to tell me you had taken the mare, you were gone. And I knew not where. Thankfully, Olwyn found me only moments later, or I fear what would have happened."

She kissed him. "But naught did, Raynor. Everything was as it was meant to be. Have you realized that we no longer have to live under the threat of what Harrington might do? Willow is safe from him for all time. And though she was frightened by what occurred today, I believe she is going to be fine. Why, when I left her a few minutes ago, she was resting peacefully and spoke with relief that the bad man would not try to take her again."

"Nay, he will not," Raynor growled, a hint of anger in his voice as he remembered. "'Twas a fitting end. And now that Hyla has been captured by my men, there is her punishment to consider."

Elizabeth put her finger to his lips. The past and Nigel were dead, and she resented even one more moment of their future spent on thinking of him. "Now is the time for us, Raynor. No more can he harm us. Hyla will wait until morn."

"Aye, you are right." He rolled her on her back and kissed her then, long and hard. And deep inside her, Elizabeth felt a stirring of warm desire. She sighed against his mouth, her hands disappearing in his hair as their embrace grew steadily more heated. In this ancient, most intimate way would they celebrate their love and life together, leaving the past behind them.

Insistently she placed her hands on his shoulders and urged him onto his back. With sweet deliberation, she knelt to cover his chest with hot kisses. His fingers tangled in her hair as he whispered in the darkness, "Elizabeth, I love you. I love you. My heart is yours, now and for always."

At long last, she knew it was true.

His heart belonged to her.

Her own heart thrummed with joy.

And as she explored his body with her lips and hands and tongue, she resolved to be worthy of that care. In the years to come, she would show him all the love and devotion he deserved.

* * * * *

Harlequin® Historical

WOMEN OF THE WEST

Exciting stories of the old West and the women whose dreams and passions shaped a new land!

Join Harlequin Historicals every month as we bring you these unforgettable tales.

RUGGED. SEXY. HEROIC.

OUTLAWS *and* HEROES

Stony Carlton—A lone wolf determined never to be tied down.

Gabriel Taylor—Accused and found guilty by small-town gossip.

Clay Barker—At Revenge Unlimited, he *is* the law.

JOAN JOHNSTON, DALLAS SCHULZE and MALLORY RUSH, three of romance fiction's biggest names, have created three unforgettable men—modern heroes who have the courage to fight for what is right....

OUTLAWS AND HEROES—available in September wherever Harlequin books are sold.

HARLEQUIN ®

PRIZE SURPRISE SWEEPSTAKES!

This month's prize:

BEAUTIFUL WEDGWOOD CHINA!

This month, as a special surprise, we're giving away a bone china dinner service for eight by Wedgwood**, one of England's most prestigious manufacturers!

Think how beautiful your table will look, set with lovely Wedgwood china in the casual Countryware pattern! Each five-piece place setting includes dinner plate, salad plate, soup bowl and cup and saucer.

The facing page contains two Entry Coupons (as does every book you received this shipment). Complete and return *all* the entry coupons; **the more times you enter, the better your chances of winning!**

Then keep your fingers crossed, because you'll find out by September 15, 1995 if you're the winner!

Remember: The more times you enter, the better your chances of winning!*

*NO PURCHASE OR OBLIGATION TO CONTINUE BEING A SUBSCRIBER NECESSARY TO ENTER. SEE THE REVERSE SIDE OF ANY ENTRY COUPON FOR ALTERNATE MEANS OF ENTRY.

**THE PROPRIETORS OF THE TRADEMARK ARE NOT ASSOCIATED WITH THIS PROMOTION.

PWW KAL